WARRIORS & HEALERS

H.J. Brues

Dreamspinner Press

Published by
Dreamspinner Press
4760 Preston Road
Suite 244-149
Frisco, TX 75034
http://www.dreamspinnerpress.com/

Warriors and Healers

Cover Art by Paul Richmond   http://www.paulrichmondstudio.com
Cover Design by Mara McKennen

ISBN: 978-1-61581-288-2

Printed in the United States of America
First Edition
December, 2009

eBook edition available
eBook ISBN: 978-1-61581-289-9

To my father,
who never stopped asking me
"When are you going to write a novel?"

To my mother, who wrote such beautiful letters.

And to Marta, who always knew.

Chapter 1

JEFF raised his head once more to check the arrivals on display in front of him. The plane was due in a few minutes, right about time to get rid of the board on which the new doctor's name was written in big, black block characters. "Ugarte," it said, and he had been wondering what the right pronunciation for that could be. At least the man's name was Daniel, so there was still a dignified way out of it, even if the Spanish accent didn't stress the same syllable at all. That could be easily forgiven, he hoped, especially if the doctor was just a typical NGO volunteer, all beard, sandals, and easygoing, brotherhood-of-man attitude.

Jeff had played his last hand with a phone call and still could not believe the famous NGO had acknowledged his plea for help and sent in a doctor right away. Not that the medical situation of his people wasn't shameful or disastrous enough, but Jeff's reports had been passed from government agency to government agency without so much as a polite dismissal. So it came as a surprise when just a phone call had brought them money, supplies, and, most importantly, a well-trained doctor, even if he was only to stay for a few months. It was a beginning, and the publicity he could get from having an NGO consider theirs a critical situation might shame the local authorities into doing something just to save face.

He only hoped the man could win his people's trust in such a short time. Jeff knew how their minds worked and was reasonably afraid they would shut him out, no matter how much they really needed a doctor. Maybe the fact that he was a foreigner, and European at that, would help, especially if Spaniards had that brown-skinned, dark-haired image their neighbors across the border sported.

The loudspeaker announced the incoming flight. Jeff had done all he could, no point in worrying anymore. He walked to the gate with that look of grim determination on his face that had earned him the respect of his people and usually came in handy in crowded places, making passersby steer clear of him just as they were doing now, as if he were a force of nature suddenly cut loose in the small county airport.

DANIEL grabbed his case and started walking, more slowly than he intended, but his body didn't seem all that cooperative after a twelve-hour flight, three plane changes included. Not that working late the last few days helped much—as Raúl had pointed out—but it wasn't an office he worked in; he couldn't just up and go, leaving a bunch of papers on his desk. *You don't have to kill yourself to keep others in good health*, his best friend had told him, voice tight with anger, but Daniel knew he wouldn't be able to sleep if he didn't do all he could. He might have been overdoing it lately, though.

After Estela left, he had taken extra shifts to keep his mind busy, making true what she'd said he was: a twenty-four-hour, house-call doctor with no time for career advancement or medical research. *Medical research?* Raúl had snorted. *Bet that's what she claims she's been doing with that plastic surgeon.* Daniel had tried to give him a stern look, but sometimes the way his friend berated Estela helped, no matter how wrong he knew it to be. Made him feel less guilty, less hurt.

He changed the laptop bag from shoulder to shoulder. Damn, he felt so tired. At least he had taken Raúl's advice, or rather command, the way he had looked at Daniel with those I-know-better, big-brother eyes of his before saying: *No war, no disaster area this year.* He didn't think he would have made it with camp facilities this time, the way he was dragging himself about like a too-heavy attaché case.

Funny, they had just the right job for Raúl to approve of, in the least expected of all possible places. It was going to be weird, really weird. Just to think of the name of the social worker he had to contact made Daniel shake his head. Christ. How was he supposed to call someone "Redbear" without feeling he was insulting the man? It wasn't simply that he had to face a culture somehow alien to him; he had done that before. The problem was this time he couldn't help bringing with him a lot of what he imagined to be simple clichés about life on an Indian reservation. He sighed. They would have to be a little patient with him, but then again, they were on the same team, everything should be just fine. Right now, all he could hope for was someone waiting for him outside the gates, even if he had to pretend that giving the guy some animal's name did not make him expect to be punched in return.

PASSENGERS started spilling out of the sliding doors. Jeff searched tired, expectant faces, holding the cardboard sign gingerly away from him. He felt like a tour leader waiting on a bunch of tourists. Not that anyone would travel that far to visit a reservation that didn't even house a casino, but the embarrassed feeling was there all the same. He just hoped nobody he knew had business at the airport that day.

People carrying cases passed by him, but so far, no one looked the way he expected the foreign doctor to look. Maybe he was clinging to stereotypes there, but he figured his own looks entitled him to do so. He couldn't hide what he was, never tried to. In fact, he always made sure one or two of his favorite stereotypes were right in place before leaving home.

Today he looked especially typical: his long, black hair falling unbridled past his shoulders, flannel shirt slightly open to show Grandpa's medicine pouch, well-worn jeans hanging rather loosely on his lean frame, dusty cowboy boots on his feet. Surely the doctor wouldn't have a hard time spotting him among the crowd, if he ever made it through the gate. Shit. What was keeping the man?

Jeff let his eyes wander over the passengers and almost gasped aloud. It had been a long time since he'd last seen anyone, either man or woman, so overpoweringly attractive. The guy definitely stood out. He wasn't particularly tall, yet the way he moved, the way his clothes fit his slender body, the way everything he wore—case and shoulder bag included—had been carefully chosen to look casual and still elegant, all of it spoke of a kind of background completely alien to this godforsaken corner of the country. Not to mention the effect it was producing on Jeff, an instant knot of desire melting his brain right then and there like the nearby explosion of a supernova. Sweet Lord Jesus. The man had one of the most beautiful faces he'd ever seen: features exquisitely drawn on a fair, flawless complexion, sensual lips, big green eyes staring with an intensity that made Jeff's throat go dry when their gazes met.

They stood like that for a moment, eyes locked in some kind of staring-down contest that the stranger seemed to lose as his gaze focused on the cardboard sign in Jeff's hands. Jeff forgot to even feel embarrassed; he was too busy keeping his knees from giving way under him. Then the stranger looked up and Jeff had to blink twice to be sure he was seeing right.

There was a smile on the man's face, no doubt about it. And it wasn't a smirk, either. It was a full, disarmingly sexy smile, the kind that makes you turn your head to confirm that you are the true recipient of such wonder. Jeff didn't turn around, though, because the stranger had started walking toward him and he was frozen in place, the cardboard held tight in front of him as some kind of protective shield.

"Hi, I'm Daniel Ugarte."

It took Jeff some time to process that single sentence, so much so that the man had to point to the board with the big name on it.

"That's me," he said, his voice a little uncertain this time.

Jeff shook himself out of the trance and offered his hand.

"Jeff Redbear. Welcome to the States."

He could have slapped himself. What an original introduction. The man didn't seem to care, though. He appeared truly happy to meet him, or to be there, or whatever it was that made him smile so brightly. Maybe that trait was the only one that matched his expectations. He seemed to be nice in a mushy-missionary kind of way. Or rather, that was what Jeff's growing reticence tried to make him believe.

It happened every time he met interesting white people, which wasn't that often, anyway. He felt threatened. Of course he knew it was irrational, but he couldn't help it. He had built the courage to navigate through an all-white world from a well-proven notion that the culture he had inherited was in many ways superior to the dominant one.

He was honestly proud of who he was, and having seen too often what came out of despising one's own roots in an ill-conceived effort toward assimilation, he felt grateful. His identity was solid, and comfortably so. Yet when something from the other world caught his attention, he felt as if he were about to betray his people, and all his defenses went into red-alert mode.

"I really appreciate you coming to pick me up. I feel like the perfect textbook example of jet lag."

There. That was it. Of course the man was happy to find someone waiting for him after what, ten, eleven hours locked up in a shaking metal box? And there he was, being a total jerk. He fumbled for something to say.

"Have a good flight?"

Great, Jeff. How lame was that?

"Yeah, quiet all the way. Still, by the fourth Bruce Willis movie, I was ready to try my hand at skydiving."

Jeff chuckled in spite of himself. "Could have been worse. Last time I took a Greyhound bus, I had to watch the first half of *Dances with Wolves*. Twice."

The doctor laughed. Up close, his eyes were amazing. Never imagined green eyes could get that dark. Jesus. He'd better get a grip on himself. He was going to be stuck with the man for some months. He couldn't afford to keep drooling over him all the time.

He bent to grab the doctor's case, just to hide his embarrassment, but the man wouldn't let him, so he ended up carrying what appeared to be a laptop. Of course. Jeff had been told the guy was some bigwig at a famous hospital, director of the pediatric emergency department or something like that. He probably expected the reservation to have Wi-Fi or at least proper ADSL facilities. Yeah, he was in for a big surprise. The nice doctor would probably faint when Jeff showed him the place they had refurbished for him to work and stay in.

As they walked toward the exit, Jeff realized he was still carrying the piece of cardboard and dumped it unceremoniously into the first trash can he saw.

Brace yourself, city boy, he thought as they marched to the parking lot, almost snorting as he remembered the state his pickup was in after the storm last night. He couldn't wait to see the doctor's face when he realized his fancy clothes had to touch that muddy piece of rolling junk.

Chapter 2

DANIEL looked out the pickup window. The landscape was an arid succession of small, naked hills, contours blurred in the early afternoon heat. It was beautiful, in a desolate kind of way, and made him feel small, or rather would have if the truck owner hadn't already been so intent on showing him how insignificant he was. He wondered what he had done to piss the guy off.

From the very beginning, Redbear's black eyes had stared him down from the high seat of his outstanding cheekbones. And the way he had discarded the cardboard with his name? Christ. He might as well have stepped on it. Daniel wouldn't have felt worse. Redbear his ass; Redcoyote should be the proper name for the man.

He turned to look at Jeff. The social worker had a stunning profile. Deep chiselled features, sharp eyes and thick, black hair, smooth skin. He was lean and tall, and everything about him had an air of tense concentration that made him appear dangerous.

Daniel smiled. He could imagine his gay friends raising eyebrows at him. Well, as he always told them, he was straight, not blind. And to that Miguel Ángel would always respond, patting his shoulder with *Yeah, yeah, just you wait and see what happens when the right hunk crosses your path. You won't know what hit you.*

For all Daniel knew, he was ready to agree with his friend. He'd always believed Freud's innate bisexuality made sense, but his own upbringing seemed to have been very effective in defining his sexual orientation. If Estela had left him, it had nothing to do with their sex life, which had been pretty satisfactory from the start. *No, it's simply that she never ever loved you,* Raúl would say, with that resentful look he always got when mentioning her.

Aw, man. Daniel had promised himself not to think about Estela till it stopped hurting, and there he was again. He was hopeless.

"Your English is very good. Where did you learn it?"

Jeff's voice startled him. What now? The man was trying to be nice? It was driving Daniel crazy, the way he swung from utter contempt to politeness.

"I went to college in England."

And at that he could almost hear Jeff's brain cringing. Terrific. He didn't know what to say that would not dig his own grave even deeper.

"Don't worry. Soon I'll be mixing prepositions up and letting some French words slip in...."

Shit, shit, shit. He might as well tell him he could read Japanese, kanji and all; it would sure help.

"Was your family living there?"

Daniel stared blankly at him.

"In England, while you studied there."

"Oh, no, it was just me."

"Boarding school?"

"Yeah, British cliché all the way, from uniforms to cricket."

"Sounds funny."

Sure. Paradise on earth: alone in a foreign country with classes in a foreign language and a bunch of snotty kids never allowing you to forget you weren't of British descent. Which, in spite of Daniel's fair complexion, put him on the same level of college underlife as the Hindu, Arab, and Japanese kids studying, or rather, hiding there. Yet even those kids went home for the holidays. He wasn't that lucky. Had it not been for Raúl's parents, he would have spent even Christmas in the empty, gothic dorms.

Was it his imagination or Jeff was looking at him in an odd way?

"I seem to have developed a strange case of fish-and-chips allergy, though."

Redbear's face showed an almost smile.

"Me, it's lemon college cafeteria jelly I'm allergic to."

"The kind that tastes like pine air freshener?"

"Yep, that kind exactly."

Now he was smiling. That really was something to see, the way the corners of his eyes lifted, losing that predatory stillness that made his stare so scary.

The road got narrower and the pickup bumped along its cracked surface. They hadn't passed any other cars for some time now, and Daniel wondered if they were taking an alternative, less-used route.

"Is this the main road into the reservation?"

Jeff snorted. "Guess you could say so, if this reservation had any 'mains' to it."

Daniel wanted to roll his eyes at the patronizing tone, but he understood what Jeff felt. People who worked every day in depressed areas had to deal with a lot of frustration and lashed out at the slightest pressure. Wasn't Daniel's fault, but he could relate to it.

He imagined the whole situation that had brought him there was the reason behind Jeff's hostile behavior. In his place, Daniel would have been mad; he always was when having to deal with bureaucracy back home. Still, he couldn't help sensing something almost personal in Jeff's righteous resentment, and *that* he wasn't going to take too kindly. It wasn't his fault if life sucked.

"Like the landscape?"

He looked at Jeff, searching for any sign of mockery. His face betrayed no emotion, so Daniel thought he was swinging to the polite side again.

"Yeah, kind of reminds me of a region back home where rocks also get these tortured shapes. You can travel through miles of barren-looking land without meeting a single soul, and yet feel the place is full of life. It sure has its own sort of beauty, much like those almost empty Zen gardens have."

Jeff was eying him oddly again. Maybe it was the way Daniel spoke, hands moving in front of him to stress his points or maybe it was his choice of words. He couldn't quite read Jeff's countenance, and it was really vexing. Made him feel like a brainless parrot.

"Truth is, I know little about your country.   What is it like?" Redbear asked.

Daniel let his breath out in a huffing sound that had Jeff smiling at him.

"Difficult question, huh?"

Daniel smiled back. "Well, it's just that Spain can look really different depending on where you are, much like this country does. It has all the shades, from coastal blue to forest green, snow-white to desert brown, and people change accordingly, in character as much as appearance, so you can never really tell what Spain or the Spaniards look like." Daniel frowned. "That just sounded like a brochure from the Tourist Board."

Jeff's laughter came as a nice surprise, the more so since he appeared to clam up every time some kind of emotion threatened to alter that stoic expression of his. "So, what kind of Spaniard are you? You don't strike me as the 'desert-brown' type of guy."

It was Daniel's turn to laugh. "That's true. I've been taking so many night shifts lately that I'm rather on the snow-white side right now. My family comes from the north, anyway, that's why we tend to be light-eyed and whitish, but my skin gets easily tanned. Come summer, I end up looking like a black cat."

He shut his mouth abruptly. In his experience, Americans were quite sensitive in the skin color department, and he guessed it wasn't particularly wise to keep babbling about his complexion in front of a Jicarilla Apache. Daniel turned a contrite look toward Jeff, only to find dark eyes set on him with genuine curiosity.

"You are not from Madrid, then?"

"No, I live and work there, have for some years now, but I was born up north, in Navarra."

"Planning to go back someday?"

"No."

Jeff seemed to wait for him to elaborate, but as the silence stretched, Daniel felt uncomfortable. That was a topic he loathed to broach with strangers, yet he did not want to sound rude, so he was ready to add something when Jeff spoke again.

"Don't think I could do that. Always felt out of place whenever I had to leave here."

"What about university?"

"Well, it sure was interesting in its own way, but not enough to get me hooked. If anything, it just confirmed my belief that it's here I belong."

Daniel looked at the social worker as if he were seeing him for the first time. Working as a volunteer, he had often met the likes of Jeff, people who had the opportunity to leave behind impoverished environments but refused to do so out of a feeling of community, clearly knowing where and by whom they were needed the most. It always filled him with a sense of awe, and more often than not, envy. He himself had never felt linked, bound, connected. He had severed his family ties before they smothered him, lived in a city where everyone was a stranger, worked in a big hospital where patients had no names but symptoms, and spent the odd month with people all over the world he never got to see again. He wished he knew where *he* belonged.

"Truth is you don't really need to leave here to broaden your horizons."

Daniel cocked his head at Jeff, gauging his expression until Jeff's hand moved to cover the empty landscape stretching miles and miles ahead of them.

"As you can see."

Jeff said it so seriously that Daniel's laughter broke out in spite of himself, relieved to see a smile tugging at the corners of his companion's mouth. Maybe it wasn't going to be that difficult after all; maybe they could get along just fine, the two of them.

Chapter 3

SEAN MCCALLUM stood facing the empty square from behind his office window. Why there should be a bench and a small fountain just in front of the sheriff's headquarters completely escaped him. But there it was, enticing him to go out and soak in the early-morning sun.

His gaze had been drawn to that bench from the very first day, and still, after a month, he couldn't help staring out the window, watching that empty piece of iron and wood. It sort of matched his actual condition: a lonely thing utterly out of place, just sitting there waiting to be useful.

When he'd met the former sheriff, he'd understood why the Bureau of Indian Affairs had been so intent on lobbying for someone used to dealing with ethnic issues to cover the post. The man was the perfect cartoon image of those fat, mean, old cops who filled their mouths with tobacco and nasty words, those who, having spent their whole lives in a place surrounded by Apache, Hopi, Navajo, Ute, and Tohono O'odham reservations, stuck to a vocabulary for people that ranged from "colored" to "Injun."

Sean had felt that just removing the guy would bring a much-needed change, but he had been naïve as to its extent. He had expected people to see the difference right away and flock to him for help. Maybe if sheriffs were elected into the post there and not appointed, things might have looked brighter for him, since people would have had time to get to know him. But probably not. Probably they'd have rather kept the mean old bastard they were familiar with rather than electing a total stranger.

Having never lived in a diminutive place like this before, Sean was not used to the amount of mistrust he had to swim through everyday. He'd always known some people just don't like cops—apart from the ones who had a vested interest in avoiding them—and of course expected a certain reticence to him, being too Irish-white in a multiethnic community, but he'd never counted on being outright dismissed as a stranger. For all the good he was doing, he might as well have come from outer space.

So up until now, the lonely bench outside his office had been the perfect metaphor of his own situation. But lately there was another reason for him to start his working days contemplating the empty seat: it wasn't empty anymore.

A few mornings ago he had been startled to discover someone actually sitting on the bench, at such an early hour he would have thought it likely the man had spent the night there. But he had been startled one more time by the guy almost jumping off the bench and running out of the square as if all hell was after him.

The following day Sean stood on watch by the window, waiting to see if the man would come again. As he waited behind the glass pane, sipping his coffee, he went through mental pictures of the people he already knew, the town being so small he was sure he had already met almost everyone who lived there at least once. Still, he couldn't imagine who among them would display such a keen interest in fitness as to trot in and out of town that early in the morning.

At last, a real case to lay his hands on, he thought with a chuckle. And right then he saw the lonely figure of a man making his way down the street at a fast pace. Sean studied his stance and the cadence of his long strides and concluded the guy was not the usual weekend jogger you could find on big-city sidewalks. He ran as if he had been doing it for years, probably even professionally. That intrigued Sean. Gossip of a professional jock living there would have reached even him, so maybe he was not so much a sportsman as someone whose job required a good physical condition. A firefighter perhaps? No, the town only had volunteer firemen and the closest proper fire department was about sixty miles away. Too far to come running from. A cop? That could probably be it. With so many different jurisdictions crisscrossing the land, there were all sorts of law enforcement officers, from Customs Patrol to every kind of tribal police you could name. But just as the man approached his window, Sean could see there were no ethnic features he recognized, apart from the too-obvious Caucasian ones. FBI then? They certainly came down there a lot, what with so many borders and bureaus of this and that, but somehow he doubted it. Sean was half hidden in the unlit office, but a cop would have spotted his silhouette and looked up at him to gauge the threat.

The runner didn't seem to pay much attention to his surroundings. He just stopped to drink eagerly from the small fountain by the bench. Then he straightened and stretched his limbs in a totally unself-conscious, catlike way that made Sean smile. He finally sprawled on the bench with gusto, as if the rigid woodwork were covered with cushions.

Today he looked spent. Maybe he had run longer or faster than yesterday or maybe he was tired from work. Yet, there was something fetching about him. Even the abandon of his posture seemed only to add a languid note to a general picture that Sean struggled to confine into one word. The guy was certainly attractive: pretty face, nice body and all, but there was something far more all-encompassing, some kind of natural, almost animal elegance that had little to do with the clothes he wore.

Coming from a line of sturdy Irish men and at six foot two himself, Sean had always envied the easy stance of lighter-built folks, his own body a too-obvious presence to ignore. He had tried to make the most of its awkward mass by training it into a well-honed tool but still couldn't help admiring shorter, lithe guys like the one resting on the bench in front of him.

The man had been motionless for some time now, so much so that a sparrow had taken him for another of the square landmarks, fearlessly hopping about his sneakers. As the runner slowly cocked his head to watch the bird, Sean could get a full view of his profile and caught him smiling at the little one's advances. The new sheriff found himself chuckling. He already liked the guy, though he couldn't name any sensible reason why he should. Didn't even know who the stranger was, to begin with. By the costly look of his nicely fitting tracksuit, he could only tell he was an outsider. Maybe that was the crux of it: he longed for a fellow alien to share his loneliness with. Or maybe there was far more than that to it.

As the sparrow took flight and the runner lifted his face to follow the bird, Sean thought there was something quite enticing about the guy. He looked nice in a way his own mother would approve of, but as much as he seemed agreeably dependable, his eyes had a touch of mischief to them that spoke of a humorous, unpredictable character. He definitely wanted to know more about the guy and would have gone out to talk to him right that moment if the stranger hadn't stood and left just as fast as the sparrow had.

Sean promised himself he would meet this runner the next time he came into town to sit on what Sean had taken to thinking of as his own personal bench.

Chapter 4

JEFF parked the pickup down the hill from his uncle's home. He needed the long walk to sort things out in his head.

His first reaction upon hearing the wild rumors had been to storm out of his office and drive like a fury along the contours of the mesas that pointed the way to old man Charlie's lot. Now he wasn't so sure about the motive behind his righteous anger.

He knew the way of it, how someone might say something plain and simple just to have it turned around in someone else's words till it grew into a monster of a tale belonging to no one in particular. And he certainly knew his uncle. He probably had made the most innocuous of comments, something along the lines of the doctor having soulful eyes and steady hands, something he could easily see overcooked into the guy being some sort of ancient warrior come back to life in the body of a white man.

Had he gone out of his way just to chide his uncle for something Jeff knew he had no control over? Or was there something else he didn't want to acknowledge?

People spread their silly notions about other people all the time and it never bothered him, not even when it was his own person they were rambling about. Why was this instance any different? Whatever fantasy people had chosen to believe about the doctor, it was at least good they knew he was there and probably would make them curious enough to go and pay him a visit. That was surely his uncle's intention in the first place, and Jeff was beginning to suspect that what really chafed him was the fact that his uncle had chosen to praise the man. It was as simply and pathetic as that: he hated the thought that his favorite relative had given any mental space to the same white guy who was already plaguing too much of his own, reluctant, thoughts.

Jeff shook his head. If he could be reasonable about anything concerning Daniel Ugarte, he would have said Uncle Charlie was right to praise him. He remembered vividly the moment he had shown the doctor the place they had readied for him. Exhausted as Daniel was from the journey, he had only given the most cursory of looks at what would be his spartan living quarters and begun right away opening packages of medical aid, sorting them out, moving pieces of equipment, and even going as far as to disinfect every surface that had already been cleansed so that the place could admit patients at any moment. And all the while he'd had an air of absolute concentration about him, as if nothing existed beyond the walls of that ramshackle building—or rather, nothing beyond what he envisioned the place had to look like to serve the purpose he had in mind.

Jeff had been so swept away by Daniel's enthusiasm that he didn't even remember having offered to lend a hand. It had come naturally to him, not even noticing he hadn't reeled at the thing he hated above all else: being told what to do. Small wonder Daniel led an emergency-room team in a big hospital. He could imagine him in the most chaotic of night shifts, all exhaustion drained from him as he moved about dispensing calm efficiency, supervising twenty different tasks to completion without a single angry word. Jeff was sure he even managed to spare a wink and a smile for the children he had to tend to. And having received some of those smiles himself, he knew the man could just about melt rocks by sheer warmth, which was probably the reason Jeff was now stomping uphill like a stubborn mule.

That whole afternoon with Daniel had been incredible. He had listened to the guy and found him intelligent, had laughed with him, talked to him, looked into his eyes, and thought he understood. On top of all that, and no matter how hard it was to acknowledge it now, he had let his gaze linger on Daniel's body, following every movement of his long limbs, feasting his eyes on the exposed, tender skin of his nape, wanting to leave teeth marks on his white neck, to cup his face and bite those fleshy lips till they bled. Daniel didn't just turn him on: he made him hungry. And that was a private shame Jeff had to bear.

When he found out the doctor's name was on everybody's tongue, he just couldn't put up with it, no matter how different from his own he knew their fantasies to be. The man was his personal battle, a one-man challenge.

Jeff reached his uncle's house with a self-deprecating smirk on his face. He had just discovered his reason for being there had nothing to do with his uncle.

The door opened even before he knocked. Aunt Helena appeared in front of him with her old, beaming, wrinkled face. "Now this is really a sight to see," she said with her hands on her hips. "A Redbear walking all the way to this humble hut."

Jeff chuckled. "That's only 'cause he smelled your cooking. You should be more careful of the kind of wild animals you draw near."

"Don't worry, red bears are not wild, just grumpy, and this old woman knows a thing or two about handling them."

Still laughing, Jeff took the diminutive lady in his arms and hugged her fiercely, lifting her tiny feet off the ground. "Let go, you big bully!" she said in mock anger as her nephew put her back down. Jeff loved his aunt's banter. She had a keen intellect and a sharp tongue that had earned her the nickname of "Ear Breaker" among his mother's family, a none-too-subtle way of reminding her she would always be the unsophisticated Navajo in a proud Apache clan.

Marrying into the Apache hadn't been easy. Her father had said they were a bunch of drunkards and opposed the marriage doggedly. It didn't help much when he learned one of the Redbears had actually died in a car wreck while driving drunk. Not that the Navajo didn't drink themselves to death, too, but Helena being his only daughter, he wanted her to at least marry within their station, not so low down the scale that her family would be ashamed to bring her husband into their household.

And the Redbears themselves hadn't been much better. They always referred to the Navajo by the old Hopi derogatory name "Head

Breakers," meaning it was so far beyond their ability to make bows and arrows to kill their enemies, they had to split their skulls open with a hard blow to their heads.

When the wedding finally took place, it was a paltry ceremony with some sullen Apache faces and no Navajo to be seen except the stubborn little bride.

That was the true reason behind their living arrangements, in spite of all the talk about the great view from the hill: it was simply a question of distance from any relative of whatever branch of their families.

The child Jeff had been was unaware of the circumstances surrounding the marriage. Not until he was well into adulthood had he learned about the cause of their isolation and the price they had paid for it. He just loved staying in that house on the hill. The journey to get there, the emptiness of the landscape, the big silence enveloping the outer walls, the mysterious shaman ways of his uncle, the strange customs of his aunt, the tales she told—so different from those he heard in the crowded, noisy household of his mother's clan—all made the visit an adventure he always looked forward to. So when his mother had moved to town, taking only her daughter with her, he was all too happy to be left with his aunt and uncle to notice he wasn't going to see his mom and sis for a long time.

Coming from a background where people always ran to catch up with the changing ways of the outside world and never quite made it, where school taught boring things to children who couldn't find any use for them and couldn't quite grasp the chances they were supposed to offer, the little house on the hill had been a magical refuge for Jeff. Traditions had appeared exotic there, not restraining. Far from closing him off from the world, isolation had opened a new world for him, and one that was much more attractive than the other, which he would always be kept from reaching. So when the time came for Jeff to descend the hill, he carried baggage with him that allowed his eyes to capture the truth behind the bright lights of the big, white world.

By then he was ready to learn other deeper, hurtful truths and accept them for what they were. It was about that time that he'd found out his father had been killed in a car accident along with the drunk driver, who happened to be his brother-in-law. Jeff understood then why his mother had tried to escape from a place that drove men into alcohol and early deaths, only to discover small-town white men were no better, never finding inside herself the strength to either move on or back, just moving about from job to job, from man to man, from alcohol to drugs.

Jeff had learned other disturbing realities about the people closest to him. He discovered the house on the hill was not so much sanctuary as it was exile. He learned that Uncle Charlie's obsession with healing came from his inability to deal with sickness in the isolation of that house where he saw his own child die and had barely managed to keep his wife breathing the long miles to the nearest hospital. Aunt Helena had survived, but she would never have a child of her own.

By the time Jeff learned all those things, he had been brought up to understand what they had meant to the people involved, how they had shaped them, and how the ripples of those events had reached the quiet shore his own life peered from. He was able to grieve then, and yet be thankful, for every loss carried a compensation, as if to balance the final outcome that was him. One of his uncles had killed his father, yet every one of his remaining male relatives loved him as if each one was his lost father. His mother had abandoned him, yet she left him where he could have a true home, knowing as only a mother could that he wouldn't have survived what her daughter did. He had lost his sister for years, yet of all her relatives, she chose to keep in touch only with him, being proud of her brother instead of resentful of whatever chances he got. His aunt had buried a son because she never had the support of her family, yet she took care of another woman's child, hiding her bitterness behind a playful mockery that taught Jeff how to smile at dreadful things. His uncle blamed himself for almost losing what he loved most, yet instead of drowning in his guilt, he decided to take fate in his hands and love even more, adopting his nephew as if he was the child he lost and learning all there was to learn to prevent the sky from falling upon his roof.

"And what are you making that face for?"

Jeff came back from his thoughts to find Aunt Helena looking disapprovingly at him. "Me? What face am I making?"

"What face?" she mimicked him. "The same face your uncle makes when he thinks he just saw Changing Woman."

Jeff laughed. She always dismissed her husband's mystical quests. *He tries so hard to look beyond,* she used to say, *that his eyes cross and all he sees is his big Apache nose.* "And where is my uncle now?"

"Oh, so you've had enough of your aunt already…."

"No, I never have enough of her, so I'm gonna deal with my uncle for two seconds just to spend the rest of the day with you." He paused. "That is, of course, if you feed me decently."

"So says the man who cooks in a box."

"It's not a box, it's an oven."

"If that thing is an oven, your uncle is a hawk."

"Aunt Helena!" Jeff tried to pretend outrage but couldn't stop the corners of his mouth from lifting. His aunt wagged a finger at him.

"And then, boy, I would sure have trouble feeding *him* decently."

Jeff's laughter echoed in the small room. He just couldn't help himself around his aunt.

"Shhh, he's gonna hear you, the man has the ear of a bat."

"Well, I'm not the one calling him names."

The small woman whacked his arm with surprising force. "I'm entitled to call him dog if I want to, but you must respect your elders and keep a straight face, you big lump of a man."

"I'm sorry, Auntie, but I'm an Apache and I don't know better."

Her aunt gave him a playful shove. "Go pester your Apache uncle, then, he is back there with that pond-eyed kid."

"Pond-eyed kid?" Jeff repeated, but his aunt was already waving him away before disappearing into the kitchen, so he headed for the back porch, where he knew his uncle loved to sit. He remembered the times he'd sat there with him, the hard landscape spread around the house, his uncle's voice breaking the all-encompassing silence with the stories he used to teach the ancient wisdom of their people.

He found those stories amusing, thrilling even. Uncle Charlie knew how to tell a tale, his voice changing with the plot, his pauses always significant. And he sure knew when to stop the storytelling for the day. Jeff smiled, remembering how he would rush through his chores just to go sit on the back porch and hear a new installment of his favorite hero's adventures.

He pushed the door open. His uncle sat in his old recliner, exactly as he used to do back then, his head resting on the wood, eyes closed, his voice flowing softly in his mother tongue.

Jeff's eyes wandered about, looking for his audience. And just as he had done when he was a boy, someone had moved the other chairs to expose the wooden floorboards where he used to sit or lie back on. Someone lay now just like he did those days, but the body resting on his uncle's porch was that of an adult, and a white adult at that.

Jeff did a double take before believing his eyes. He knew it was Daniel lying there, but he found it hard to process that knowledge. What was the doctor doing in his family's house, and why on earth was his uncle speaking to him in a language he couldn't possibly understand? He felt rage building inside him. The damn white guy was creeping into his life like a sneaky lizard, treading on the most cherished of his private realms.

His uncle was looking at him now, concern all over his wrinkled face. Jeff only glared at him before slamming the door and stomping back out through the house. He didn't even stop when his aunt called after him; he just couldn't wait to descend the hill and jump into his pickup, as if all of hell was on his heels. And sure it was, but not exactly on his heels. His mind was swirling like the trail of dust clouds he was leaving behind.

How could Uncle Charlie? Him, of all people? Jeff couldn't help replaying the images in his head: Daniel on the pine wood floor, his tawny hair on a cushion, a cloth covering his eyes the same way it had covered Jeff's on the occasions his uncle chose to train him in the most secret ways of healing. He was not to become what his aunt called a singer—it was not in him—but still, he had felt special when his uncle trusted him with small doses of that precious knowledge. It was never a given thing; he had earned that trust day after long day of struggling to become someone his blood would never be ashamed of. And now his uncle had decided to break that trust and defile the secret teachings of their people? Did he truly believe that saying them in a language that wouldn't be understood spared him from any responsibility? Didn't he remember the power was in the words themselves more than in the meaning they conveyed?

Jeff tried hard to recollect what his uncle had been saying to Daniel. He had been so busy restraining his anger that the words had flown in and out of him like empty noises. Something about corn bread maybe. He couldn't quite remember. It might have been just that, harmless talk about one tradition or another. But why not use English then? If it was safe to speak about it, why not let Daniel understand? Unless of course Daniel *did* understand.

Jeff laughed aloud. He slowly released the tight grip on the steering wheel. He was overreacting, and it was easy to see why. Same reason that took him up the hill in the first place.

He knew his uncle well, knew what he wouldn't stand for. Once again, this wasn't about Uncle Charlie. It was about jealousy.

The moment he thought it, Jeff had to step on the brake hard. He was dumbfounded. He understood now that all his anger wasn't about wanting to keep his shameful attraction to Daniel hidden and so resenting every intrusion that hampered him in the grim task of fighting his feelings away. No, it was far simpler than that: shame or not, he just couldn't put up with sharing what he wanted only for himself.

Chapter 5

DANIEL wasn't much into running that morning. His head still pulsed with every step he took, but he could feel he was already on the way down from the big roller coaster that was his migraine.

"You sure you're all right? You don't look so good."

He didn't turn to look at Sean. The less the man saw of his face, the better. He knew he was pale as a ghost, big, dark circles under his bloodshot eyes. But he hated talking about his problem. That people knew he had them made him sicker than the migraine itself.

"Yeah, I'm fine. It's just a headache."

They ran in silence for a while. He liked it, running with Sean in the early light. The big, blond sheriff was a fellow exile, and they had hit it off from the beginning. Not that Sean was difficult to get along with anyway, being straight-talking and humorous, but the fact that they could relate to each other's situation was what drew them to share more than they usually would have with someone they'd just met. So they got together as often as they could, given the nature of both their jobs, and they talked as if they had just been rescued from isolation cells. Laughed a lot, too, something Daniel really needed after Estela.

"You have migraines, don't you?"

Daniel stopped cold in his tracks. He couldn't believe his ears. How on earth had Sean found that out?

"Oh, come on, don't make such a surprised face," Sean said, retracing his steps to where Daniel was standing in awe. "I'm a cop, remember?" he added with a wink and a smile.

But Daniel couldn't smile back. He was panicking. His heart raced in his chest, the pain behind his eyes banging in his skull like a hammer, cold sweat trickling down his sides, fear making him sick like nothing else could, not even a migraine.

"Daniel, what…." Sean moved toward him, concern plain on his face. Daniel put out a hand, retreating a little. He couldn't bear the thought of Sean seeing him like this, getting closer to him, having to look into his eyes and see what was in them right now. Shame rose inside him like bile, and he had to turn to the nearest tree for support. Dizziness swept over him and he threw up, holding onto the rugged trunk for dear life.

He thought he heard Sean say something, but he just couldn't make the words out. His vision blurred and he shut his eyes to stop everything. He would have stopped breathing if he could.

"…deeply."

Deeply? What…? His eyes went wide. The tree wasn't there anymore, but Sean was. Not that he could see him, but he definitely felt his strong arms around him, pressing his body against that big wall of muscle that was his chest. He felt fear rushing once again through his veins.

"Breathe deeply now, Daniel."

The voice resonated inside him and he couldn't help reacting to its commanding tone. He inhaled deeply, fear receding with the rush of oxygen. "That's right, keep breathing."

Daniel felt the hands shift on his body and his legs giving way under him. But he never hit the ground. He was gently deposited on it, his head lifted to rest on a tracksuit-covered thigh. He opened his eyes to find Sean looking down at him.

"Better now?"

He desperately searched those blue eyes for any trace of disgust and found nothing but concern and affection there. He blinked. Yeah, it was definitely affection he was seeing, but how? Why? He struggled to find his voice. "I'm sorry, Sean," he stammered hoarsely, his throat rasping like sandpaper.

"Don't be silly. It's not your fault."

Daniel had to smile at that. Raúl always said the same, but he did it in a mock-analyst voice that had both of them instantly laughing. Yet Sean had said it in a serious way, like he meant it. Not that Raúl didn't mean it, but they knew each other too well not to be embarrassed by that kind of self-help talk.

"Did I say something funny?"

He gauged Sean's expression. He wasn't angry, just curious. "No, sorry, you were very... kind."

Sean snorted. "Don't go all polite on me now, doc."

"Well, you sure took kindly to my puking session before."

"Oh, I was a safe distance away; it's that pine over there who's mad at you."

Daniel laughed out loud and his head throbbed in response. He lifted his hand to his temple, but Sean stopped it midway.

"Let me try something," he said, and before Daniel could react, he put his hands over Daniel's eyes, thumbs pressing on the sore spot between his brows and nose. Daniel gasped as Sean's other fingers spread over his skull, the pressure surprisingly comforting on his aching brain.

"Feels good?"

"Hmm."

Sean chuckled. "Sounds like a yes to me."

As the hands moved to massage his scalp, Daniel almost let out a moan. It was amazing how such big hands could be so gentle.

"Tell me, when did you start having migraines?"

No. Not now, not that. He shut his eyes tightly, trying to make the question go away.

"Daniel?"

The hands on his head stopped. He didn't want them to, didn't want to lose that soothing touch. He tried to say something. "Wednesday."

"That's not what I meant." But the hands started moving anyway, so Daniel kept quiet. It was a while before Sean spoke again.

"So you've been in this kind of pain for three days now." There was no question to it; he was just stating a fact. "Wonder how you people manage to go on with your daily lives."

Daniel opened his eyes. "What do you mean 'you people'?"

"My sister has migraines, too, and, apart from the hours she spent hidden in the dark, she was always there helping my parents cope with all us five boys, headache or not. She's just like you, all fragile-looking but tougher than steel."

Daniel smiled to hide his confusion. He felt relieved, almost giddy at the pride he heard in Sean's voice. He tried to joke his way out of the subject. "Hey! Who are you calling fragile? You wanna try some of my hidden jujitsu moves?"

Sean smirked. "Yeah? And where do you hide them in that skinny pile of bones?"

Daniel punched Sean's stomach feebly. "I'm not skinny, you caveman."

"Ouch! You think I'll go easy on you because you have a headache?" Sean said, looming menacingly over Daniel. "Think better, you skinny elf."

Daniel lifted a placating hand to him."You mean elf as in leprechaun-related?"

Sean let his infectious laughter echo in the trees about them. "No. You have the kind of eyes I fancy Tolkien's elves would have," he paused, staring at Daniel, "and you're a looker too."

Daniel blushed intensely, to Sean's amusement.

"Though I doubt the fair ones would ever go red like that, wouldn't suit their complexion."

Daniel punched him again, stronger this time. "And since when do cops like fantasy movies?"

"Movies?" Sean looked offended. "Oh, of course, Mr. Pediatrics-Emergency Room-Doctor-in-Chief here thinks it impossible for a mere cop to even know there's a book, much less have read it."

"I didn't—"

"Yes, you did," Sean said, pressing an accusing finger to Daniel's forehead, "and you were wrong. I've read the *Lord of the Rings* at least four times, the whole three books."

"I just—"

Sean's hand covered Daniel's mouth. "And for your information, I didn't even like the movies."

Daniel smiled under Sean's fingers.

"That tickles, you know."

Daniel arched an eyebrow at him.

"Okay, I'll let you speak, but only if you're gonna behave."

Daniel nodded, the sudden movement bringing the pain alive.

"Still hurts, doesn't it?"

Daniel didn't answer, didn't need to by the look on Sean's face.

"We better head home then," Sean said, putting his hands under Daniel's shoulders and lifting him little by little. He got up easily, one hand still holding Daniel in place while he offered the other to him. When Daniel took it, he pulled him to his feet with no apparent effort. "Dizzy?" he asked.

"No. Thank you, Sean." And he really felt grateful to him. He couldn't help reacting as he did to others knowing about his migraine; that reaction was deeply carved into him, imprinted almost, yet lately people had been offering unexpected responses to it.

First it was the reservation shaman and his wife, both noticing right away and fussing about him till he was comfortingly resting with a wet cloth over his eyes, the old man saying things he didn't understand as if he already knew the sound of human voices soothed Daniel more than anything else.

And now Sean. Guessing what was wrong with him, trying to make it better without once showing the kind of look Estela always gave him, that mixture of disappointment and exasperation he'd seen so many times, and not only in her eyes.

"Let's go now," Sean was saying.

"You don't have to see me home, I'm all right."

"I'm not seeing you home. You're coming to *my* home with me."

"Sean, I have to be back."

"No, you don't. It's Saturday. You should take the day off."

"You know Saturdays are busy around here."

"Yeah, but not before midnight. You need some rest now."

Daniel sighed. "I'll be fine. I'm used to it, Sean."

"You may be, but I'm not, so I'm gonna make sure you really *are* fine." As Daniel was about to repeat himself, Sean added, "And I won't take a no for an answer, Legolas."

Daniel had to smile at that. "All right, you win," he paused, measuring him. "Strider."

Sean laughed. "Strider, huh? Well, can't say I dislike it. Far better than what they sure are calling me behind my back these days."

As they made their way to town, Sean's arms around his shoulders, Daniel felt at ease for the first time in a long while.

Chapter 6

JEFF entered the sheriff's office, wondering about the whole irony of his presence there. Old Sheriff Barclay had always liked to keep him as far from that door as he could. Not that Jeff had minded. He never got much out of their snarling standoffs. And now this new sheriff wanted to talk to him as often as possible. Damn him. The guy was into meetings and briefings and a whole bunch of interagency cooperation.

Jeff thought it was a sign of the typical beginner's naïveté: all rookies wanted to go by the book till they banged their heads against one or two nasty realities. Yet now, he wasn't so sure that was the case with Sean McCallum. He seemed quite experienced and was catching up fast with the complicated network of bureaucracies swarming the territory.

As Jeff moved along the desks, he again noticed the shift in attitudes around him. The sheriff's old guard had gone into retirement now, and the young deputies had no problem in following McCallum's lead, so they all nodded or greeted him. Yeah, he could do without the glares, though he wasn't so sure political correctness on its own would make any difference.

The door to the meeting room was half-open and laughter poured out of it. One was the deep roaring laughter of the Irishman and the other he would have recognized anywhere. Shit. Seeing Daniel was the last thing Jeff wanted right now. He had been avoiding the doctor as much as he could and still wasn't ready to face him with a cool head.

The door opened suddenly and McCallum stepped out of it, still smiling at whatever joke they'd been laughing at. He visibly jumped when his eyes met Jeff's.

"God! You shouldn't appear out of nowhere like that, man."

"Sorry, was about to knock when you came out."

"Well, come on in now. I'll bring some coffee."

And just like that he left him to deal with Daniel on his own. Jeff almost cursed aloud.

"Oh, hi, Jeff."

Daniel's eyes actually lit up at seeing him. That caught him off balance, so Jeff quickly schooled his features and nodded a bland "hey." He could see Daniel's expression harden in response. Crap. He probably thought he was a jerk. And no doubt Jeff was acting like one.

"Here you go." Sheriff McCallum handed him a cup of black coffee. Yeah, he had remembered from previous times. The guy was good with details, had to give him that.

"Milk and sugar for our little baby here," McCallum said, offering Daniel a mug with what surely looked like milk to Jeff.

Daniel rolled his eyes. "Don't go all tough on me or I'll tell your deputies that you learned all you know from P. D. James."

"So go tell them. Those kids won't even know who she is. Only writer they've heard of is Stephen King."

"It would be rather scary if you'd learned anything from that one, though."

"Yeah, plumb scary."

Jeff looked from one man to the other. They seemed at ease, like old friends or even brothers would. He wondered with a pang of envy when these two had gotten so close.

"Come on, Jeff, don't just stand there. Sit down."

He did, on a chair across the table from Daniel. Jeff could feel his eyes on him. Small wonder Aunt Helena had called them pond eyes; they had that dark shade of green that still waters have, light bringing odd reflections every time Daniel moved. Jeff just wished he could drink from those bottomless ponds. Oh God.

"Now, let's see if we can get this going," McCallum said.

Jeff was grateful for the chance to keep his mind busy. Yet Daniel was too close for his comfort. He couldn't help following his hands as he spoke, those slender fingers tracing spells in the air between them, his voice incredible sexy in its rich, foreign nuances. He found himself staring at Daniel's throat, wanting to touch, to lick, to bite the delicate skin there. The sparse hair on his forearms was turning to blond. He wondered if Daniel was like his people, body mostly hairless, as the small glimpse of chest he got from his open shirtfront suggested.

Jeff shifted in his seat, trying to focus his attention on the work at hand and finding it rather difficult. Every time he actually succeeded in focusing his thoughts, he found the other two were good at what they did, minds alert and fast, quick with words, even managing to joke without losing the thread of their arguments. And every time he thought that, Jeff couldn't help getting defensive. And sure enough, right then, McCallum would pace the room as he spoke and casually rest a hand on Daniel's shoulder, or touch his arm, or shove him playfully when the smaller man made fun of him. It was driving Jeff crazy, all that good-natured petting. The difference in size between the two men made it worse, because no matter how well he knew it to be the typical, innocuous, male bonding, still he found the interaction between them arousing, couldn't help imagining those big hands on Daniel's naked skin, caressing, stroking, easily handling that lithe body to pull him into his arms and squeeze him breathless.

Then McCallum would ask him something, and Jeff's mind would be forced to land abruptly till he found Daniel listening to him, looking at him with those amazing eyes, and the whole cycle would start again like a hellish roundabout.

So when they finally went through the last report of the day, Jeff was so worked up he couldn't wait to be out of the room, the sheriff's office, and as far from the damn town as he could get. He barely waited for the others to gather all the papers still on the table. He tried to sound casual in his good-byes and marched out of there, for once glad he always wore loose pants.

Chapter 7

JEFF was still sitting in the uncomfortable plastic chair when his cell rang.

"Jeff, it's Sean. I got your message." Jeff could tell by the background noise that Sean hadn't wasted any time getting into his car as soon as he'd learned that Daniel was in St. Dennis. The sheriff's voice was clipped when he spoke to him. "What happened?"

"I found him lying on the floor," Jeff answered.

"*What?*"

"Don't worry, he's fine now."

"But what…?"

"He seems to have these awful headaches that—"

"Yeah, I know."

"You know?"

"'Course I do. For Christ's sake, Jeff, can you begin to tell me what happened?"

Jeff fought the urge to shout back at him. Sean was worried, he understood. "He'd been having a big crisis for some days and neglecting to drink and eat properly, so he just collapsed. Doctor said he's all right now, but I'm not yet allowed to go in, so I can't—"

"I'll see you when I get there."

Jeff was left staring at the phone. That man sure got on his nerves. And what did he mean he *knew* about Daniel's migraines? *'Course I know*, the cocky bastard had said. True, they spent a lot of time together, Daniel and Sean, but still. He shook his head. Who did he think he was fooling? Daniel was about to go back to his country, and Jeff had barely managed to stop avoiding him. Damn. Jeff was more familiar with the sheriff now than with Daniel, knew more about McCallum's life, was even on a first-name basis with him now.

"Mr. Redbear?"

He looked up.

"You can see Dr. Ugarte now."

He thanked the nurse and entered the room carefully, not wanting to wake Daniel if he was asleep.

He walked to the bedside. Daniel's eyes were closed, so Jeff just stood there, his hand reaching out on its own to touch that pale skin. He looked spent, almost transparent, all energy drawn out of him till he resembled one of those marble angels guarding children's graves.

Jeff's stomach clenched. He could still remember the shocking waves of emotion that had swept over him when he found Daniel lying motionless on the floor of the makeshift clinic. The thought that he might be dead had short-circuited Jeff's brain till he just couldn't think anymore, till all he could do was feel the nauseating taste of fear enveloping him. He had never panicked like that before. He was always quick to react—the more pressing the need, the calmer he became, his mind ruling out emotions so that he could concentrate on the problem at hand—but his emotions had been too strong to put them aside this time, and he couldn't stop wondering at what it all meant: the paralyzing fear first, and then when he could finally muster the resolve to kneel beside Daniel, the overpowering relief at that tiny pulse he felt under his fingers.

All the way to the emergency room he had barely managed to keep his eyes on the road, checking on Daniel every other second, watching that vein under his jaw till he didn't even need to touch it to feel it throb. The waiting afterward hadn't been any better, his mind going over every possible explanation till he thought he was going to be sick with worry. When the doctor told him it was mostly dehydration that had made Daniel faint, Jeff could only slump back on that awful plastic chair and keep air going in and out of him.

He looked into Daniel's sleeping face, searching for an answer. How could this pale foreigner get to him like that?

The soft knock on the door almost made him jump. Sean came to stand beside him, worried eyes taking in every minute detail of Daniel's form, lying there on the bed. Those inquisitive blue orbs searched Jeff's face then, asking the question before his mouth did.

"How is he?"

Daniel moved slightly, lips parting in a pained sound. Jeff motioned Sean to follow him out into the hallway.

"Doctor said he was just dehydrated, so there's no need for him to stay the night."

Sean sighed with relief.

"The analgesic they shot him is pretty strong, though. He said to keep an eye on him, 'cause if he gets so dizzy he throws up, it would trigger all hell back."

Sean nodded. "No problem, I'll take him home with me."

Jeff hesitated for just one second. "I think my place would be better; you might get a night call and have to leave him there."

"It's all right. I'll send a deputy if there's trouble."

"But—"

"No, really, there's no need for you to go out of your way to—"

Jeff inhaled deeply. "I know there's no need. I just want to do it, that's all."

Sean looked at him, disbelief all over his face. "You just want to? Come on, Jeff, we're talking about Daniel here, that white guy whose guts you seem quite intent on hating?"

"I don't hate him."

"Oh, no, you just love him so deeply you can't bear to look at him lest you burn into a pile of fuming ashes."

For a moment, Jeff just glared at the big sheriff, subdued hospital noises distinctly heard in the sudden silence stretching between them. Sean started to glare back when his eyes went wide, realization dawning on him.

"You...."

Jeff felt heat rising in his cheeks, so he turned to avoid Sean's eyes. "We better wake Daniel and get him out of here."

"Yeah, we better."

And Jeff sure didn't need to turn to know there was a smirk on Sean's mouth. God, how he hated that smart-ass cop.

As HE followed Jeff's pickup, Sean could feel a smile creeping into the corners of his mouth. That had been quite amusing, the flush turning olive skin into something not so much red as dark-yellow.

He should have known. The way Jeff was behaving was too far out of line to spring from a general mistrust of white men.

He turned to look at Daniel. His eyes were closed, but Sean wasn't sure if he was sleeping or just hiding his embarrassment. His breath didn't have that soft rhythm to it, so, embarrassed, he guessed. And small wonder, knowing him.

He had been so dizzy they'd had to help him get dressed, Sean hauling his naked body from the bed and holding him in place for Jeff to put his clothes on. They had worked remarkably well together, never once getting in each other's way, never once needing words to know what they had to do next. And Daniel had been shuddering in his arms, eyes tightly closed, his skin so cold Sean feared his hands would be branded into it like hot iron. Seeing him so vulnerable made Sean ache all over, and it took all his willpower not to pull him to his chest and squeeze some warmth into him. Jeff wasn't making it any better, the way he donned each piece of clothing as if it was part of some ritual, silently worshipping every inch of Daniel's body he happened to touch. So Sean didn't even wait for shoes, he simply scooped Daniel up into his arms and walked out of there, drawing stunned looks all the way to the parking lot.

Daniel had called out his name in protest, struggling faintly to be let down till a new wave of dizziness struck and had him leaning heavily into Sean. And the way *that* made him feel, the sudden pressure against his chest, Daniel going limp in his arms, surrendering to his embrace…. It had almost made him growl.

Jeff's truck came to a stop. Sean took in the one-story house, the porch, the curtained windows. It had an old look to it but seemed well-kept, almost lovingly so. Jeff opened the door on Daniel's side and crouched there, waiting. Daniel opened his eyes, looking around.

"Where are we?" Daniel asked, his voice so low it was almost a whisper.

"My place." Jeff was not quite smiling, but his face had an openness to it Sean had never seen before, not with Daniel about, anyway. "Can you walk to the porch or shall we ask the big guy for a hand?"

Daniel almost jumped out of his seat before realizing he was barefoot.

"Not so fast, stranger," Sean said chuckling. "No need to walk on stones for us." He eased his way out of the car and went around it to Daniel's door.

"Bring him in, Sheriff."

Now Jeff *was* smiling, the bastard. Daniel cursed in Spanish as Sean bent to pick him up.

"Stop grunting and hold on to me, Doc." Daniel cursed louder this time but flung his arms around his neck all the same. "Good boy," Sean said as he carried him through the door Jeff held open, only to receive a smack to the back of his head. "Getting better already? That's good. We might not have to undress you after all," Sean drawled.

Daniel made a strangled sound.

"Be careful, Sean," Jeff said, opening the door to a small, cozy bedroom, "I hear Spaniards are vengeful people."

"Are they now?" Sean eased Daniel's feet onto the floor. One moment he looked ready to punch the lights out of him, the next his legs wobbled and he reached out to Sean for support. Those hands felt so good on him, Sean's voice came out hoarse.

"Don't worry, I got you now, Doc."

Jeff rummaged in a chest of drawers and came back to them, flannel pajamas in hand.

"I can put those on, you don't have to...." Daniel's eyes went from him to Jeff, pleading. The whole situation would have been comical if Sean didn't feel the unease in Daniel's voice.

Jeff must have felt it, too, for he went all serious as he spoke. "Daniel, please, don't be ashamed. You're still gonna be dizzy for some hours, and we cannot risk you getting another migraine." Sean could feel Daniel tense in his grip. "You have to understand, helping you is not a nuisance we put up with, but something we want to do, willingly." They kept silent for a moment, Jeff's words sinking in.

"You *want* to undress me?"

They burst into laughter, the three of them, laughing so hard their sides hurt.

"I'm afraid we do."

"Willingly."

"God, you make me sick," Daniel muttered.

From then on, whatever they said or did only made them laugh harder, so that when they finally managed to put Daniel to bed, they felt so weak they had to lean into each other for support.

They left the room like a pair of drunks, arms around shoulders, staggering all the way with silly smiles upon their faces. Sean ran a hand absently along Jeff's back and felt the shorter man shudder. Their eyes locked, faces suddenly serious, almost dangerously so.

Jeff shifted his body to face him, his arm leaving his shoulder. Sean caught his wrist in midair, never once taking his eyes from Jeff's. They were pitch black now, those eyes. He could feel the strong pulse throbbing under his fingers but couldn't let go, feeling an urge to press harder, to leave marks on that dark skin. Jeff licked his lips, and that was all it took. Sean pounced on him like a hungry lion.

He forced his way into Jeff's mouth, and teeth surged back at him, scratching his lower lip. Jeff's hips rolled against his, pressing their groins together. Sean moaned into the kiss, feeling Jeff buck in response. He ran his hands down to cup Jeff's ass and squeezed hard, lifting him off the floor. Jeff's muffled cry resonated down his spine, his cock bulging against the zipper. God, the man was pure sex, tight body wriggling, rocking, grinding into him as their tongues battled furiously, all the while making strangled noises that were driving him crazy.

Sean should have been surprised at the bruising rawness of their want, but he had stopped thinking the moment his eyes met those dilated pupils. He was starved and so was Jeff. They couldn't be gentle right now, badly needing the sting, the friction, the hurting roughness. Sean hadn't even let go of Jeff's wrist, and Jeff didn't seem to mind, the fingers of his free hand tearing at Sean's shirt, craving naked flesh.

Sean's knees gave way and they fell to the floor with a heavy thud, Jeff on top of him. He rolled to pin him down with his weight and felt the lighter man arch to meet his need with his own luscious desire. He was so lithe, so pliant it made Sean want to bend Jeff forcibly, try out his limits. Sean grabbed a handful of thick black hair and pulled Jeff's head in to nibble at his already swollen lips. Jeff held his ground, hands fumbling with Sean's belt, managing to unbuckle it and unzip his pants without stopping the suction on Sean's tongue. His cock flapped against Jeff's thigh, the tip wet with pre-come.

Sean let go of Jeff's hand to undo his jeans, pulling them and Jeff's underwear harshly down, scraping dark skin all the way to his ankles. Jeff hissed, his cock bobbing in sudden freedom. Sean yanked at one worn-down cowboy boot and then the other. He got rid of Jeff's pants and rolled his T-shirt out of the way in one swift motion. Jeff tore at it till he shook it off, till he was stark naked under Sean's gaze, all that hot olive skin stretched out for him, hungry for his touch. He took just one moment to unbutton his shirt and throw it away, Jeff's hand immediately running up and down his taut belly, petting, teasing, his legs spreading under him, wanton and needy, almost begging for him.

Sean didn't even remove his pants; Jeff's fingers were cupping his ass and pulling him down. He groaned when their bodies clashed, heat radiating from them in scorching waves, his nostrils flaring at the acrid smell of their arousal. He didn't think it would take much longer, the way their hips bucked in a frantic rhythm. He took a brown nipple in his mouth and sucked hard. Jeff bit his own lips to keep his cry from coming out, digging his fingers into Sean's hips, bruising and unrelenting, urging him for more. Sean ground faster into him, harder, gasping at the way Jeff's hips lifted to meet the pressure. He felt his climax approaching and reached down to take Jeff's head and bring those parted lips to his, groaning into that sexy mouth as wetness splashed all over their bellies and chests, Jeff bucking madly just one beat after him, teeth sinking into his flesh and actually drawing blood into the kiss.

They stayed like that for a while, bodies shuddering, mouths tasting, licking, muffling moans and whimpers. Then Sean rolled over and sprawled on the floor by Jeff's side. They kept silent, hearts slowing down little by little.

"Didn't know you were gay."

Sean chuckled at the hoarseness in Jeff's voice. Didn't think his would sound any different, though. "Too butch for the part?"

"No, too Irish Catholic."

"Guess I'll burn in hell for this," Sean paused, "but man, was it worth it."

It was Jeff's turn to chuckle. "Yes, it was. Though I'd have never expected it to get so…."

"Wild?"

"Rough."

"Yeah, guess we'd been dying to tear at each other's throats for some time now."

They laughed quietly.

"That and too much pent-up frustration."

Sean turned to look at him. "You mean over Daniel?"

"Yeah, and I'm sure he doesn't even have a clue."

"You bet he doesn't. He'd be a few thousand miles away by now if he had."

"Will be that far pretty soon anyway."

"I know."

They lay in silence for a moment before Jeff spoke. "What are we gonna do?"

"Beats me."

"Have to do something."

"Yeah. We'll think of some solution. We're good at that."

"Are we?"

Sean looked into those black eyes staring mockingly at him and smiled. "Who could bring down a plan concocted by a treacherous Apache and a twisted Irishman?"

"A straight Spaniard?"

Sean laughed. "Yeah, maybe."

"Guess we'll have to do with maybe."

"Guess we will."

Chapter 8

JEFF felt Sean's eyes on him as he donned a fresh T-shirt. Amazing how such cold blue eyes would let out that kind of heat. "Sorry, I haven't got any clothes your size."

"It's okay, look better in uniform, even rumpled as it is."

Sean did look good in that uniform. Made him appear wholesome, powerful. "Look better *without* the uniform."

Sean laughed that rich, infectious laughter of his. "Never thought I'd hear you say something like that."

Never thought so himself, but then again, even Jeff's most twisted fantasies came short of the reality they'd put themselves into, pouncing at each other, biting and tearing like animals, never minding hurt, craving it, the sharp, painful sting of pleasure.

"Must be some case of double personality."

Sean arched his brows. "Double personality, my ass. You were showing so many faces I was starting to believe those tales about shape shifters your people tell."

Jeff let out an incredulous laugh. "Shape shifters? You never cease to amaze me. Where did you get that one from?"

The big man glared at him. There was no humor left to his expression. "I amaze you because you dismissed me as white trash the moment you saw me, just like you did with Daniel. Except that with

Daniel, you even felt the need to rub it in his face, your opinion of him."

Jeff tried to say something but found he couldn't, really. Sean was hitting too close to home, or at least to what his guilt told him was the truth.

Sean's glare softened somewhat. "Guess it made you mad, the way you fell for a white guy."

Jeff sighed. "You don't get it, Sean. The problem is not that I dismissed you or Daniel. Problem is I didn't. Couldn't."

Sean looked at him for a second. "Sure, I get it. I'm gay and I'm a cop. I know everything about acting defensive."

It somehow eased Jeff, knowing that Sean understood, and the words were out of his mouth before he could even think. "You're smart."

Sean looked dumbfounded. "Whoa! Was that praise I just heard from those lips?"

Jeff felt the flush coloring his face with the urge to hide away, but Sean closed the space between them and reached out a hand.

"Praises sound good on those sexy lips," he said, running a finger over them.

"Hmm. Guess you mean those *sore* lips."

Sean laughed as he pulled Jeff to him. A large hand stroked his back leisurely as Sean nuzzled his neck. "You smell great. Edible."

That deep voice vibrated along Jeff's spine, making him shudder. Sean tensed, muscles rippling, wrapping him, squeezing, hurting. He felt that harsh need building again in his belly and thrust forward, hands grabbing Sean's hair and pulling his head down for their mouths to feed on each other. Didn't know what it was about Sean that made him so aggressive. Could be his size, making him feel he had to fight him for survival, could be the way Sean reacted to him, hard and demanding, as if he knew he could take it, want it.

Sean cupped his ass and pressed their bodies together. They both moaned into the kiss and it made them laugh, the sound throaty and comical enough for them to let go and look at each other.

Jeff studied Sean's face, the blue-gray eyes searching his in wonder. Yeah, it was amazing, the way he could feel the attraction deep in his bones, the way he knew Sean felt it too.

Sean kneaded his ass, hips rolling to provide friction. Jeff hissed, his smile going feral. And just then, when his cock was starting to fill against Sean's thigh, there was a distant, muffled yell and a thud.

They froze, bodies still pressed together. And suddenly it hit them, the reason they were alone together in the first place. They raced to Daniel's room, finding the bed in complete disarray, pillow crumpled against the headboard, sheets spilling over one side to pool on the floor where Daniel lay in fetal position, grabbing handfuls of cloth in his fists, shivering violently on the wooden planks.

Jeff's stomach clenched. He needed to see Daniel's face to know what was happening to him. He came closer, hands reaching out to touch him, when Daniel flinched visibly. It hurt, that small gesture. And it hurt the most because Jeff knew it wasn't personally directed at him. It was the sort of blind rejection he'd seen again and again over his years as a social worker. It was the universal language of abuse, one shared equally by men and beasts. But Daniel simply didn't fit into his previous experience—was in fact *against* his previous experience.

Sean put a hand on his shoulder, pulling him back from his thoughts. "I need you here now, Jeff."

He nodded. Sean was right. Questions could wait; their priority was getting Daniel to trust them, to let them help. They needed to make him understand he was safe, out of harm's way.

Sean sat beside Daniel on the floor, his back to the wall, and lifted Daniel bodily to sit between his legs. Daniel held on to the sheets, desperately trying to resist Sean's pull. He growled something in Spanish, his body shaking, wriggling to get free. Sean grabbed his wrists firmly to stop him, but he only made it worse, Daniel going outright mad, kicking, yelling, thrashing, struggling with such desperation that Sean could barely restrain him. Jeff couldn't bear to see him like that, the ache in his heart throbbing like an open wound. He knelt in front of Daniel and grabbed his head with both his hands, forcing him to keep still.

"Look at me, Daniel. It's okay, it's me, Jeff." Daniel's eyes moved fast, clearly not registering anything he saw, hell-bent on getting free, not acknowledging names or faces but threats. "Daniel, stop." Sean pulled his hands to his sides forcibly, and Daniel just growled, struggling to move his arms, his head, in their grip. "We don't want to hurt you, Daniel. Stop." Daniel actually bared teeth at him, all but snarling, and Jeff just couldn't take it anymore, the pain of it all. "*Stop it now!*" he yelled at the top of his lungs, digging his fingers into the skin underneath them.

Daniel's eyes went wide with shock. In the sudden silence that followed, Jeff could hear them panting, sweat dripping from their exhausted bodies. He eased the pressure on Daniel's head, moving one hand to pull light brown hair from his flushed face.

"It's all right, Daniel, it's over now."

Daniel blinked, eyes finally there, knowing, understanding. He tried to look away, but Jeff wouldn't let him.

"Come on, Daniel, it's us, you don't have to worry about anything."

Sean let go of Daniel's wrists, thick arms wrapping around his chest to pull him back gently. Daniel offered no resistance this time. He just leaned into Sean and closed his eyes, head resting on his shoulder.

Jeff looked up into Sean's face. He was frowning at the marks he'd left on Daniel's wrists. It made him look for his own marks, and he found them, clearly visible—red handprints on Daniel's cheeks and jaw. Jeff felt Sean's eyes on his and saw the same question in them that was troubling him. What could have triggered Daniel's reaction, made him jump from the bed, in a fear so deep he couldn't recognize them, just needing to run and hide from whatever it was he'd seen in his head? Was it the drugs they'd given him, or did they just sharpen deep, old feelings, memories of feelings?

"Daniel?" Sean's voice was calm, soft. Jeff nodded to him. He knew it was now they should ask questions, now that Daniel couldn't find the strength to avoid answers, to hide the truth. And he knew it would hurt. "Daniel, what happened? Why were you on the floor?"

He took a moment to answer, his voice a rasping murmur after all the yelling. "Dream."

"You had a nightmare? Is that what you mean?"

Of course Sean knew that's what he meant, but he wanted Daniel to stop being monosyllabic, force him to explain.

"Hmm."

Sean wasn't discouraged by that. He kept on asking. "What was it about, the nightmare?"

Daniel shifted in his arms, visibly uneasy. "About home."

Sean looked up at Jeff, frowning. It wasn't a good start, if it meant what they both thought it meant. "Are you talking about your family home?"

Daniel opened his eyes and tried to pull away, but Sean held him firmly in place. Daniel almost grumbled in frustration. "I'm okay, Sean, let go."

"No."

Daniel inhaled deeply, obviously trying to keep anger under control. "Please let go of me now. I don't like this."

"Neither do we, but you have some explaining to do."

Daniel looked from him to Jeff, fear creeping into his eyes. "Look, I'm sorry about this… this…." He struggled for a word, his usually fluent speech deserting him. Jeff knew the signs: he was panicking. Everybody did, when forced to expose the ulcers of their pasts. Yet there was no other way out of it, and Jeff was well aware they had to be insistent, cruel even, to help him. Daniel seemed to sense it in the way they were looking at him and tried his best to find an explanation that would buy him some time. "I know I must have frightened you and I'm sorry, but I'm fine, I swear I am. I'm just not used to the analgesic they gave me. Dreams seemed too real and I woke up disoriented, didn't know where I was, and then you stormed in and held me down that way… It just felt like… like a threat to me. I'm really sorry, never meant to lash out at you like I did. I'm sorry." His eyes went suddenly wide. "Have I hurt you? Are you both okay? Did I…?"

Jeff stopped him with a raised hand. "You didn't hurt us, but we might have hurt *you*, the way you fought us."

"Left prints all over you, bet you're sore here," Sean said, sliding his hands along Daniel's forearms to touch his abused wrists. The moment his fingers grazed the reddened skin, Daniel shuddered. Sean moved away quickly, an apology starting to form on his lips when something seemed to hit him. Jeff raised his eyebrows questioningly, but Sean just gave him an *I'll show you* look and closed his hands around Daniel's wrists, wrapping them completely in solid flesh handcuffs. He might as well have run electric shocks through him, the way Daniel's body arched, hands clenching into fists, every muscle under his skin painfully tensed, his breath quick and shallow, anxiety widening his eyes until his face was a wild mask of panic.

His own reaction surprised Jeff. He had to fight a powerful instinct to protect Daniel, to take down the man who was harming him. He felt so ready to attack that when Sean finally released his hold on Daniel, he couldn't wait to pull him away from the hurting hands, his own fingers running soothing strokes over Daniel's shoulders and back, his voice mumbling incoherent words of comfort, bodies a safe distance apart, only gentle touches letting him know he was there. It wasn't long before Daniel broke down with a sob.

Jeff gathered him carefully in his arms, almost trembling from the urge to comfort and heal him. Daniel hid his face in his shoulder, heart-wrenching sobs shaking his body. Jeff let the pain flow out, just rocking him gently while he made hushing sounds, the time for words already over.

Daniel's breath was becoming stable now, finally relaxing into his arms. Jeff placed one hand under his chin and lifted his face to look into his eyes. They were darker now, a nighttime ocean of tears looking back at him. He pressed his lips to the white forehead, and Daniel closed his eyes, the tenderness of the gesture seemingly undoing the last trace of resistance left in him. Encouraged by his surrender, Jeff kissed his eyes, tongue briefly tasting the salty flavor of the skin on his cheeks, before kissing his way down to the corners of Daniel's mouth.

He took his time there, bringing his fingers up to caress the fine skin while his lips moved about, small pecks never quite on target till Daniel's breath came out in a ragged sigh. Then his mouth closed over Daniel's in a gentle, chaste kiss.

Daniel's eyes flicked open. He tilted his head to look searchingly at him. Jeff returned the look, breath quickening, hoping with all his might it conveyed the intensity of feeling that flooded his veins. And somehow it must have reached him, because Daniel looked taken aback, pressing a hand to Jeff's chest and pushing lightly to widen the distance between them, as if to gain some perspective. Jeff forced himself to stay still, waiting. He ached for more contact, the warm hand on his chest bringing alive every nerve, all his body itching with anticipation, barely managing to restrain himself. But he had to. He didn't want Daniel to think he was just trying to comfort him, didn't want Daniel to even imagine he'd do anything out of pity.

Suddenly there was something else in his field of vision, and he took reluctant eyes from Daniel to check on it. Sean was now by their side, kneeling on the floor. Jeff blinked. How could he have forgotten Sean so completely? For a moment there had been only Daniel; everything else in the room discarded as a mere distraction from the real focus of all his thoughts. And now Sean was there, too, his solid presence hard to ignore as his blue eyes flickered from Daniel to him. And there was something in those eyes that made Daniel's hand on his chest feel almost unbearably warm, heat spreading from the slender fingers to reach every corner of his self.

Sean held out his hands to touch both Daniel's nape and Jeff's upper arm. Daniel shuddered at the contact. Jeff let his body lean into it, knowing he would need the extra support if the intensity of feeling rose any higher. And it certainly looked as if it would, the way Daniel hummed when Sean's fingers spread to cup the back of his head, the way the hand on his own arm stroked his way up to his shoulder and down his back. It was all Jeff could do not to moan, but he couldn't help himself when Sean loomed over him, hot mouth covering his, tongue breaching to entwine with his own, big hand moving to the small of his back. When Daniel's hand stroked his chest, Jeff actually whimpered.

Jeff's hands found Daniel's waist and pulled him closer. He heard him gasp when their bodies pressed together, Sean leaving Jeff's mouth to nuzzle Daniel's white, delicate throat.

Jeff took Daniel's parted lips between his, letting his tongue explore the inside of that sweet mouth he'd been dying to taste for ages now. The soft noise Daniel made as he responded to his kiss went tingling all the way down his spine, making his cock strain against his jeans. And then Sean was licking both their necks, tongue lapping over their connected jaws and up to the corners of their mouths, wetting their lips any time they barely parted to meet again with Sean's taste all over them, making them lose track of any boundaries between their touching bodies, the sensations traveling through Jeff's nerves so intense, he knew he couldn't stand it for long. Daniel didn't seem to be taking it any better, the way he arched his back, pressing his erection against Jeff's bucking hips, needy noises escaping his throat every time Sean's lips sucked under his jaw, Jeff's tongue buried deep in his mouth. So when Sean ran a hand over his jeans front, palm first, Jeff just lost it, his cry drowned in Daniel's kiss, hips moving out of control till he felt Daniel shuddering with him, against him, Sean's hand never stopping the long strokes till they collapsed against his broad chest.

Sean held his ground, supporting their combined weight with no apparent effort. Jeff didn't remember the last time he'd felt so at ease, lying boneless and carefree in someone else's arms. He was about to close his eyes when the notion hit him.

"Sean, you haven't...."

Sean only smiled sheepishly.

"You have?"

"Damn, you guys looked so hot I never needed to touch myself. Hasn't happened to me since I was a horny teenager."

"Yeah, guess the whole thing was rather—"

"Fucking intense." Daniel cut in, voice so husky and face so serious that Jeff and Sean had only to exchange one look to burst into raving laughter. Daniel's flushed skin went almost purple with embarrassment, making them laugh harder. "Oh, shut up, you hyenas," he said, trying to push his way out of their embrace, only succeeding in bringing them down to the floor with a big thump.

"Shit. I think I need a doctor right now," Sean said, rubbing his sides as if they hurt.

"Yeah, you might have been laughing yourself to death too much lately," Daniel said.

Sean turned to look at him. "You know, you are cute when you get mad."

"Oh, please," Daniel said, trying to lift himself from the floor before Jeff and Sean both pulled him back down between them. "Wipe those smug smiles from your faces, you assholes."

But he was smiling himself as they rolled toward him, arms and legs wrapping around him like ivy.

Chapter 9

DANIEL'S mind was not on the music. His favorite Shostakovich, a one-night-only performance by a great foreign orchestra, and he was barely paying attention. Laura had bought the tickets, she and Raúl always conspiring to force him out, to distract him, but he just couldn't help it, his mind kept going back to the reservation, to those last weeks before he left.

Everything had changed so drastically in those few days, he couldn't stop wondering. As the time to leave drew near, he hadn't wanted to go home. It was a first, in all his years of volunteering. Probably it was because he was always sent to the worst places, being as he was used to dealing with emergencies, but this time the situation had been completely different, in every sense. He had experienced what it was to be a doctor in a small community, knowing every one of his patients, learning their names, their family relations, talking to them calmly, following their cases, sharing a bit of their lives. It had all been incredible.

After the first days of awkward distances, they had flocked to the clinic as if they had decided, as a group, that he could be trusted. Many of the first patients, in fact, only suffered from a bad case of curiosity, but even that had been fun for him.

In his years of practice in big hospitals, patients flowing in and out with no time to catch their names, he had always missed the human touch. He craved the long-run perspective on their cases, wanted to see his own decisions bear fruit over the months; he wanted to actually see that what he did served a purpose. Not that he couldn't see the use in what he usually did. He knew it saved lives, but still he missed the slow transitions. He wanted to see his patients go through illness and leave it behind, wanted to know what they were like when they were healthy, normal people.

So he had started wondering if he could find a way to stay on the reservation for more time. The last weeks he had been considering so many possibilities it had brought about the worst migraine he'd had since his arrival. It lasted more days than usual, and still he couldn't stop going over plans and making decisions, so lost in his thoughts he didn't follow the basic rules: eating something even if his stomach churned, drinking a lot even if it made him feel sick. That time, however, he simply had too much on his mind to be bothered with things his body rejected in the first place. That's how he ended up in a foreign hospital bed. And from then on, everything went down the drain.

Jeff had found him, lying on the floor like a Victorian damsel prone to fainting. And the forever-condescending, derisive Apache had instantly changed gears into full social-worker mode since Daniel was not so much an annoying white man as someone in need of help. And damn if he hadn't needed his help.

The sumatriptan he took for his migraines always made him dizzy and cold to the bone, but different brands had different components, small changes that his body reacted aggressively to, and whatever it was the hospital gave him had aggravated his usual weak state till he was no more than a pathetic, shivering wreck, unable to even dress himself or stand on his own two feet.

To his undying shame, Jeff and Sean had had to dress him and carry him as if he were no more than a baby. But of course, that hadn't been enough, no; the drugs had to give him hallucinations too, bringing a sense of the most hair-raising reality to his usual nightmares.

He had often visited that room in his dreams, but it had never been that detailed, that close, that perfect. It was all there: the stark, pulsing light, his father's collection displayed over the walls with barely any room left for him but that which he dreaded the most, the small bare expanse where that piece of junk stood waiting for him, hands open to receive him and keep him there, as it had kept many others over the centuries.

In the dream he had seen his father, the contempt in his eyes as he looked down on him, as he instructed his brother on the right way to deal with weakness. And then there was only the pain, the fear, and the darkness, so cold and hard against his chest that he'd tried to run away, only to find he was still in darkness when he opened his eyes and someone was holding him painfully down to prevent his escape. It just drove him mad. He hadn't known what he was doing till Jeff cried something out, digging his fingers into his face to keep him still. When he finally realized where he was, what had happened, he'd wished he was dead.

He had closed his eyes, willing himself to disappear, and then Sean started asking questions. And as the questions hit closer and closer to home, Daniel had felt anger rising inside him. They had no right to pry into his most private memories—or at least that was what he had tried to convince himself, anger hiding what he was truly afraid of: the disappointment he couldn't bear to see in their eyes.

They must have seen through him anyway, for Sean found the way to bring all his defenses down in one single motion. He only had to hold his wrists firmly. That was all it took. And he lost it.

He could have yelled forever if Sean hadn't let go of him, if Jeff hadn't almost yanked him from Sean's hands. Maybe at that point there really wasn't anything he could do to make it worse. Anything but crying. Shit. That was the most pathetic thing ever. Of course, he was drugged and sick, hadn't had a decent meal in twelve hours, and had awakened from a nightmare to find himself restrained so, yeah, he had all the excuses in the world. But crying, for Christ's sake, crying. That was beyond shameful.

Sean and Jeff were professional helpers. Their natures couldn't resist the pull of a distressed soul, and he sure had flashed all the warning signs: fainting, crying, even going berserk on them. What were they supposed to do, the social worker and the good cop? They tried to comfort him.

Guys being guys, comfort became sex. *That*, he wasn't ashamed of. Right. He was a little freaked out, to say the least, but not ashamed. He'd always believed men were naturally bisexual, but jumping from theory to practice had been quite the shock. Not at that moment, though; it all went like spontaneous combustion, with no hesitant first tries, no smooth transitions: one minute he was straight and the next he was making out with two guys, just like that. Of course the morning after had been a whole different story. And he still hadn't found the answers to any of the questions that came tumbling down on him.

Alone in Jeff's spare bed, he had felt lost, wondering why it had happened. Was it just because he needed the comfort? Would it happen under other circumstances, with other men? And what about Sean and Jeff? Were they gay? They'd never broached the subject, and Daniel was pretty obtuse when it came to telling where people's attraction lay. He hadn't known what to do next. Should he apologize? Wouldn't it look like he was ashamed? He finally opted not to, just because he thought there was nothing shameful in it but the vulnerability on his part that had prompted Sean and Jeff's response. He convinced himself that there wasn't more to it than that: friends wanting to help. And if he'd had any doubt left, he got his answer soon enough.

They didn't exactly act awkward, but they never once mentioned what had happened. Those days, Daniel had been too busy preparing for his departure to even give it a second thought, but when they finally saw him to the airport, he realized he had only seen them once or twice since then, always concerning reservation matters. Even there, shaking their hands good-bye, they had gone silent, almost avoiding each other's eyes till Sean said, *Please think about coming back, will you?* His tone was so casual that if his eyes hadn't betrayed a little emotion, Daniel would have thought he had dreamt ever kissing those lips that now dismissed him so nonchalantly.

Jeff hadn't said anything, but Daniel could see he was fighting words back. Problem was he couldn't tell whether it was the intensity of feelings or just utter shame stopping him.

When the plane took off, Daniel was surprised to feel disappointed. What was he expecting? He had acted pitifully and received compassion in return. There was nothing more to it.

After some weeks went by without any news from them, Daniel

knew for sure he had been right in his appraisal of the situation. Then he made every effort to discard all his previous projects and decisions. Going back there was no longer a possibility, not one he could afford.

For some time he had put his mind so completely off the subject, he even forgot about the wheels he had set in motion before his migraine episode had ruined everything. So when the letter from the hospital board arrived, he had to read it four times before understanding what it said. It was all in plain Spanish, the board accepting his petition for a sabbatical since they not only considered that his years of excellent work entitled him to it, but also the interest in his research project.

He remembered having made some phone calls, but since he hadn't been contacted about the matter, he thought there was no need to even mention his change of heart. Yet the board probably believed he was trying to be unobtrusive, his lack of interest actually working in his favor. And now he was trapped.

He had met with the board, tried to convince them he wouldn't mind waiting a bit longer, but they seemed to consider his project and the cooperation with the NGO too beneficial for the hospital's reputation to let go of the opportunity. His insistence only made his own reputation as a hard worker grow in their eyes, and so they kept thinking a reward was in order, to tie him to the hospital's future.

So there wasn't really a way out of it now. This concert—the one he wasn't listening to—was, in truth, his last chance at leisure before getting ready for the dreaded journey. Most of the time he was calm enough to believe he could focus on his work there as much as he did here. The doctor in him knew his experience would be put to good use and that he'd be happy about it. But most of the time wasn't all of the time.

He still thought about Sean and Jeff, and even when he didn't, he surprised himself by appraising other men, wondering whether he found them attractive, sexually attractive, and then wondering to what extent it made him different. Could people tell? Did it show on his face? It was driving him crazy, especially when it all came down to assuming that maybe he'd been deluding himself, thinking he hadn't been gay all this time. Of course, then it would be easy to explain why

Estela had left him, no matter how satisfactory their sex life had seemed at the time. Maybe he just wanted to believe it to avoid feeling even more the failure.

He didn't know what to think, didn't know himself anymore, and the utter loss of control was turning his life upside down. The old nightmares were back with a vengeance, and his migraines were so frequent now they didn't seem as much an ailment as a personality trait.

Daniel had to do something before he returned to the reservation. He needed to get his control back, needed to be someone his patients could trust, someone his friends would not be forced to look after. He would only be there for a year; he surely could manage not to shame himself. He always did, was in fact a master at it: getting in and out of people's lives like a professional burglar, never breaking anything, never leaving any traces, walking on tiptoes around them, an aseptic mask on his face, just taking away what they didn't need, what was hurting them even if they didn't know what it was. He could do it one more time. He only had to be careful to not let his guard down and to never let his weakness show.

When he felt Raúl's eyes on him, Daniel turned to look at him, a smile on his face to let him know everything was all right. The reins of his life were back in his hands, and he would not let go of them, not anymore, not ever again.

Chapter 10

HERE he was, back at the airport again, save this time he knew exactly what the doctor they were expecting looked like. And yes, Sean was waiting with him, moving back and forth like one of those big bears behind the bars of a zoo cage.

"Will you stop rocking? You're driving me crazy."

"Sorry, I just can't... I don't...."

Jeff had to smile at his stammering companion. "I know," he said. And he did, he really knew what Sean was feeling, the uncertainty of the last months mixed with a bit of anxiety and large doses of expectation, all of it revolving wildly inside him as if instead of butterflies he had a whole bunch of crows fluttering in his stomach.

It had been difficult, those months after Daniel left. They had only discussed it once, the answer being so obvious: they could not, should not, pressure Daniel to come back. His life, his career, his friends, his family, all that was thousands of miles away. They had no right to even suggest they wanted him there with them. Besides, what would be the point? He might be able to spend a few more months on the reservation and then what? Would they tell him what they felt? Did they even know what it was or how Daniel would react to it? They only had that weird night at Jeff's place to judge from, and the circumstances surrounding it weren't exactly normal, to say the least. Sure, Daniel hadn't rejected them, but maybe he just needed the comfort. And maybe it was just his need that drove theirs, maybe that was all there was to it.

"What's on your mind?"

Jeff turned to look at Sean. His eyes were red, purplish circles drawn under them. It had been a busy night in town and it showed. "Same old what ifs."

"I'm sick of those," Sean muttered.

"Yeah, me, too, but I can't help myself."

Sean's tired eyes studied him for a moment. Jeff liked the way he always paused to consider him, as if he thought what he did not say to be as important as his actual words. "You're not sure anymore we did the right thing?" Sean asked.

"Well, Daniel only warned us he was coming a week ago. That about says it all."

Sean sighed. He looked less imposing in plain clothes, but what he chose to wear revealed more of his body, strong legs hugged by tightly fitting jeans, solid chest stretching a long-sleeved sweatshirt in deference to the cooler winter weather, but his bomber jacket was left in the car, as it was most of the time, since Sean seemed to radiate heat as he walked. Even as he stood there now, Jeff felt his presence in the air around him, almost as if he could see the undulating heat waves coming from his body. It made him want to reach out and touch his burning skin, lay his hands on him to cool him down. Not that he needed an excuse to touch Sean. He had been doing that a lot lately, any time, any place, or rather, all the time, everywhere. It was like an addiction and, much like addicts, they always told themselves it wouldn't happen the next time, and it always did. They focused on the work at hand, but once it was finished, they couldn't wait to lock whatever door there was between them and the rest of the world and go at it like deprived castaways. And it was still violent. No matter how many times their bodies tried to fulfill the need, they never took the edge out of it.

There had been tenderness only that one night, and only because Daniel was between them, channeling their raw hunger into something that was more complex and yet sweeter, the destructive power of nature turned into beautiful electric light. But Jeff was beginning to doubt that miracle would ever happen again.

"You think he'll be angry at us?" Sean asked.

"I almost wished he was."

Sean waited for him to go on, and it made Jeff smile. Sean seemed to be catching more and more native traits as the months went by, and not wanting to interrupt was one he had easily adopted, probably because he was already a good listener.

"What?" Sean finally asked.

"For a moment there, you just acted like a big, white Navajo."

Sean gave him a dubious look. "Is that your polite way of calling me a dumbass?"

Jeff rested a placating hand on his arm. "No, I was trying to praise you, you dumbass."

Sean laughed, vibrations reaching Jeff's fingers, making Jeff even more aware of the contact. Their eyes locked, suddenly serious, and Jeff had to swallow hard. They were so anxious about Daniel that their bodies were even more wired than usual.

"Damn," Sean muttered in a coarse whisper.

Jeff just nodded, his hand slowly tracing the contours of Sean's arm before letting go. "We'd better...."

"Yeah."

They smiled guiltily at each other. There never was an agreement to conceal what was going on between them. They never actually talked about it, but they both acted like it was something they had to wait out, that might well disappear with time. Right now, it was just an itch they had to scratch. Nothing more.

The first passengers were now spilling through the glass doors. They had positioned themselves some distance apart, far enough so as not to be in the way, but not so far they didn't have a good view of the gate. Then again, spotting Daniel was no trouble at all, the way he stood out easily among the plain crowd. As always, it wasn't a question of size—he was, in fact, surrounded by taller and bigger people—but still he drew attention, heads turning at his every step.

There was something different about Daniel this time, though. He seemed sharper, his movements brisker, full of purpose, the expression on his face more focused and determined, concentration giving a hard edge to his beautiful features. His outfit contributed to the military air about him, everything meant to proclaim vacation was over and he was in for the real work.

He wore his hair shorter, in a spiked crew cut that made his eyes stand out even more. Made him look thinner, too, fine bones clearly traced under his now paler skin. Or maybe he *was* thinner, Jeff thought with a pang of anxiety. He checked what he could see of Daniel's body for some evidence, but winter clothes didn't allow much exposure.

Daniel was wearing cargo pants, a woolen turtleneck and hard leather boots, all in strict black, as if he was in some kind of medical special ops, the image completed by a costly looking, metallic gray parka, full of straps and pockets of every size. He looked like a well-trained expert in something secret and dangerous or a movie star ready to shoot on location.

Jeff was glad of the distance. He didn't even dare look at Sean, though he saw movement from the corner of his eye. He must have waved at Daniel, because he had suddenly stopped pushing the cart with his cases to look in their direction. Jeff felt himself trembling for the judgment in those green eyes, knowing his first reaction would be the most meaningful, the most spontaneous.

They stood like that for a moment, just looking at each other, and then Jeff saw the change in Daniel's expression, felt it deep in his chest as Daniel's eyes softened, a smile brightening his face. It didn't matter that Daniel then averted his look to fumble with the cart. Jeff knew what he had seen, knew it was strong enough to wipe away every other thought that interfered with his primal need.

"Guess I'm back," Daniel said in a terse voice as soon as he reached them.

Sean laughed at that. "Guess you are. Took you long enough, though."

Daniel's eyes widened slightly, but before he could say anything, Sean pulled him into a bear hug that made his parka creak loudly. Jeff could see Daniel's body tense at the contact, arms hanging rigid by his sides.

"Missed you," Jeff whispered, his voice so emotion-ridden he barely recognized it as his own. Daniel turned to look at him, Sean's arms loosening their grip just enough to give him room but still clutching possessively at him.

He looked into Daniel's eyes, seeing confusion there. Jeff didn't know if he was surprised at his words, the emotion they conveyed, or the fact that it was him who uttered them. Anyway, it stung, making the desire to prove himself almost unbearable.

His fingers closed on Daniel's arm, pulling lightly. Sean must have felt his urge, for he gave Daniel a gentle shove that sent him right into Jeff's arms. He had somehow managed to slip his hands under the open parka, and Jeff could now feel Daniel's body under his fingers. He moved them along Daniel's sides, almost counting his ribs. He was definitely thinner. That notion brought a tightness to his chest he didn't know how to handle.

"You've lost weight," Jeff finally managed to say.

As Daniel pulled apart from Jeff's embrace, he saw embarrassment in his face. "Maybe, I don't know, been really busy lately."

"A lot of work or a lot of things on your mind?" Sean asked casually.

"Both, I guess." Daniel made a dismissive gesture with his hand. "You know me, the more hectic things become, the more I think them through. Just my luck to be working emergencies."

Sean laughed, but Jeff was sure he hadn't missed the evasive maneuver.

"I hope you brought your pickup, Jeff, 'cause this time I'm not traveling light." More evasion. Daniel looked tired but also nervous, his eyes wandering from Sean to Jeff without lingering.

"No, we came in Sean's heavy horse."

Sean smacked Jeff's shoulder. "He's just envious of my new car," he said to Daniel.

"You call *that* a car?" Jeff scoffed. "Can't begin to imagine what you drove in the city."

"A racing horse, that goes without saying."

They stopped their banter, the look on Daniel's face giving them pause.

"What's wrong, Daniel?"

He quickly averted his eyes. "Nothing, sorry, I was just surprised."

"Surprised?"

"Yeah, when did you two…."

Jeff's heart missed a beat. He knew? Was it that obvious? He searched for something to say and was relieved to hear Sean answer.

"You mean when did this cocky bastard stop looking down his Apache nose at me?"

Daniel smirked. "I meant when did you start getting along."

"Just what I was saying."

Jeff took in a deep breath. So that's what Daniel meant. Of course. When he'd left, Jeff supposed he was still reluctant to give Sean any credit. Four months and a lot of sex had set that to rights. Now he could say he knew the man inside out, and literally too.

"Well, you know, time conquers all. These days I can even order him around. Jeff, stop daydreaming and pick up one of these fancy cases."

Daniel laughed till Sean's last words sank in. "Hey! What do you mean 'fancy'? They're plain, standard cases."

Sean arched an eyebrow at him. "They certainly look standard, if you'd just descended from a space shuttle."

Jeff lifted one of the metallic-looking cases, surprised to find it much lighter than he expected. "Wow, he definitely took the shuttle. I can't feel the gravity pull on this one."

Daniel rolled his eyes. "Of course you don't. It's just fancy plastic, you dummy."

They burst out laughing, happy to see Daniel felt comfortable enough to follow the joke. Jeff wanted to recover the open-hearted, sweet guy he knew Daniel to be, and those first awkward moments had made him doubt anything would ever be the same as it was the past summer.

Sean picked another case and a duffel bag, leaving only a laptop and a briefcase for Daniel to carry. He tried to protest, but Sean strode purposefully away from him. Jeff smiled and blurted out, "Don't worry, we're happy there's so much luggage, it means you're staying for good this time."

Daniel blinked and Jeff hurried to correct his wording. "I mean you're going back and all, but you'll be staying for so long it's almost as if you didn't want to leave here."

It didn't sound much better now. In fact, it sounded worse, by the look on Daniel's face.

"I mean—"

Sean turned his head without even stopping. "You'll have to forgive him. He never quite managed the language of the white man."

Jeff glared at him but was relieved to see Daniel smile.

"He means we love having you here, the longer the better, so we'd be delighted if your luggage was even heavier, 'cause it'd mean you'd be staying for good. With us." Sean had turned to go through the airport exit glass doors, so Jeff couldn't see the look on his face as he said that last bit. Daniel couldn't either, and he seemed disconcerted.

"If it's a question of weight, I can always sit on one of the cases and make it much heavier for you," Daniel offered.

Sean didn't even turn this time. "Nah, it wouldn't make any difference. You're skinny."

"I'm not."

"Yes, you are," Jeff agreed with Sean.

"Says the scrawny Apache."

"I'm not scrawny. I'm… lanky."

"He is not lanky. He sure has long legs on him, but lanky guys are not that pliant. He's strong, too, has good muscle definition. So he's more on the wiry side," Sean said as he put his load in the back of the SUV.

They both looked at him in surprise. Jeff felt a tinge of pride at his words. Not for the image they conveyed of him, he didn't much care about it either way, but because they were spoken from an intimate knowledge of his body, and the casualness in Sean's voice meant he took that knowledge for granted. It was the kind of talk a man used to describe what he owned, and, appallingly enough for Jeff, it felt good being so appraised.

Sean turned around to pick up the rest of the luggage, but the look on both their faces stopped him cold. "What?"

Daniel inhaled deeply. "Well, I guess I'll say this again, and I'm not talking about getting along this time. When did you two…." His hand made an undetermined gesture, but they took his meaning only too well.

Sean looked at Jeff, the question plain in his eyes. Jeff shrugged tersely. They had never considered telling Daniel because they never talked about what they had going. It was not an issue, just a thing they did, like washing the car or putting on clothes every day. It was not conversation material, but Jeff knew hiding it from Daniel would only break the thin line of trust that might still be left between them. Speaking about it, though, would probably give it an importance it completely lacked. There was no way out of it now, so he just hoped he would take it well. The last thing they needed was more awkwardness between them.

"It's your fault, Daniel."

Jeff's eyes widened. He could hear Daniel's sharp intake of breath. Shit! What was Sean thinking?

"You left us to our own devices when we didn't even know how to handle each other, so we just got down to the basics, reckon'd body language was the thing for us since words came out wrong all the time. Wouldn't have happened if you'd been here to translate."

A mischievous grin tugged at the corners of Sean's mouth, making it all sound like a joke, but Jeff knew better. That was a hell of a way to say one truth after the other without really telling *the* truth, the one with a capital T.

Jeff looked admiringly at Sean and was rewarded with a flash of white teeth. The big man had an easy way with people Jeff could only envy. And he surely knew how to smile. It took years off his ruggedly handsome face, making him look the charming frat boy all over again. Daniel wasn't smiling, though, and Sean went all serious, too, exchanging a quick, panicked look with Jeff.

"Is this gonna be a problem for you?"

Daniel held his gaze for a long moment before replying. "You mean do I have a problem with interethnic, cross-border, interagency, cop-civilian, mismatched, same-sex couples?" He paused. "Don't think I have. It being my fault and all."

Jeff felt a fierce urge to hug Daniel, but it was Sean who acted on his feelings, big arms wrapping the lithe body and squeezing tight. The vision put his senses in overload, his whole self aching to join in, to share the deep wave of affection that threatened to burn out of control and turn into something else. Then Sean shifted, one arm still holding Daniel tight while the other pulled Jeff close.

God. Jeff didn't remember ever catching someone's scent the way he was doing now, as if trying to memorize every nuance so he never lost track of his mate's whereabouts. And of course he couldn't possibly remember any other time when his mate's scent had been a blend of the distinctive smells of two male bodies.

"Who are you calling mismatched?"

Jeff's eyes shot wide open. Daniel stepped back a little to look up at Sean.

"Now don't give me that innocent look. You said we made a mismatched couple, you know you did."

Daniel chuckled. "So you finally got to that. A little slow, I must say."

He started to move away from them, but Sean's arm held him in place. "Don't think you're going anywhere till you explain yourself, you sneaky lizard."

"I didn't mean—"

"Yes, you did," Sean and Jeff said at the same time.

Daniel's smile was a sight to see, his eyes traveling from one face to the other, Sean and him trying as best they could to fake anger.

"No, really, what I was trying to say is that you're quite different, opposites even, but, well, looking at you up close, the contrast just enhances each other's good points. You certainly make a good couple, really."

"Yeah, sure."

"Honestly," Daniel insisted.

"You know, saying that while you snort kind of spoils the effect."

They burst out laughing, the kind of laughter that makes a person weak all over, finding more reasons to laugh in every silly word or muffled noise, bodies doubling and leaning into each other for support until they were completely wasted.

"Not that I mind, but we must look weird, laughing like crazy in the middle of a parking lot," Sean said.

"Not quite befitting a sheriff."

"Especially if he's holding onto an Apache and a guy from outer space."

"Hey! Spain is not *that* far away!"

"Maybe, but you're still an alien."

"Yeah, but when I say E.T. I'm just meaning *emergency team.*"

When they finally got into the car, they plopped down into the seats, the three of them as exhausted as if they had all traveled across the ocean. Yet Jeff could tell they were happy, or at least that's how Jeff felt, pleased to see the same tired smiles in the others' faces.

He knew they had just made it through the first stage, but everything would come in due time. The important thing was that they had Daniel back, in more ways than one.

Chapter 11

SEAN poured coffee into three mugs. None of them matched, like most of the things in the tiny kitchenette. The rest of the apartment wasn't much bigger, just the dining room and the small bedroom with a minuscule bathroom to one side of it.

He hadn't made up his mind about moving out, though most of his stuff was still packed in boxes. Of course he knew this wasn't the place for him, but something he couldn't quite explain kept him waiting for the right moment to make the decision. Even before Daniel came back, there were a lot of things to sort out in his life: he needed to be sure he was staying, needed to find out what it was they were doing, Jeff and him, needed to be sure of what he wanted.

With Daniel there, the situation was far simpler, in a way. He clearly knew what he wanted, yet he wasn't at all sure he could get it, so again it was a question of letting the troubled waters settle down before plunging in headfirst. Meanwhile it was just a comfortable arrangement, the owner of the old shop below so happy to have a cop there Sean almost paid no rent, allowing him to save for the kind of house he'd really like to live in.

He loved the feeling of open spaces, rooms where you could move about without bumping into furniture, high ceilings where a guy like him didn't have to be constantly reminded of his height. Yet growing up in a big family made him quite able to adapt to cramped spaces, the more so if it was people and not furniture crowding the rooms.

At times like these, he could enjoy all the benefits of small houses, following the conversation as he readied coffee, taking just two steps to place the mugs in front of Daniel and Jeff.

"And this is the last case," Jeff was saying as he opened a folder. "William Chinosa."

Daniel made a disgruntled sound. "Not him again, please."

William—Billy Chinosa as they all knew him—was a peaceful, good-natured man who wreaked havoc every time he touched a bottle. Daniel had explained to them that alcohol triggered a psychotic disorder he could otherwise keep under control, his unobtrusive personality helping him cope with his lot in life till alcohol-induced delusions showed him an altogether different world.

The problem was everybody knew he was a good guy, so they simply steered away from him when he was drunk, and even when his frenzies got out of hand and he destroyed tables, glass panes, or car tires, they never once pressed charges. They knew Billy would work hard to pay for the damages he'd caused, so the cycle repeated itself over and over again.

"What was it this time, what did he break?"

"Oh, he didn't break anything."

"He didn't?"

"Nope. He just… how did they put it…" Sean opened his own folder on the case. "Oh, yeah, he *defiled the most cherished symbols of our cultural heritage*."

Daniel stared, uncomprehending.

"You know that lovely bronze group in front of the town council?"

"The one supposed to portray border life as a cultural melting pot?"

"That one. Well, he kind of used it as his personal toilet."

"Shit."

"Exactly."

They tried to keep a straight face after that, but didn't succeed for more than two seconds.

"He said it was his own contribution to the melting pot."

Daniel's disgusted gesture made them laugh harder.

"Oh, but don't worry, he was very clean about the whole business. He even used toilet paper."

"Pity it was the mayor's campaign poster he grabbed for that purpose."

"I bet that's what really got him into trouble," Daniel said.

"Nope, what *really* did it was saying the mayor wouldn't mind kissing one more ass."

It was good to laugh with them, as it was good to work with them, just simply to be with them. Over the months, the time they spent together had grown exponentially, so much so that they even ran together now, the three of them.

Every morning Sean started his warm-ups in front of his office, looking south till one or, if he was lucky, two shapes appeared in the distance. They only established a time to meet, not a day, for something could always come up, their jobs being as unpredictable as they were. Yet with three runners the chances of training alone were far less, and a lot more fun when they all made it.

Daniel was back to his old self, and he seemed genuinely happy with the progress of the reservation health center. People simply loved him. They trusted him completely and did their best to help any way they could. Besides, since Jeff had dropped any reticence he might have harbored before, communication between all the parties involved in the project was smooth, everything working like a well-greased wheel.

Sean didn't delude himself, though. He knew there was a solid wall Daniel had built to keep them out, both Jeff and him. He never spent the night at either of their places, no matter how late they finished, no matter how bleak his living quarters at the health center became as winter grew colder. He never once mentioned his migraines either, though it was obvious to them why he would stop running three days in a row. The morning after he always had some work-related excuse, and they just let it go, not knowing how to handle it without hurting Daniel or freaking him out.

Of course they knew they had to do something, as time was running out, but they were so afraid to lose what little they had, they always ended up looking the other way. Yet, since it wasn't in their nature to ignore challenges for long, they were growing increasingly frustrated, and it showed in the desperate way Sean and Jeff went over each other every time they were on their own. The violent attraction between them hadn't relented a bit. Truth was, they weren't even trying to tame it, since it was their only way to vent the angry resentment at their uselessness.

"Come on, stop laughing. We have a serious problem here."

"What? How to clean the melting pot?"

Daniel backhanded Sean's head. "That's exactly the problem. Nobody thinks Billy can be dangerous. He's just too funny."

Sean sobered a little. "You believe he's dangerous?"

"I'm sure he is. Paranoid delusions are not to be taken lightly. He may be a good guy, but I for one can't begin to imagine what he would do if he ever felt threatened."

"Can it be treated?" Jeff asked.

"Sure. Trouble is, I can't medicate him if he's going to get drunk as soon as he leaves the clinic."

"So he must go through a detox program first."

"Exactly. And no one is going to make him do it unless a judge sentences him to it."

"Which can't happen as long as people don't press charges."

"That's it," Daniel confirmed.

They kept silent for a few moments.

"I think you're the only one he'd listen to, Daniel."

Daniel snorted. "As if I haven't tried."

"You have, but never when he is drunk," Jeff said.

Daniel looked at him for a second and then his eyes went wide. "Your uncle told you!"

Jeff tried to suppress a grin while Sean looked from one to the other. "What are you talking about?"

Daniel rolled his eyes. "Ask Redcoyote over there."

Jeff cackled. "Sorry, Daniel, I can't help it."

Daniel crossed his arms in front of his chest.

"Come on, guys, I want to know," Sean said.

Daniel kept glaring at Jeff. "Tell him. Enjoy yourself."

Sean could see the mischief in Jeff's eyes, no matter how serious he tried to look.

"You know Uncle Charlie is teaching Daniel some Jicarilla basics," Jeff said.

"Yeah, I know," Sean said.

"By the way," Jeff said, looking at Daniel now, "he told me you were getting the knack of it pretty fast and—"

"Don't even go there. Flattery won't make it any better."

"But it's true!"

Daniel raised an admonishing finger at him.

"Okay, whatever, fact is Daniel was there giving his first Jicarilla speech when in comes Billy and says: *So that's where you got your magic from, you old fox.* My uncle, of course, asked him what he meant, and Billy then pointed a finger at Daniel. *You've had Naiyenesgani hidden all this time, speaking English and pretending to be a foreigner to fool us.*"

"Naiyenesgani? Isn't that an Apache hero?"

"Not just an Apache hero, *the* Apache hero. Everybody knows him; even other nations have stories about him."

"Well, not to gainsay Billy, but Daniel here doesn't look much the Apache," Sean said.

"That's what Uncle Charlie tried to make him see. He told him his magic wasn't powerful enough to turn a Jicarilla into a pale, green-eyed, light haired man."

"And that convinced Billy?"

Jeff beamed. "He said, of course Naiyenesgani's colors had all washed down when the monster first swallowed him and swam deep into the lake. Who wouldn't have gone white at that!"

Sean laughed. Daniel was shaking his head, but he could see there was a smile on his lips.

"Well, I'll try to talk to him again, see if I can impart some ancient wisdom," Daniel said.

Jeff nodded. "That'd be nice. Just try to look fierce while you are at it."

"Look fierce? Daniel? Those terms can't go together in the same sentence," Sean said.

Daniel narrowed his eyes at him. "Are you calling me a wimp?"

"No, I'm just saying you're too sweet-natured, and it shows."

Daniel turned to Jeff. "He's calling me a wimp."

Jeff tried hard not to laugh. "Look here, big guy, if you keep insulting the cultural hero of my people, I'm gonna have to beat some sense into that hard skull of yours, no matter how sweet he happens to be."

"Oh, shut up already, you two," Daniel groused. "And, by the way, nobody has ever accused me of that before, so just stop making fun of me."

Sean's smile went sour. Nobody had ever told Daniel he was sweet? Well, they were sure teasing him, but that was so obviously true that Sean had to wonder at the kind of affective background Daniel had had. He looked at Jeff and saw him frown. He could tell he was reaching the same conclusion.

"What now? What are you making those faces for?"

Sean wasn't about to tell Daniel what they were thinking, so he just said the first thing that came to him. "Maybe it's not such a great idea for you to talk to Billy."

Daniel went deadly serious. "When I told you he was dangerous, I didn't mean I was going to shake off my responsibility as his doctor. I never back away from things that must be done just because there's danger involved."

Shit. Now he had made Daniel mad.

"That's not what I—"

"I was just stating a fact so that you both know it, since we are working together in this, but I don't need your protection, I can stand on my own two feet."

Jeff whistled. "You sure you don't have some Apache blood in you?" Daniel shot him a murderous look.

"Don't know. Mother always said she couldn't ask father 'cause he disappeared every night through the western gate and she was always asleep when he came back through the eastern gate every morning."

Jeff laughed and explained it to Sean. "Naiyenesgani's father was the sun."

"Yeah, and my father was just like him: if you tried to get close, you only got burned." There it was again, the bitterness in Daniel's voice when talking about his family. Sean couldn't focus on it, though; he didn't want the misunderstanding to settle between them.

"Look, Daniel, I never meant to imply you needed protection. I know you're no coward, or weak, for that matter. You are strong, or rather, more than strong. You are...." Sean fumbled for the right word until Jeff cut in.

"Resilient."

"What?" Sean asked.

"Daniel. He is resilient. Strong people can take wounds and keep on living with them. Resilient people heal."

Daniel opened his mouth as if to say something but closed it just as fast. For a moment he looked lost, his eyes roaming all over the room to avoid meeting theirs. Then he placed both hands on the table and lifted his head to look at Sean. "I know you meant no offense, Sean. It's all right. I'll speak to Billy when he's sober, but I'd like you to try and convince people to press charges the next time, explain to them it would do Billy good, make them know it's not jail he's going to be sent to unless he goes on like this and finally hurts someone. And you, Jeff, should do the same with tribal cops, though Billy tends to keep his drinking sprees off the reservation. That's all we can do for the time being."

Sean and Jeff nodded.

"Then that'll be all for today."

"Are we dismissed now, sir?"

Daniel gave him a playful shove. "I'm a civilian here, you big brute."

"Maybe, but you sure know how to order us about, must be in your blood." Sean noticed the panicked look crossing Daniel's eyes at his last words and he hurried to add, "You being a king's son and all."

"There are no kings in Apache mythology," Jeff said. "The sun is more god than king."

"Oh, don't get into lecture mode with me. I was talking about elvish kings here."

"Elvish? You mean those unsavory, smallish creatures?"

Sean could tell Daniel was enjoying the exchange, laughter shining in his eyes. "No, I'm talking about tall, slender, beautiful, wood-dwelling creatures."

"Ah, you're quoting that racist book."

"Racist? *The Lord of the Rings*?!"

"Well, what would you call a book in which the braver the warrior, the blonder he gets, the wisest beings known as 'the fair ones' not because of the quality of their justice but for their *skin quality*?"

"Nordic?"

They laughed.

"That sure explains a lot. Always wondered about the ring fetish in such manly men," Jeff said.

"Treasure-hoard mentality."

"Maybe, but elves wore them too and they weren't particularly greedy."

"Or macho-looking, for that matter."

"Should've known. You just found a way to call me a wimp again."

They had to laugh harder at Daniel's mock anger. The earlier tension was forgotten, but Sean knew work was over for the day and Daniel would soon be wanting to head back home. He tried to make it last a little longer.

"Hey guys, you hungry? Mrs. Chambers brought me stew enough for a party of ten, and she's a wonderful cook."

"Oh, that's right, you saved her Bobby," Jeff said.

Sean growled. Wasn't too proud of that one.

"You saved her son?" Jeff snorted, Daniel arching an eyebrow. "Her husband?"

Sean rolled his eyes. "No, Daniel, I didn't save any relative of hers."

"Strictly speaking," Jeff muttered.

"Shut up, Redcoyote." Sean saw Daniel smile, for it was usually him who gave Jeff that name. "Okay, I just saved her cat. There being no firemen around, it was the only decent thing to do."

He could tell Daniel was fighting back laughter. "You took a ladder to a tree and all?"

"We don't keep any ladders. Had to use the resources at hand."

"*Underfoot* would be the right word in this case," Jeff said.

"Shut up."

"Underfoot?" Daniel asked.

"Well, he climbed on top of a patrol car and…"

"Don't you dare."

"…and sort of used it as a trampoline," Jeff explained.

Daniel bit his lip.

"I caught the damn animal, that's all that matters," Sean said.

"In the first try?"

"You want some stew or not?"

"How could we refuse a pillar of the community…?" Sean pounced on Daniel, lifting him bodily from the chair and throwing him onto the nearby couch. Then he straddled his hips and proceeded to tickle him mercilessly. Daniel laughed, wiggling under him. God, he loved the sound of that laughter, could live on just that for months on end.

"Jeff, please, take this grizzly off me!"

Jeff smiled from ear to ear. "Thought you'd never ask."

Sean didn't even see him coming before strong fingers landed hard on his own ticklish spots. He tried to back away, but Daniel caught his wrists and held him in place.

"You're playing dirty here! I'm outnumbered," Sean said, laughter weakening his every effort to get loose. Not that he was trying too hard, anyway, just enjoying the firm touch of Daniel's slender fingers and Jeff's dark ones finding ticklish areas he didn't know he had. Daniel surged suddenly from under his legs, pushing him till his back rested on the couch, Daniel moving up to straddle him in turn.

Jeff hooted the Apache way. "You've conquered the bear."

Sean laughed in spite of himself. Daniel's weight felt good on him, strong runner's thighs pressing against his hips. He was glad Daniel still held his wrists, for he felt an unbearable urge to run his hands along that back and down to the small, tight butt sitting on him.

"Guess I should take some trophy. What would you recommend?" Daniel asked.

Jeff gave his stretched-out form a once-over, eyes glinting.

Oh, he was so paying for that as soon as Sean could get his hands on the slim Apache.

"Well, paws make good keepsakes…." Jeff suggested.

Daniel lifted one of the hands he held and studied it seriously.

"Nah, too thick on the bones, would need a saw to do the job."

"Hey! No saws allowed! I'm a pillar of the community, remember?" Sean yelped.

"A pillar of the cat community, you mean."

Jeff snorted. "Fangs could do nicely too."

The bastard was still focused on hunting trophies. Daniel looked down at him, smiling. "I'm afraid this bear's too old to have any good teeth left." Sean growled.

"Then you should at least eat his heart," Jeff said.

"Oh no, he already did that," Sean said too quickly. The confused look Daniel gave him made his chest ache. He thought he heard Jeff swallow and couldn't take it anymore. He thrust his weight to one side, making Daniel lose his balance and pulling him down to the floor with him. He then used the momentum to flip the light body so that he was on top of him and grabbed his hands, pinning them down firmly with his own weight.

And suddenly it all went wrong, Daniel almost yelling at him. "Let go!" He wrung his hands furiously, fighting to get free, his eyes intent, panicked. Sean made the mistake of trying to calm him instead of loosening the grip on his hands, and Daniel lost it. He growled something in Spanish and shoved him with all his might, wrenching his wrists from Sean's fingers so violently as to leave marks on his pale skin. Then he crawled to the nearest wall and sat with his back to it, hugging his knees tightly, breath labored, never once raising his head to look at them. Sean made a move toward him, but Jeff's hand on his shoulder stopped him.

"We would never hurt you, Daniel." Jeff's voice was calm, soothing.

Daniel's reply came muffled, the sound almost lost between his knees. "I know."

They kept silent for a moment that seemed endless to Sean, but still Jeff shook his head when he looked at him. Sean could have growled in frustration. It was breaking his heart to see Daniel like that; he desperately needed to touch him, make him know they were there for him. Yet he could tell Jeff was right. Daniel was acting like a cornered animal, and he would only pull farther away if they pressed him.

At last Daniel lifted his head, though he avoided their eyes as he spoke. "I'm sorry. I know you meant no harm, Sean. It's just that I can't bear... being restrained." Daniel made an attempt at smiling apologetically but didn't quite succeed, his lips quivering before returning to a flat line.

"Who used to restrain you?" Jeff's voice was neutral now, but Daniel hid his face between his knees and went silent. "It was your father, wasn't it?"

Sean looked up at him in surprise. Of course. It had been there all the time, how could he not have seen it before? And by the wide-eyed look Daniel was giving Jeff, he was right on the mark.

"What did he do? Tie you up, as punishment?" Daniel's features closed at Jeff's words, eyes narrowing. Then he took a deep breath and started getting up from the floor. "Daniel...."

"It's in the past now, Jeff. Just let it stay there."

"You're still reacting to it now, it's still bothering you."

Daniel glared at him. "Oh, excuse me for not being—what did you call it?—*resilient* enough for you."

He strode angrily to the door but Sean intercepted him. "Don't leave like this, Daniel."

Daniel almost spat the words at him. "Like what?"

Sean arched an eyebrow. "Utterly mad? Completely pissed off? Angry as hell?"

Daniel's lips moved just a tad upwards. Sean gave him a full smile and landed his fingers on Daniel's shoulders. "Come on, come back here. Talk to us."

Daniel let Sean steer him back to the couch and sat down beside him. Jeff was still sitting on the floor and he now crossed his legs, resting his hands on his propped-up knees, dark eyes following their every move.

"Hope you don't start chanting or something, Sitting Bear." Daniel really smiled now, and Sean could see relief in Jeff's eyes. The worst wasn't over, but he knew they had delayed it for too long. It was about time to get to the root of it.

Sean turned to face Daniel, his hand still touching sharp bones under soft, woolen fabric. "Now, please tell us what happened. What it is that made you so… reactive?"

Daniel smirked humorlessly. "You mean so frightened."

Sean kept his face straight. He couldn't bear Daniel's self-deprecating tone. "Whatever you want to call it. I'm not avoiding words to make you feel better. I just think there's nothing to be ashamed of."

"It was outright panic, Sean. All you did was touch my wrists and I went berserk. How is it not something to be ashamed of?"

"Well, a rat bit my leg when I was five and now I always lose it when I see the gray bastards. Should I be ashamed, then?"

"Of course you should." They both turned astounded faces to Jeff. He shrugged. "I mean as a pillar of the cat community and all…"

Sean threw one of his slippers at him. "Is that an Apache trait, killing your enemies with bad jokes?"

Jeff threw his slipper back in response. Sean caught it in midair and put it back on his foot. Then he turned once again to Daniel, his eyes serious now, pleading. Daniel held his gaze for a moment.

"Sean, I don't think…."

"Please, give us a little trust, we're your friends."

"There's nothing that you can do about it."

"We can listen," Jeff said.

Sean felt Daniel's body tense under his fingers. "You don't have to; I'm not one of your cases."

Sean almost gritted his teeth at the resentment in Daniel's voice. Jeff looked hurt, as if Daniel had slapped his face. "Is that what you think?" Jeff's voice was low, menacingly so. "That you are a case to me, that I act out of compassion or even duty? That I want to pry into your secrets to write some report, to get something published?"

"Don't know. Do you?" Daniel's voice almost broke. It was him who looked hurt now, and Sean bit his lip, realization dawning on him. They had been so intent on not pressing Daniel that they had led him to believe they didn't care. Shit. He was so used to seeing them helping people that he took their interest for professional zeal. Small wonder he felt betrayed. What would he himself have thought if two guys fussed over him, had sex with him, and then acted as if nothing had happened, never calling him in four months, even when it was not likely that he would ever come back to them? How could they've been so stupid?

Jeff stood and walked over to Daniel, grim determination in his eyes. He crouched in front of him and cupped Daniel's face in his hands, forcing him to keep his focus on Jeff. "Now listen here, Doc. I don't know how it goes for you, but I never take my cases to my own house, much less put my tongue in their mouths." He paused. "And I seriously doubt the sheriff here goes touching his suspects to make them cream their pants."

In the silence that followed, Sean could count his own anxious heartbeats. Jeff's hands hid Daniel's expression, so he didn't know what he was thinking, how he would react to Jeff's harsh words.

Then Daniel just whispered, "That's gross."

And they broke out laughing, Jeff's hands sliding from Daniel's face and resting on his thighs, almost clutching at them for support, he was laughing so hard. Sean reached out for Daniel's head and let his hand rest there, needing the contact, wanting so much more but not daring to go any further. It felt so good just touching his soft brown hair, sensing the delicate curve of the bone under his fingers.

When their laughter died down, Jeff looked up into Daniel's eyes.

"What I was trying to tell you—"

The phone rang so loudly Sean almost jumped in his seat. He swore aloud as he picked up the receiver. Whoever was calling had better have a damn good reason to be phoning right then. "McCallum," he barked.

One of his deputies' voices came to him and he could tell by her subdued manner that there was real trouble, knew he would have to leave as soon as he heard the whole story. He turned to Jeff and Daniel to meet their expectant eyes.

"Okay. Be there in...." He still wasn't used to living across the street from headquarters, still gave in to the old habit of calculating transit delays. "I'll be there."

He hung up with a resigned sigh. "Have to go now."

"Anything serious?"

"Nah, but it's gonna take some time to check it out." Sean looked at them, gaze lingering on Daniel. "Why don't you stay the night? We'll talk when I make it back."

Of course, Daniel shook his head. "I can't. I promised to see Salazar's kids first thing tomorrow, before they leave for school."

Sean exchanged a look with Jeff. "Daniel, we have to talk. Even if you don't want to, there are things we have to tell you, things we should have made clear to you a long time ago."

Daniel's eyes traveled from him to Jeff and back again.

"All right. You do that, but not today. I seriously can't."

It didn't escape Sean how quickly Daniel had grabbed his offer of them doing all the talking. It was fine by him. They wouldn't let Daniel off so easily; once they got him to listen, he was going to answer some questions himself. Jeff seemed to be thinking along the same lines, for he stood and told him to leave.

"Don't worry. We'll hold him to his word. Gonna have that conversation no matter what," Jeff assured him.

"Hey! I'm still here, you know."

Sean ignored Daniel deliberately. "Right. Just do me a favor and feed him some of Mrs. Chambers's stew before you take him home. He gets skinnier by the day." He feinted to avoid Daniel's smack, laughing. As he reached the door, Sean turned to look at the two men standing in front of him. They were both of a height, both light-framed and slender, but the similarities ended there. All the rest was sheer contrast.

Jeff's olive skin looked dark brown beside Daniel's paleness, his blue-black hair making Daniel appear blond. As they returned his gaze, the lamp light threw shadows on Jeff's eyes, showing black pools trained on Sean's every move, while Daniel's irises were fully illuminated, a watery green so light they looked almost transparent. Even their smiles had a contrasting quality to them, Jeff's hard features framing a foxy kind of smile, Daniel's soft ones drawing a sweet curve on his lips. They made quite a picture, almost the biblical illustration of darkness and light, angel and demon, warrior and healer. Almost... the all-encompassing effect broken by the mischievous spark in Daniel's eyes and the tender look Jeff was giving him. Oh yeah, that angel was up to no good, and the demon by his side had too gentle a heart to even engage in evil thoughts.

Sean felt his own heart melting, a foolish grin spreading on his face. He knew he would be the happiest guy on earth if it was just that picture he saw every time he opened the door to his home.

Chapter 12

"WHAT'S wrong?"

Jeff lifted his head to look at his aunt. "Nothing. Was just distracted, that's all."

Aunt Helena's eyes narrowed. "Sure. Food on your plate is so distracting, what with pursuing peas and all, it can be mind-blowing."

He had to smile in spite of himself. "Okay. I was giving some thought to…. It's nothing serious, just things I have to sort out."

It was his uncle who spoke now. "Maybe saying it aloud might help. You know you can talk to us about anything."

"I know, Uncle Charlie, it's just that—"

"Oh, don't you be so snotty and spill the beans already."

He chuckled, his uncle shaking his head at his wife's bluntness. "What if it's something personal?" Jeff said, smiling.

"I changed your diapers, boy, can't get more personal than that."

"You have a point there."

His aunt raised an eyebrow, waiting.

"All right. I'm worried about Daniel, that's it."

Uncle Charlie nodded silently, but Aunt Helena didn't let go. "What's wrong with him?"

"Well, he's sort of... I couldn't call it hiding, but he sure is keeping things from us, important things, kind of shutting us out."

"Us?"

"Sean and me."

His aunt looked pensive. "Always wondered," she said. "That kid can smile so sweetly with those eyes so full of hurt."

Uncle Charlie nodded again as he spoke. "He's a true healer, that one is, puts his heart out every single time. Still, he can't heal himself, keeps thinking he'd better protect people from him, keep them at arm's length."

Jeff shouldn't have been so surprised, but it had been a long time since he'd last spoke with his aunt and uncle about serious things. He'd kind of forgotten how inquisitive they were, how wise. He felt like a kid all over again, laying his problems in front of them, desperately in need of their guidance.

"We can't seem to get it right with him, no matter what we do. We tried to let him be and he ended up thinking we didn't give a damn, so we pushed our way instead and now he's avoiding us. I swear I can't stand it. One minute he's on his best-friend behavior and the next he comes up with a lame excuse to run away from us lest we notice he's having one of his migraines."

"Migraines?"

"Yeah, he suffers from these brain-shattering headaches that can last days, and he knows we know, yet he'd rather die than let us see he's in pain."

"Oh, but you can surely tell. It's all over his face, those pretty eyes of him going all cloudy."

Jeff looked at his aunt, dumbfounded. "You knew?"

"What kind of question is that? Of course we knew! He's had to lie out there in the shade with a damp cloth on his eyes more than once, your uncle telling him stories to make him forget the pain...."

Jeff almost laughed, remembering what he'd thought that time he saw Daniel lying on the floor by his uncle's chair, how jealous he'd been. God. Could he get any more stupid than that?

"But why on earth should he be ashamed of being sick? He's a doctor, for Christ's sake."

"Have you asked him?"

"Sure. He says he's used to dealing with it on his own but, by the way he reacts, I'd say there's much more to it than him simply trying not to be a bother."

"Well, if he was any other man, I would have thought he didn't like showing weaknesses, but I reckon that doesn't apply to Daniel. Never once heard him telling that bullshit you men are so fond of."

"He's just polite, Aunt Helena, doesn't mean he wasn't brought up the same way we all were, same 'boys don't cry' shit and all."

"We never taught you that. Proof is you've become a two-spirits."

Jeff looked at his uncle's serious face and feared he had offended him. He was about to apologize when his aunt snorted unceremoniously. "You might be losing your memory in your old age, Charles Redbear." His uncle glared at her. "Oh, don't give me that look. You were always telling this boy how brave Apaches don't do this or that. You are as bad as any other father I know. And don't use that dreadful word for Jeff. He likes men as well as women, and that only makes him smart. That's all there is to it."

Jeff laughed. His aunt had never liked the word some Native Americans had chosen to more or less mean gay. Being a Navajo, with all their ritual aversion to dead things, she couldn't hear "spirits" without imagining a bunch of evil ghosts. He patted his aunt's wrinkled hand and turned to his uncle. "You raised me well, Uncle Charlie. What you taught me gave me a solid ground from which I could judge what people said or did outside this house. But I don't think someone like Daniel was that lucky. I believe he's had to fight down every single notion he was taught and, the more I know him, the more I suspect he was taught the hardest possible way."

"You think he was…."

"Yeah. Took me long enough to realize it, him being so open, so caring, and coming from a rich family, but I've dealt with too many abused children not to see the signs."

Aunt Helena covered her mouth with her hand. His uncle looked worried. "Are you sure?" Uncle Charlie now asked. "Has he said anything that makes you think…?"

"No, but that only confirms what I'm saying. People who suffer that kind of abuse keep it to themselves 'cause they feel ashamed, can't help thinking it was somehow their fault, can't get over the notion that they're flawed. Guess it's difficult not to believe you're worthless when your own parents tell you so."

"That poor kid."

"He's not a child for you to pity, you silly woman. The young doctor is a fine man, and his soul is as strong as they get, so don't you go disrespecting him."

Jeff gaped at his uncle, disbelief written all over his face. What had gotten into the man? He looked really angry, hands closed in shaky fists on the table, eyes narrowed into black slits, glaring madly at his wife.

To Jeff's surprise, Aunt Helena nodded, her voice lowering. "That he is, a fine, strong man." Jeff couldn't believe his ears. Aunt Helena placidly taking a rebuke from her husband; well, that was a first. "But you know, the stronger the man, the more he thinks he can battle things on his own, so you'd better stop respecting him from afar and move your sorry Apache ass to help that kid."

Jeff fought down laughter till he heard his uncle chuckle.

"Should've married a Hopi. I hear they make good, silent wives."

"Yeah, but they can't cook for shit."

They laughed over their masterfully cooked lunch. He knew his uncle never regretted marrying his aunt, and not just for her cooking skills. Even her banter he appreciated: as blunt as she could be, still, she saw clearly through everything and wasn't afraid to speak her mind. Uncle Charlie always took her advice. He did so now, turning to Jeff.

"Why don't you invite Daniel over someday you're both free? We could use the sweat lodge."

That was a good idea. The atmosphere of the sweat lodge spurred confidences easily. Daniel would relax there. Jeff knew he trusted his uncle. Maybe he could let go with him, let himself be guided. His uncle was good at that; it was worth a try.

"You should invite that big sheriff too."

"Oh, don't meddle in our affairs, Helena. It ain't a social call we're talking about."

Aunt Helena rolled her eyes. "Of course it isn't. That's why you should invite him, you old fool. I swear sometimes you make me wonder what you use your eyes for. Can't you see how close he is to Jeff's heart? Can't you see how both have that kid in their hearts?"

Jeff almost choked on his food. "Aunt Helena!"

"What? Are you telling me you don't care about those two?"

Jeff fumbled for some way out of it, but he had never lied to his aunt, mostly because he knew she would always find out. "How did you…?"

"Oh, come on. You should listen to yourself. It's always Sean this and Sean that. And the only times you've brought the sheriff here, what was that we all ended up talking about?"

Jeff smiled. "Daniel."

"There you have it."

He shook his head. Guess they were obvious, the two of them. And just as the thought sank in, his smile froze. "You think anyone else might have noticed?"

"Nah. Look at your uncle here. He's supposed to be inquisitive and all, and he didn't have a clue." She paused. "Wouldn't hurt to be careful, though."

Jeff nodded. Up until now he couldn't have cared less what people thought, but it was different now. This was someone else he could bring harm to, someone more important to him than his own reputation or well-being.

Surprising as it might be, he'd rather die than hurt Sean or Daniel in any way. He almost chuckled. If someone had told him that he'd put some white guy before everything in his life, he'd have laughed in his face or even punched his lights out, insulting as the mere suggestion would've been.

"Well," Uncle Charlie said now, "guess you'll have to bring the sheriff too."

"And warn your uncle well in advance 'cause he's gonna have to widen that tiny entrance the lodge has."

He laughed. "Sean is not *that* big, Aunt Helena."

"So you say, but I wish I'd known what his ma fed him. Would have made a true red bear out of you."

"Are you implying I'm small?"

"No, but you're scrawny."

He smiled. "That's what Daniel says."

"Oh, he's one to talk. That kid is so pale and thin he's almost transparent. Should know better, too, being a doctor and all."

"Yeah, he doesn't take much care of himself."

"Then you should. You're two to one, couldn't be that difficult, even if you had to tie him down and force-feed him," she said.

Tie him down. Jeff shuddered involuntarily, remembering how Daniel had reacted to being restrained. He could only begin to imagine what his father had done to him.

"It's gonna be all right, Jeff."

He looked up and tried to give a reassuring smile. Yeah. It was going to work out. Wouldn't know what to do if it didn't.

Chapter 13

SEAN handed Jeff the keys, enjoying the surprised look on the Apache's handsome face.

"No need to be showing me the way when you can drive us there yourself."

"You sure?"

Sean laughed. He knew the right thing to say to stop all that hesitation. "What, you afraid of big cars?"

As he expected, Jeff snatched the keys out of his hand and got into the driver's seat, almost slamming the door closed after him. Almost. Still couldn't help being careful around Sean's SUV, still looked too brand new to him in spite of the coat of dust and the fresh scratches on the paint. It wasn't an easy country for cars, or people, for that matter.

He took his seat by Jeff and turned to look at Daniel. "Got your seat belt on, Doc?"

Daniel rolled his eyes. "Yeah, Sheriff, I'm all safe and cozy back here."

Sean laughed but couldn't deny that was exactly what he wanted, to keep Daniel safe and cozy by their side. Well, that and a few more things he shouldn't be thinking right now, especially not when Daniel looked so sexy, sprawled on the backseat. Though "sprawled" was too coarse a word for the elegant abandon of his long limbs. Damn the guy for always looking like a poster boy, no matter how relaxed the posture.

As the car started to move he turned to face the road, only to catch Jeff staring into the rearview mirror.

"Focus, Redbear," Sean said, chuckling when he saw the flush on that olive skin.

It was a fine spring afternoon, and he felt elated to be out with Jeff and Daniel for reasons other than work. Sean was thankful to Jeff's uncle for providing the occasion they had been waiting upon. And most thankful that he had thought to include him in something he didn't expect the old shaman to like sharing with whites. He had believed it was Jeff who suggested he should be there too, but Jeff had just shaken his head when he asked, not caring to explain further. It was fine by him. No matter the reasons, he was really glad to be there. He just hoped it worked, since they were running out of time.

"Is there anything we should know before we get there?" Daniel asked. "I mean, so as not to make fools of ourselves."

Jeff flashed a smug smile. "Oh, don't worry. Whatever the preparations, you're still gonna make fools of yourselves. You can't help carrying it in your genes."

"How very funny."

Sean threw Jeff a look. No reason to make Daniel self-conscious about it all. It might spoil the effect they were aiming at. Jeff seemed to understand, for he quickly added, "No, really, Doc, there's nothing to worry about. Just think of it as if it was a sauna we were about to step in, a place to relax and get some hazardous waste out of our systems."

"Blow some steam, so to speak."

"No, Sean, it's not gay baths I'm talking about."

Sean felt heat rising in his cheeks. "That's not what I meant, you righteous bastard. And just so you know, I've never even been to one of those."

"I have." They both turned wide-eyed looks on Daniel, the car swerving on the dirt road before Jeff regained control of the wheel. "Don't look so shocked, it was just a private party." And then Daniel must have understood how that sounded, for his hands did a nervous dance in front of him as he hurried to explain. "I mean it was a friend's birthday and we rented a sauna to spend the day together...."

"Daniel, you're making it worse by the moment."

It was Daniel's turn to blush and they just had to laugh at his embarrassment. "You are mean."

"Nope, just worried about your virtue, you being so clueless and all."

"I'm not clueless."

"Oh, yes you are," Sean and Jeff said in unison, exchanging knowing looks.

"He's even cuter when he pouts."

"I'm not pouting!"

In the silence that followed Sean could see Jeff fighting back laughter as Daniel started to realize what he hadn't denied in his outburst. "Can we drop the subject, please?"

"The one about you attending a private party at a gay sauna, or the one about you being cute?" Sean asked. Daniel just covered his face with his hands, Jeff cackling openly by then. Sean reached back and patted Daniel's head. "Sorry, Doc, just kidding. You're not cute at all."

Daniel dropped his hands to look at him, eyes narrowed in suspicion.

"Big man's right, you're not cute, no way," Jeff added. Daniel looked from one to the other. "You're simply..." Jeff said, exchanging a look with Sean.

"Beautiful!" they almost shouted before their voices broke into roaring laughter.

Daniel tried to stare them down, but didn't quite manage to keep a straight face. "Should've known if I crossed the ocean the natives were gonna make fun of me."

"We're not making fun of you."

"No, just using me to release some tension." Daniel must have seen the look in his eyes for he added hesitantly, "That didn't sound quite right, did it?"

"Well, it did sound right." Sean paused. "For a gay sauna private party."

"God, I'm clueless," Daniel muttered.

They laughed so hard Sean didn't know whether it was the road or them that made the car bump. When they got to Charles Redbear's place, he was feeling so weak he thought there was no need of a sweat lodge. If he got any more relaxed he would have to crawl his way home.

Sean sobered a bit when he saw Jeff's uncle standing in front of the house. The man looked like a picture from old times: long mane of gray hair falling past his shoulders, dark eyes narrowed against the afternoon sun, countenance unreadable. He didn't move as they left the car, just stood there, tall, proud, waiting for them to come to him. Sean had to admire the commanding energy that radiated from him as he fixed each of them in a severe stare. He was used to smaller guys having to look up at him, but even as he did, Jeff's uncle still managed to stare him down. Under those unwavering eyes, Sean just felt like a lost kid begging for guidance.

It wasn't until Daniel said something he supposed was a Jicarilla greeting that the stern face opened into a warm smile. Then he was back to the harmless grandfatherly figure, but Sean already knew better. He wouldn't make the mistake of underestimating the man.

"Where's Aunt Helena?" Jeff asked as they followed his uncle inside.

"Oh, you know her. She said she'd leave us to our *all-boys pajama party.*"

Sean let out a surprised laughter. "She's quite a character, your wife."

"That she is. That woman always has something to say. In fact, she left a word for you, too, said to tell *the big sheriff* to come visit more often and bring *that kid* along so she can feed him properly."

Jeff chuckled. "That'd be you, Daniel."

"Yeah, your aunt is on a crusade to fatten me."

"Wonder why that is." As Daniel glared at him, Sean felt Charles's eyes roam from one to the other, and he couldn't help the wild notion that the man knew. He blushed slightly under those inquisitive eyes, trying to convince himself he was imagining things.

"Well, shall we begin then?" Charles asked.

They all nodded and Jeff started to strip, leaving his clothes in a neat pile on a chair. As they followed his example, Sean was relieved to see Jeff and his uncle left their boxers on, because it would surely prove too much to be around both Daniel and Jeff in the nude. He tried to walk in line with them as they followed Charles out of the house; he didn't want to risk even a look at their half-naked bodies. It wasn't that they were there for. The purpose of the ritual, or whatever they called it, was to provide a setting where Daniel felt safe to uncover his past. Sean had to stay focused on that goal.

He lowered his head to step into the dimly lit interior of the sweat lodge. It was a simple wooden structure with no openings except the small door that Jeff closed after him and a smoke hole in the ceiling above. Sean's eyes had to adjust to the scarce light filtering through the cracks in the wood planks and coming from the low-burning fire they now sat around. Charles poured water over the coals with a ladle and clouds of steam went up with a swishing sound. As he poured more water, the air became thick and wet, waves of heat enveloping them like clammy fingers. He then extracted some yellowish powder from a pouch and threw it every which way, each movement preceded by a flow of words that had the cadence of a prayer. Time took on a different texture, floating about like a slow, suffocating breeze that couldn't leave the small space, but just went round and round in the same, never-ending second.

Jeff stirred the coals in the fire pit and the heat rose even more. He looked into Jeff's eyes for a moment and felt a different kind of warmth in the pit of his stomach. For all his fierce native looks, Jeff had a caring nature Sean was always delighted to discover, especially when all that care was lavished upon him. He nodded slightly to let Jeff know he was fine, hoping his eyes would convey the wave of affection that wrapped him like a blanket. He saw Jeff's chest rise as he took a deep breath, dark skin shining with sweat, black eyes never once leaving him. His whole body felt the need in those eyes, heat rising almost unbearably, pouring out of him in fat droplets of sweat, a deep flush reddening his skin, blood filling his cock instantly.

Sean couldn't seem to care, though. There was something special about the lodge atmosphere, some kind of protective cocoon where nothing mattered, or rather everything did, but on a different level.

He held Jeff's gaze and let his own need flood him. He wanted that man. He wanted to bury his hands in that lush hair, trace those chiseled features with his fingers, taste the sweat that ran down that taut body, cover every inch of that tanned skin with his lips. He wanted all that and still he wanted more. He could see it clearly for the first time. He wanted that man as he wanted the thick air that burned his lungs. Mere contact would never be enough; he needed to swallow, claim all that Jeff Redbear was and make it his, breathe him in and let him take over every single cell of his body, give himself over to him and let his strong hands rebuild him into something new.

As a monotonous, repetitive chant filled the air, Sean remembered they weren't alone, he and Jeff. His consciousness registered vaguely the shaman's presence, but he didn't quite manage to disentangle himself from Jeff's eyes. It was all right, anyway, for the shaman knew. He was sure of that now. And Daniel knew too.

Daniel. He almost said the word aloud, felt it traveling along his body in a new wave of scorching heat. He turned his head, somehow knowing that Jeff followed his gaze till it rested on Daniel, where he sat beside Charles. Sean's mouth went suddenly dry, his heart slamming against his ribs. All the light in the room seemed to flow into those huge eyes that now glittered with a feral glow, much like those of a prowling hunter. The near darkness gave Daniel's skin an impossibly solid white hue, sweat glistening on its slick surface like pure marble. He was an otherworldly creature captured in the shaman's spellbinding chant, but the look in those extravagant blue-green eyes was all too human in the intensity of feelings it conveyed. There was heart-warming affection that Sean's body absorbed like the water he thirsted for. But there was also longing and hurt, most of all hurt, as if the object of his affection was out of his reach because he really was the creature he now looked like, too alien to belong, too inhuman to be loved. Pain flowed from those eyes like steam, making the air heavy, difficult to breathe. Sean was appalled, unable to understand how

Daniel managed to go on living when he found it so hard to even breathe in the mere reflection of that pain Daniel's eyes projected. Sean's whole body itched with the urge to wrap Daniel in his arms, to protect the exquisite creature that he was until his wounds healed, until he was back to his whole, powerful self, and then just sit waiting at his feet like a faithful dog, begging for a touch, a look, a smile, anything his master would throw at him.

Daniel. Now he did say the word aloud, voice so heavy with meaning that he heard Daniel gasp, his body shuddering as if he had touched him. His reaction traveled through Sean's burning body right down to his cock, which now throbbed, aching for release. He felt feverish, sweat trickling down his face like silent tears, chest hurting with every labored breath he took. Daniel gave him a concerned look and turned to say something to Charles. And just the knowledge that he worried about him was enough to send shivers down Sean's spine, the bubble of emotion growing so much inside him that he felt he was about to explode. The moment he thought he couldn't take it anymore, heat pressing against his chest like a solid wall, crushing him breathless, the door burst open and a gust of cool air rushed into the lodge.

There was someone at the door, but the light was suddenly too bright for him to distinguish who it was. He just heard a meaningless stream of shouted words, heard Charles responding while his heat-addled mind told him it was Jicarilla they were speaking. He wasn't that far gone that he didn't catch the threatening note in the intruder's voice, though, so he tried to stand and block the stranger's advance. A wave of dizziness swept over him, forcing him to sit back down and quickly shut his eyes to stop the room from swirling. Then he heard the urgency in Daniel's voice. His lids flicked open just in time to see a blur of white skin as Daniel tackled Charles, bringing him down the very moment he heard the unmistakable sound of a gun being shot.

When Sean saw the intruder move, he lurched forward, praying his body would respond as he needed it to. His weight landed limply on the stranger's legs and the man fell with a muffled cry. Just as Sean saw Jeff moving toward them, something hit his head with a sickening crash, and his world exploded into brilliant shards of pain before he sank into darkness.

Chapter 14

JEFF flexed his fingers. His wrists hurt, the tight rope chafing his skin every time he struggled to loosen it. No luck so far, but he had no idea what else to try.

He turned to look at Sean's motionless body. He was white as a sheet, blood crusting his blond hair and leaving a trail down his right cheek. But still Jeff saw the soft movement in the big man's chest and could only hope it was just a concussion he was dealing with.

He lifted his head to check on his uncle. The old man nodded, his gagged mouth making a small reassuring sound only Jeff was close enough to hear. He felt rage flowing through his veins, his wrists screaming in pain as he clenched his fists. The whole damn idea of the sweat lodge had been the worst stupidity ever. He knew it wasn't his uncle's fault, but right now he couldn't forget it was *his* idea that had them where they were, couldn't ignore it was him Billy had felt wronged enough by to point a gun at and pull the trigger.

Jeff closed his eyes as he felt his rage turning quickly into guilt. What right did he have to blame his uncle when he himself had been so absorbed in his own feelings he hadn't even noticed what the heat was doing to Sean? Damn. The guy was the fucking sheriff; he could have stopped Billy with just one finger if Jeff had only taken care of him, seen how dizzy he was, given him some water, put out the fire. Shit. Even about to faint, Sean had managed to topple Billy, while Jeff, even with Billy down, hadn't been able to take the gun from him. Even then it had been Daniel who saved the day, Daniel who had already taken a bullet for his uncle.

Jeff realized he had shut his eyes and opened them wide. If he hadn't had a cloth in his mouth he would have cursed himself aloud. They weren't dead yet, none of them. There was no time to wallow in self-pity. He was the only one in the room who wasn't wounded or old, the only one who could do something if the occasion presented itself. But he had to be focused to do it. There might be only one single chance, and it all might depend on him.

He tuned in Daniel's voice again. He was still trying to put some sense into Billy, had been for what seemed like hours now, his tone steady and soothing, just talking calmly as if it was a recliner he was comfortably lying on, giving some simple, unimportant advice to a confused teenager. And that was exactly what Billy looked like right then, no matter how close to thirty he really was. The Apache was short and thin, his black hair gathered carelessly with an elastic band, his clothes hanging from his shoulders and hips as if they had been handed down from an older, bigger brother. His attitude was more than a little incongruous, his eyes fixed on Daniel in reverent worship while his fingers held a loaded gun. He was listening sheepishly now, only from time to time putting in some crazy notion or other that Daniel tried to bring down carefully, never risking another outburst from the deranged man.

Daniel's head was propped up on a cushion, on one arm of the couch, his stretched-out body covered by one of Aunt Helena's colorful Navajo blankets. He just seemed to be resting, except for the pale hand pressing a cloth against his shoulder. His face was pale, too, purple circles forming under his eyes.

Jeff felt a dull ache in his chest. At least Sean was out of it, but Daniel was there, bleeding, in a pain he could only begin to imagine, knowing the lives of all depended on what he said next. And Jeff heard him try one more time, fighting against all hope, till his last breath if it need be. God, but the man was brave.

"Billy, we can't go on like this. Sean needs a doctor and so do I. You know the bullet is still inside."

"Can you feel it? Does it hurt?" Jeff almost rolled his eyes. Billy still believed Daniel was some kind of warrior-god, immune to pain or any other human flaw.

"Yeah, it hurts, and it can still cause enough damage that I might die from it."

Billy cocked his head. He seemed to be gauging Daniel's expression, trying to decide whether he should believe him or if it was some kind of test he was putting him through. His eyes went wide as he realized something. "The bullet," he said, slapping his own forehead in what would have been a comical gesture under very different circumstances. "It's a thing we never had before the white man brought us all his evil ways. Of course it's hurting you. It must be removed."

"Yes, it must. So take me and Sean to the emergency room. They'll see to it."

Billy stood and Jeff felt hope growing inside him till he opened his mouth. "I won't let them put their filthy hands on you. I will do it."

Oh, God no. His stomach lurched, fear and desperation rushing through his blood. If that man put a knife to Daniel, there was no telling what he could do to him.

"You can't do it. You're no healer."

Billy stopped, doubt plain on his face. Jeff silently prayed for Daniel to go on like that, to follow the bastard's twisted logic.

"I know your intentions are good, but your hands might harm me even more."

Billy hung his head down. "Yeah, they're polluted now. I touched a gun, a white man's instrument of death."

"There's still a healer in this room."

The Apache looked up, his head turning toward Jeff's uncle. When his eyes rested on him, Billy's face changed, rage curling his lip into a snarl. "That's no healer!" he growled, his hand rising to point the gun at Uncle Charlie. "He is a traitor to our blood. He deserves to die the worst of deaths, he—"

Jeff tried vainly to move, his mind racing, desperately searching for some way to stop Billy till he heard Daniel's commanding voice.

"Billy!"

Jeff looked up. Daniel was standing in front of Billy, his face stern, his posture so straight he looked taller than usual, his eyes so fierce that Billy recoiled visibly, his raised hand dropping to one side.

Daniel had let go of the cloth pressing against his wound and blood poured freely down his naked chest. His voice faltered a little, but he held his ground, eyes gleaming in a too-pale face. Now more than ever Jeff understood what Billy saw, the battle-hardened god Billy knew Daniel to be.

"It wasn't Charles I was talking about. Have you forgotten I'm a healer too? Do you think any other than me could fix this mess?"

The Apache actually mumbled an apology, eyes on the floor. He was back to his best behavior, no trace left of the raving madman he'd been just a moment before. It was disconcerting and more than a little frightening.

"Now give me that gun and help me with this."

Billy raised his head and Jeff crossed his fingers, his mind repeating *please, please, please* as a silent prayer.

"No. It's evil. It will harm you."

Jeff let out the breath he was holding. It would have been too easy. But still Daniel tried and he wondered how he managed to even stand.

"Then drop it somewhere, I can't do it all myself."

Billy shook his head. "I have to keep an eye on them; they might try to steal you one more time."

"Billy, they're tied, the three of them, and Sean is unconscious. They can't do anything."

Billy shook his head stubbornly. "They can...."

Daniel staggered and Billy grabbed him before he fell, the gun pressing flat against Daniel's skin. Jeff felt anger rising inside him. How dare that son of a bitch touch him, put a gun to that immaculate skin? He didn't know how, didn't *care* how, but he knew that if Billy touched Daniel just one more time, he was going to kill him.

Daniel sat down on the couch, his head falling back to the headrest. "Now, Billy," he said, his voice once again firm. "I'm going to trust you with my safety, and you'd better not let me down."

Billy fell headfirst into the trap. "You know I will protect you with my life."

Daniel kept his voice stern. "See that you do, 'cause you'll have to put all your senses into it."

"I will do anything you need me to do."

"Right. Now, go untie Jeff." He raised a finger before Billy could start to protest. "He's the only one who can bring me what I need to remove the bullet *you* put in me, so give me no more bullshit and untie him. I need his help, and I need you to keep me safe. You must keep an eye open for me, see that he doesn't try anything funny."

Billy nodded and walked to Jeff, eager to comply. Jeff's heart raced in his chest. His chance had come; he wasn't going to waste it.

Billy crouched beside him and pulled at Jeff's shoulder, to have better access to his tied hands. As he did, Jeff lifted his head to look at Daniel. Their eyes met and Jeff was surprised to see him mouth "wait" as he jerked his head in Sean's direction. Jeff felt shame heating his cheeks. Daniel thought he couldn't take Billy on his own, thought he needed to wait for Sean to help him. Well, he had tried before to take the gun from him and the results were more than obvious. But still….

Billy was taking his time as he tried to undo the knots without letting go of the gun. Jeff's eyes roamed to Daniel again. He had a pained expression now. The bullet must be hurting like hell. Wait. Was he actually rolling his eyes at him? He mouthed another word, something like "ooze." He frowned his confusion. Then Daniel lifted an imaginary glass to his lips, and it all became clear to Jeff. "Booze." That's what he meant. Of course. That would be the perfect chance, the one he would have to wait for, since Daniel had meant to point Billy to him, not Sean. He felt grateful for the gag, otherwise he would have broken into giggles. He was so relieved to know Daniel didn't consider him utterly helpless.

He saw a hint of a smile in Daniel's eyes as Billy gave a final tug and his rope fell to the floor. Billy pressed the gun to his nape.

"Now don't you do something stupid or I'll blow your brains out, you hear me?"

Jeff nodded. His wrists throbbed with the sudden rush of blood, but he didn't dare rub them. He raised both hands slowly to the cloth in his mouth and pulled it off.

"Get your ass moving," Billy said, nudging him with the gun.

He didn't need any more encouragement. He crossed his legs for leverage and stood, hands still up as he walked to Daniel. He felt a pang of anxiety as he looked down at him. Daniel's eyes were dull with exhaustion, pallor spreading over his body like frost. He appeared too weak to even press the already soaked cloth to the wound, just managing to hold it more or less in place. And still his voice came out full of authority as he assumed his role once again for Billy's sake.

"I'm gonna need some bandages, cotton wads, silk or nylon thread, and alcohol."

Jeff recognized his cue. "I don't think Uncle Charlie keeps alcohol for wounds. Would whiskey do?"

"Yeah, anything stronger than beer should do it." Jeff nodded, keeping his face blank. "Now, Billy," Daniel added, "the next is a little bit dangerous, so you better watch out." Billy actually straightened, eager to appear ready and alert. "I need a knife and a needle to be put to the flames till they're red hot." Billy nodded his understanding. "That's it then. Follow Jeff and see that he gets everything."

Jeff started to move but stopped when he saw Billy hesitate. He was eyeing his uncle and Sean in a suspicious way. He tried to distract him. "Are we doing this or what?"

"Shut up!"

Billy was now looking at the rope he'd left on the floor and Jeff swallowed. He couldn't be thinking that. No way. Daniel must have guessed it, too, for he tried to urge Billy away. "Come on, Billy, I have to take the bullet out."

That seemed to decide the man. He started moving toward Jeff, so Jeff, in turn, started walking toward the door when he heard Billy bark. "Stop, you motherfucker!"

He turned around, tried to look surprised as best he could. "What now? We're not getting that stuff?"

"Bring me that rope." No. God, no."I said move!"

He went back to the place he had been sitting in and bent to pick up the discarded rope.

"Billy, what are you doing? I don't need any rope." Jeff could feel Daniel's effort to sound calm.

"I must do this," Billy said. "You're too trusting. Still reckon they're your friends."

Jeff fought the urge to say something, knowing Billy wouldn't listen to him, knowing he would only make it worse.

"C'mere and tie him."

"Billy, don't do this." Jeff stood frozen, waiting for a miracle. "Billy, I'm too weak to move. Trust me on this. Go and bring me what I need. I'll just lie here and rest, that's all I can do."

Billy shook his head stubbornly. "You're too kind for your own good. I must protect you. They'll take advantage of you again." He now turned to Jeff and glared at him. "Tie him! Now!" Billy closed the distance between them and pressed the gun to Jeff's temple. "Move!"

"Calm down, Billy. Jeff will do as you say, just don't use that gun anymore."

God, Daniel. He lifted his pale hands for Jeff to tie them, big green eyes looking up at him. There was fear in those eyes, and he knew it was sheer panic Daniel was fighting back, but there was something else there, too, and Jeff felt a knot in his stomach when he saw the look of grim determination on those soulful eyes.

Jeff took a deep breath and reached out for the hands that were offered to him. That small contact was enough to send shivers down his spine. Daniel's skin was cold to the touch, his long, slender fingers twitching a little in his grip.

"Tie him or I swear I'll kill you!" Billy hollered, leaving Jeff no other chance than to put the rope around Daniel's wrists, trying as best he could to keep his fingers on the cold, white skin, willing his touch to be steady and comforting, willing his eyes to show Daniel what his heart felt, the whole density of the feelings he had been holding back for months now pouring out of him into a look that held Daniel in place, hanging onto it as if for dear life, his breath coming shallow and fast, cold sweat shining on his brow.

Jeff tied the knots slowly, his eyes never once leaving Daniel's as the slim body started to shake. Damn Billy. Jeff fought with all that he was to keep the rage down, to hold still, just watching Daniel tremble as he struggled to keep calm. Daniel shut his eyes and all Jeff could do was squeeze those pale hands hard, make Daniel feel he was not going to let go of him, not this time, not again, not ever. His voice came out in a hoarse whisper as he called Daniel's name. He barely registered Billy's movement from the corner of his eye, heard him say something he didn't bother to understand. All he cared about was the man shaking in front of him, the beautiful, marble-white face he longed to cradle in his hands and kiss still, the green eyes that now looked up at him with something akin to despair. As his hands were yanked off Daniel's, he mouthed the words carved into his heart, and stumbled in the direction of Billy's hard shove, turning his face just in time to see Daniel's eyes widen as his message hit home.

Chapter 15

IT FELT good, those cold fingers touching his brow. Sean opened his eyes and had to close them again to block the light out. It must be late for the sun to be so bright. Must have overslept too, for his body felt stiff. Whose fingers were those? Jeff's? Nice, the way they stroked his hair. He cracked his lids open just enough to see, to focus on the profile of that face hovering over his. Daniel. He blinked. Daniel? He tried to say the name aloud when Daniel's lips pressed to his and all he could do was moan into that sweet mouth. He moved his hands to reach him and was shocked to find they didn't budge, something hard holding them in place. He jerked his head up and the world swerved sickeningly, pain stabbing his skull as if a nail was being hammered right into the bone.

Daniel's arm cushioned his head before it hit the floor in a rather awkward movement, just as if Daniel's hands were... Oh my God. Memories rushed to his brain, images flowing back in quick flashes of seemingly unrelated events, yet he understood, knew what the pain in his head meant, knew Daniel had put his lips on his because he couldn't use his hands to keep him silent.

He was so close now he was able to hear Daniel's breath, and he didn't like its labored sound. He tried to move, but Daniel pressed his body against his, keeping him still. Then he felt him shift, carefully resting Sean's head on the floor and moving away from him.

Sean struggled to ignore the throb in the back of his head and opened his eyes again. He almost let out a frustrated curse. Daniel was kneeling beside him, panting hard, his naked skin as white as his boxer shorts, forehead resting on his tied hands. He was fighting his own wave of dizziness, fighting to stay conscious in spite of the blood trailing down his chest, fighting to keep sane in spite of the rope chafing his wrists.

Sean couldn't help a groan escaping him, the sound low and desperate. His whole body ached with the need to reach out to Daniel, tear that rope away and wrap his arms around him to support his weight. Daniel must have heard him, for he dropped his hands to look at him. Their eyes locked, conflicting emotions flowing between them till they seemed to understand exactly what the other felt, what needed to be done.

Daniel finally nodded. Sean didn't dare move his head, but he forced his body to roll so he was lying on his chest. Daniel gave his fingers a light squeeze before moving to work on the rope, and that small gesture made Sean's throat constrict. He took a deep breath to steady himself. As his heart slowed down, he distinctly heard Jeff's voice coming from a distance, as if he was in another room. A strained voice answered him, one Sean didn't have trouble recognizing as Billy's. Shit. So it was Billy who had caused all this mess. Fuck. It seemed only days ago that Daniel had warned them about something like this, but he never imagined it would happen so soon or catch them so unprepared. He never even thought it would be them Billy attacked. Damn the sweat lodge. If it wasn't for its weakening effect they could have easily taken Billy down. They were four to one, even with the gun the odds were clearly against the intruding party. Just their damn luck to choose that day to have a go at some crazy ritual.

Jeff's voice sounded louder then, and Sean had to wonder if he and Billy were coming back their way. It was taking too long for Daniel to undo the knots. Not that he'd ever tried to untie anyone with his own hands bound and a bullet in him, but Sean guessed they weren't going to get another chance like that. Daniel seemed to be thinking along the same lines, for the tugs he was giving the rope became urgent, desperate.

He heard Jeff say "Think we got all the stuff" and knew they were coming back in mere seconds. Daniel only had time to roll him to the side and leave before Sean heard their footsteps. Shit. Would Billy notice anything out of place? Had Daniel managed to go back to where he was before? The rope was still in place and Sean didn't dare to try its resistance. He kept still, eyes shut, waiting, listening, praying.

JEFF put the knife carefully down, Billy's eyes following his every move. He should have seen it earlier, the way those bland eyes turned into something wild when the man got any amount of alcohol in his system. *Should have known better.* And yet he was so used to drunks mostly harming themselves that he wasn't prepared to face someone like Billy. Should have known, though, for it was a drunk driver who'd killed his father, even if he was family and hadn't hurt a fly before.

Billy was eyeing the whiskey bottle now, had been for some time before he took knife and needle and almost melted them in the stove's little blue flame.

"Think we got all the stuff," he said, the man's eyes leaving the bottle reluctantly to look at him. Daniel's idea might work, for the whiskey was proving to be a good distraction.

Billy motioned vaguely toward the living room, so Jeff picked up the tray and marched back to Daniel. As soon as he crossed the door, he noticed something was wrong. Daniel was sitting in the same position, head resting on the couch, eyes closed, tied hands in his lap. Yet something was amiss, something he couldn't quite place. He came closer with the excuse of the tray he was carrying, and as he bent to put it on the low table, he noticed the quick rhythm of Daniel's breath. He froze. Was he still fighting panic? Was he in shock? And then a third possibility came to him. No way. He couldn't have….

Billy moved closer to the couch and before he could get any nearer, Jeff took Daniel's hands. "I'm going to untie him now," he said in his best no-bullshit tone. Billy grunted but stood where he was, just watching him. Daniel's eyes opened, head moving to face him. He looked spent, even paler if that was possible, the green in his eyes appearing subdued, opaque. Yet there was no fear in those eyes, and Jeff felt relieved.

Daniel let out a shaky breath as Jeff undid the knots, the sound touching something deep in his chest, making him ache. He had to stop this madness right then. If he waited any longer, Daniel's life would be in danger—if it wasn't already at risk.

"Jeff, I need you to clean the wound. You brought the whiskey?"

He nodded, turning to reach for the bottle. And sure enough, Billy was ogling it, tongue coming out to lick his lips. Jeff poured some of the dark liquid to soak a cotton wad, the smell coming out of it pungent and heady. He just hoped Billy couldn't resist it.

"Is it strong? 'Cause it won't do, otherwise."

Jeff felt a warm wave of pride at the way Daniel's brain was still working in spite of all he was going through. He hurried to follow his opening. "Wouldn't know, could never tell the difference."

Billy made an impatient sound. "Gimme that bottle!"

Jeff's heart raced, his mouth going dry. It was now or never. The moment Billy's head tilted back to take a long swig from the bottle, Jeff lunged forward, one hand reaching for the gun as his knee went up to hit Billy's groin.

There was a muffled cry and then he was falling on top of Billy, the bottle crashing against the wooden floor. He never let go of Billy's wrist as he landed on his chest, but just like before, the man clutched the gun desperately, fighting Jeff's weight off with all his might, the strength coming out of that sack of bones so overpowering, that Jeff barely managed to pin him down.

He tried to move his free hand to hit Billy, but the moment he shifted, Billy's hand shot up to Jeff's throat, wet fingers sinking deep into his windpipe, choking him. He panicked. It couldn't be happening, not now, not this way. He grabbed Billy's arm and shook, the iron grip on his throat not yielding a single inch.

Jeff started thrashing madly, gasping for air, his lungs burning, thoughts spinning in his head. He knew his strength was deserting him, knew that any moment now Billy would be able to roll them over and get rid of his limp body. He was pretty sure of what would happen next, as soon as Billy was free to use the gun. And the worst part wouldn't be facing that piece pointed at him. The worst part would be knowing that the moment he died, nothing could stop Billy from marching across the room to where Sean lay unconscious, to where his uncle sat tied, to where Daniel lay bleeding. It would happen all over again, some drunken man taking everything that mattered away from him, everyone he had dared to love. And this time he would die knowing it was his own fault, knowing with his last breath that only he could have stopped it all from happening, knowing that he had failed yet again.

He felt rage filling him. Billy wanted him dead, and he could take his life for all he cared, but if he thought for a moment he was taking anything else from him, he was sadly mistaken. There was no fucking way Jeff was letting him come near his uncle or his men. Yeah, his men, both his men. If he was going to die, he might as well admit he loved not one but two damn white men. Loved them more than his own life. And right now, he was going to fight for them, to the death if that's what it took.

Jeff mustered all his strength to let go of the arm strangling him. His hand dropped to the floor, fumbling around blindly for a piece of glass. He heard his own ragged breaths as a distant sound, the fingers on his throat clutching so hard his vision blurred. His limbs felt numb and he knew he was about to faint. But not yet. He still had to do something before the final detachment swept over him. He grabbed the slick shard and thrust his arm in Billy's general direction, unable to see where he was aiming. He felt the cutting edge sink deep into his own palm as it pierced Billy's body, not knowing whose blood it was that flowed warm over his skin, whose voice was shrieking in pain. It must have been just his blood, must have been his wheezing breath ringing like a cry in his ears. That was all. That was how he was going to die, strangled by a drunken man on the floor of his uncle's house, a place so lost in the middle of nowhere that it would be half a day before anyone found their bodies. And it would be Aunt Helena, opening the door to her home the next morning to find death polluting her most sacred place. She would stand at the door, her hands covering her mouth, not daring to cross the threshold as she surveyed the carnage, just guessing from that distance how it had come to happen, how someone had first strangled her nephew and then shot her husband, the sheriff, and the reservation doctor, one after the other, without hesitation, without pause, just watching them tumble to the ground like domino pieces.

Jeff felt a last disturbing notion cross his brain seconds before it shut down from oxygen deprivation. Daniel wouldn't go like that. He would throw himself at Billy to save the others and Billy would do his best to keep him alive. Billy would protect his worshiped hero and make Daniel watch while he killed Jeff's uncle and then Sean, for his own good. Daniel would be left there, bleeding to death, surrounded by the corpses of the men Billy had killed for him, because of him. He would be lucky if he died in the first few hours, if Billy didn't decide to tie him to keep him from harm, if he didn't have to see how Billy sobered as time went by and put a bullet to his own brain when he understood what he had done.

As Jeff drifted into oblivion, he prayed there really was a hell where he was going. Yet he doubted eternity would be enough to pay for what he had done to Daniel.

Chapter 16

SEAN couldn't take it anymore.

"Would you stop pacing?"

And sure enough, Jeff gave him a stunned look. The man hadn't even realized he was doing that. "Sorry."

Sean smiled. "It's all right. You were just reminding me I can't leave the fucking bed and do exactly what you were doing."

That got him a small smile, the first one since they'd left old man Charlie's house. He patted the bed beside him. "C'mere."

Jeff sat gingerly on the mattress, and Sean reached out to graze the angry red marks all around his throat. "It hurts?"

"Nah… but I'm seriously considering joining a hard-core band."

Sean chuckled. Yeah, it was a hell of a coarse, rasping voice, would be for some days according to the doctor.

"What about your head?" Jeff asked.

"It's fine. The painkillers are doing their job. It only feels a little odd, like…"

"Like you actually had a brain inside it?"

He laughed, but he could tell Jeff's attention was not quite into the joke, his mind too busy with worry. He pressed his hand to Jeff's, softly stroking the dark skin. "He'll be all right. You know how strong he is."

"Yeah, I do know. Shit, the man pretty much saved our skins."

"You weren't so bad at it yourself."

Jeff snorted, no humor in the sound. "If you and Daniel hadn't come to my rescue, I'd have more than just a few marks on my throat now." He looked up into Sean's eyes. "But how on earth did Daniel manage to untie you?"

Sean smiled. "Well, he couldn't actually undo the knots, but he loosened them just enough. I tell you, I couldn't believe my eyes when I saw him there, kneeling beside me with his hands bound."

Jeff shook his head. "If you'd seen the look on those eyes when I tied him... he was shaking all over, and I kept remembering how he had lashed out at you whenever you held his wrists, thought he wasn't going to make it, that he'd be in shock by the time I came back to the room with Billy in tow. Jesus. I had been wondering how he managed to stay focused with a bullet in him and then that. He was just...."

"Yeah, fucking amazing."

Jeff nodded, his smile sad, concerned. Sean squeezed his hand. "You were pretty amazing too."

Jeff frowned and turned his face from him. "I was useless. That's what I was."

Oh no, he wasn't having any of that. Sean straightened in the bed and reached for Jeff when the room went spinning.

"Whoa, Sean, what are you trying to do? You got a concussion there, gotta stay down if you don't wanna be sick."

As soon as he heard Jeff say that, his stomach threatened to come out of his mouth, and he had to shut his eyes tight, darkness barely relieving the spinning motion. He heaved, warm hands shifting him, holding his head as he threw up over something he could only hope was not the floor. Then those hands rested his head back on the pillow and disappeared for just one moment before returning with a wet cloth that they gently wiped over his mouth. His eyes flicked open and met dark brown irises head on. God. The look those black coals had for him.

"Jeff." He knew his voice was all husky and needy, but he

couldn't care less. There were no words for what he was feeling, or rather there were, three simple words that he forced himself to say aloud before the intensity of the emotions rushing over him became too much to bear. "I love you," he said, knowing that, whatever Jeff felt about him, it was the right thing to say. There was no mistaking the nature of his feelings. In fact, he was sure he should have said it a long time before, shouldn't have needed to almost lose Jeff to know it.

Jeff gave him a wide-eyed stare and then pulled his hand from his and stood. Sean tried hard not to let the disappointment show on his face. It wasn't the right time for this. How could he ask Jeff to sort out his feelings when Daniel's life was still at risk? His own mind kept screaming there was no way they would lose Daniel now, but what if they did? What if he died? Where would that leave them? He might not be able to feel anything anymore if that happened, and Jeff would never forget it was Billy's resentment toward *his* uncle what had triggered all, that, and their inability to heed Daniel's warning.

"Forget I said anything, Jeff. I was just being—"

"Foolish, yeah."

It stung, the finality with which Jeff dismissed it, as if he hadn't believed for even a second that Sean might have meant every single word. "Maybe you're right," Sean spat, ignoring the way the walls forgot to keep their solid contours. "I thought I was being selfish, but I might have been just foolish, expecting you to feel anything."

Jeff looked at him hard, dark eyes angry, and just then the room went through another spin cycle and he had to shut his eyes, his stomach riding the waves with piss-poor navigating skills. When he opened his eyes again, the glare had gone from Jeff's look, replaced by deeply felt concern.

"You make me dizzy," Sean teased, smiling like a fool until Jeff looked away. Shit. What was wrong with him? He was acting all shy and embarrassed *now*? He sure wasn't when they shared a bed: Jeff was anything but shy then. He followed Jeff's tense figure till he reached the window and stopped, still not looking at Sean.

"I should make that call."

Sean felt his pulse racing and forced himself to take deep breaths.

He hated it. Had seen it happen again and again: men who didn't waver with a gun aimed at their chests but who would recoil in panic when emotions threatened to graze their thick skins. If you dared mention the L word to one of those men, they would look at you as if you'd just cursed their whole family line for all the generations to come.

"Yeah, go. If you stay I may embarrass you with more of my feelings."

Jeff glared at him and strode to the door. "Asshole," he spat with his hand on the knob, and Sean braced himself for the slam he knew would follow. Yet it never came and Sean almost smiled. Even pissed as he was, Jeff could not forget where they were and would be careful. Sean sighed. He, too, should remember. Daniel was fighting for his life. It was easy to understand that Jeff could only focus on one thing at a time and, right now, worry took precedence over every other possible emotion. Yeah, worry and probably guilt, by the way he'd reacted before. His mind was likely going over everything that had happened and wondering how the outcome might have changed if he'd only done this or that. He'd been there, too, but being that close to death always had the same effect on him: it pushed him forward, made him remember how easy it was to lose everything. And so every time Sean threw caution to the wind and went for the things that really mattered. It made him ruthless, and he had very little patience left for those who still hesitated.

He rubbed a hand over his face. If it wasn't for the fucking concussion he'd be out of the room in a heartbeat, but Sean dreaded the thought of standing on his own feet. Damn. Pain he could take, but being shown the hard way that the earth actually moved was driving him crazy.

Well, he was giving it one hour, no more. Then he'd leave the damned bed for good. He had things to do, important things to do, such as pace up and down the aisle to ICU, glare at the stupid doctors, and shake some sense into that stubborn Indian. He'd show Jeff stubborn. Now that he was sure of what he wanted, he wasn't letting go. There would be no more excuses, no guilt, no shame, no fear. And if Daniel thought dying would provide a good excuse, he was sadly mistaken. Sean would go to hell if that was what it took to bring him back, though he very much doubted Daniel would end up there, the way the man already looked like an angel.

He shook his head, smiling, and had to clutch at the mattress when the walls started the whole acrobatic show again, contorting and somersaulting like no solid surface had a right to do. He cursed under his breath and then, louder, he said to no one in particular:

"One hour, that's all you'll get from me, you fucker."

He wasn't sure you could negotiate with a concussion, but it sure kept him hostage, bound to the bed, weak and useless when he was most needed. And hurting. In spite of what he'd told Jeff, the painkillers only dulled the edges of what was probably the worst kind of pain he'd ever experienced. He'd been shot, stabbed, and punched, but not even broken bones had felt like this. Other pains he could isolate and work at ignoring, but how could you ignore it when it was your own self that hurt? Jeff had been teasing him, but it was true: now he was sure he had a brain, because it hurt like hell. Shit. Even his thoughts hurt. Hangovers were a blessing compared with this. And the worst was the inflaming silliness of it all. He was confined to a hospital room *because he had a headache?* Not that he would be caught saying so, but that was what it all came down to in the end. And it was doing wonders for his already bruised ego.

He shut his eyes, willing it all to disappear. He could do this. In an hour, nobody would be able to tell he was in pain. He was having no more of this shit, not when Jeff needed him, not when Daniel.... His eyes went wide. He lay there, stunned by the sudden revelation. Of course. That was exactly what Daniel went through every time a migraine hit him.

Sean had assumed it was like a bad hangover for him, but now he knew better. That incapacitating pain he felt was what Daniel had to put up with every so often, complete with dizziness, frustration and... yeah, shame. Small wonder Daniel never said anything about it. Sean was trying his best to hide it, and he had a concussion.

Damn. Now he understood why Daniel was so reluctant to take his painkillers. He said they made him dizzy, and Sean could perfectly relate. Every single time Daniel had to choose between this agonizing pain and dizziness. And of course he would choose the pain because it still let him do something, be in charge, not depend on anyone—though

Sean had to wonder how on earth he managed to take that kind of pain for days. He at least knew his concussion would get better and he would eventually get rid of all the vexing symptoms. Daniel's migraines were for good, and he'd been having them since he was a kid. He shivered, conjuring that image in his mind: Daniel, as a boy, hurting like this. How could a child bear it? Maybe it wasn't that bad for kids. He snorted. Yeah, sure, as if pain was related to body size. Children suffered as much as adults, but they were much more helpless. That was what made it so bad to see kids go through sickness and pain. And that was probably why Daniel chose to become a pediatrician. He sure knew what it meant to be a child with a medical condition.

Daniel. He shut his eyes, imagining his beautiful face, his pale skin, his lithe body, the grace with which he moved. He looked delicate, fragile even, but he was a fighter, had endurance and courage to throw away. That was why Sean felt so confident that he would make it. That, and his own inability to even consider losing him.

He took a deep breath and slowly turned his head to look at his watch. Ten minutes to the hour. Fine. In ten minutes he would get dressed and go out to look for Jeff and check on Daniel, concussion be damned. He'd been dawdling long enough. It was time to fight, and no McCallum was ever seen turning his back on a good fight.

JEFF let the phone on the other end of the line ring, hoping he'd calmed down by the time someone picked up. Shit. He was ready to bite some heads off. Stupid Irishman. *I love you*, he'd said, as if Jeff was the sheriff's personal equal-opportunity project. Sean loved Daniel, period. Didn't he know how it had gone since the *Mayflower*? Whites fucked Indians for the thrill but married whites. And now was no different. If Daniel had been available, Sean wouldn't have even looked his way. The concussion might be more serious than it appeared at first glance if he was confusing wild sex with love.

"*Diga.*"

Jeff almost jumped where he stood, the voice reminding him he was still on the phone.

"Raúl?" He asked tentatively, just hoping the man spoke English, because his Spanish was pretty much nonexistent.

"Sí, soy yo."

"Este es Jeff Redbear...."

The grave voice cut his efforts short. "Something happened to Daniel?"

He felt relieved he would be understood, so he went straight to the point. "He's been shot." There was a sharp intake of breath on the other end. He hurried on, not wanting Daniel's friend to put himself in the worst-case scenario. "He is in ICU right now, has been for some hours. Doctors say the bullet itself didn't do much damage, but it took us too long to bring him here, and he was bleeding all that time."

Silence stretched for only a moment and then the voice came back firm. "How do I get there?"

Jeff blinked. Twice. "I understand you wanting to see him, but I can assure you he is in good hands. Doctors are doing their best and Sean and I will be here 24/7, we'll keep you up on everything that—"

"How do I get there?"

He had to smile at that. Men in Daniel's life sure came stubborn; he should have been used to it by now. He gave Raúl directions and phone numbers, heard him move about even as they spoke, getting ready. He almost expected him to hang up on him and start running out of his home till he asked, seemingly on second thought.

"You and Sean all right? Not wounded?"

Jeff knew he was going to like the man. Already did, for that matter. "We're fine, thank you."

"I will see you there, then."

"Oh, one more thing," Jeff suddenly remembered. "We don't know how to contact Daniel's family, only had your number to go by."

He heard a noise on the other end, something between a grunt and a snort. "Don't worry, I will deal with his family."

He thought he heard sarcasm when Raúl said "his family," but he might be imagining things, given the strong Spanish accent.

"Okay then, we'll call you if something comes up."

"Gracias."

Raúl did hang up then and Jeff shook his head. The man was so worried he didn't even care to know what had happened, just wanted to be on his way as soon as possible—and a good thing that was, too, since he had an ocean and most of a country to cross. He understood now why Daniel spoke about him as he would of his own brother. Blood alone didn't make close families, his job had taught him that, but it still came as a surprise every time he saw it happen. A very nice surprise.

"What are you smiling at?"

Jeff spun on his heels and met twinkling blue eyes. Anger suffused him like a tropical disease. What did the asshole think he was doing out of bed, dressed from head to toes?

"You stupid son of a—"

The rest of his words were smothered under a big hand pressing against his mouth. "Quiet, babe, remember this is a hospital."

Jeff clenched his fists. If it wasn't a hospital he would have beat that smug smile out of him. Or maybe he should, just *because* it was a hospital: they would take care of any damage he inflicted and maybe then Sean would keep his ass in bed.

"Come on, let's check on Daniel."

As soon as the hand left his mouth, Jeff opened it to say what he was thinking, but Sean's mouth closed on him in a quick, chaste kiss. Jeff froze. For Christ's sake! They were in public! He darted a quick look around but found the aisle empty. Yeah, well, nobody had seen it, but Sean hadn't even checked first. Jeff glared at the stupid sheriff and found himself staring at a wide-shouldered, retreating back. The asshole. Was he expecting Jeff to follow him like a dog?

He was so mad his vision started to blur. When he forced himself to focus, all he could see was a firm, jean-clad butt moving hypnotically away. And then he felt defeated. Who was he kidding? Even here, in this dreadful hospital where Daniel lay dying, he wanted Sean. No matter what went on in his head, his body was so finely attuned to the big man that it would respond in earnest to his every move, like it was doing now, his feet marching on their own as soon as Sean disappeared from view, just like a dog would track his master when he no longer saw him. Shit. He couldn't afford any of this right now. Not after what had happened, and most likely not ever, but surely not now. He had to concentrate on Daniel. There wasn't much he could do to help him, but Jeff could at least be there, offer him his undivided attention. For now. When he recovered—and Jeff firmly avoided thinking *if* he recovered—he would send Daniel safely home, where he belonged. Then he would deal with Sean, put an end to the dangerous game they were playing. With a bit of luck, once Daniel went home, Sean would leave, too, and everything would go back to normal. And maybe then, Jeff would stop feeling guilty.

Chapter 17

SEAN looked at his watch. Five minutes. *Get a grip, McCallum.* Jeff had only gone to show his uncle out. He'd be back soon enough. Sean shifted in the hard plastic chair. It was childish, but he needed Jeff near. Even his sulky silences soothed Sean's fears like nothing else could— surely not the doctors. They were doing their best to avoid questions about Daniel. Just a moment ago, one of the bastards had glared at the bandage on his head and told him in no uncertain terms that he should be in his room, where he would be duly informed of any change in Doctor Ugarte's condition, should there be one. The jerk. Of course there would be a change, and Sean would be there to see it, not back in his room going slowly nuts. Besides, how many days would they keep him in observation? How long did it take for a concussion to disappear? Two days seemed more than enough to Sean, and he did feel slightly better; his head was now sore instead of achy, if that was possible. He only had to remember not to move briskly. The rest was bearable, especially for the chance to see Daniel from time to time. God. He looked so pale, so gaunt, so helplessly beautiful in the middle of all those blinking machines. The one time the nurse had taken pity on them and allowed Jeff and him to go in together, he had held Jeff's hand as they watched the slow movement of Daniel's chest. The Apache had tried to pull away, but Sean wouldn't let him, and the look Jeff gave him was so full of pain that he found it difficult to breathe.

Jeff was fighting his own demons even as Daniel fought for his life. If Daniel died, Sean wasn't sure Jeff would win. Even if Daniel lived, Jeff might be praying to the wrong gods, offering the wrong sacrifices. Then again, if Daniel lived, Sean would be strong enough to bring Jeff back from whatever hell he thought he deserved to be in. If Daniel lived.

He heard someone approach and remembered to lift his head slowly, praying it wasn't another well-wishing individual or police officer from every available agency. He smiled his relief at seeing Jeff, brown eyes looking solemnly into his. He was about to speak when he saw the tall figure coming behind Jeff. Another cop? He sure had the build for it: broad shoulders, firm body, gray eyes watching him closely. Dressed too casually, though, or rather, too elegantly casual to be any sort of cop.

"Any news?" Jeff asked, his voice still raspy. Sean shook his head stiffly, his eyes going to the purplish marks around Jeff's throat. He did it every time and every time he found his rage intact, his hands itching to punish the man who had dared to mark what was his.

"You talked to the doctor?"

"Yeah, told me no news was good news and that it was early to start worrying."

The stranger snorted at that. "Says that because Daniel is nothing of his."

Sean's eyes widened at the thick Spanish accent.

"Oh, sorry, Sean, this is Raúl."

Raúl? That almost blond, fair-skinned, gray-eyed man was Raúl? He was never assuming he knew what Spaniards looked like anymore.

Raúl dropped a leather travel bag and walked to Sean, hand offered for him to shake.

"Pleased to meet you," he said, voice and expression grave and dignified, all the way the Spanish nobleman.

"Good to meet you, too, Raúl." And it really was good, having the chance to know Daniel's closest friend, though Sean would rather have made his acquaintance as far from a hospital as humanly possible.

"Would they… can I see Daniel?" He looked tired and anxious, much like he and Jeff did, though Jeff was wearing what Sean had taken to calling his Apache warrior mask: a grim expression that was fixed solidly on his features and wouldn't allow any display of emotions.

"Not yet. A nurse will come to tell us when we can, though it would probably be just you going in."

Raúl's expression showed he understood this to mean Daniel's life was still very much at risk. Sean didn't know what to say. Whatever comfort he tried to offer would sound false, and Raúl didn't look the type to take well to polite lies.

The Spaniard sighed and slumped into the nearest plastic chair. He was very expressive, his mobile face a clear contrast with Jeff's clammed-up neutrality. Sean wouldn't have called him handsome, but he had a strong presence, and not just because he was big. He simply couldn't go unnoticed, with that deep baritone voice, those sharp eyes looking at everything with interest, white teeth flashing easily, movements confident, even graceful in spite of his size. Sean felt a little envious. He still was a bit taller and wider than Raúl, but the man was certainly big—and yet he didn't look awkward, didn't look like he *felt* awkward at all.

Raúl spoke. "Tell me what happened, please."

Jeff looked at Sean and he nodded. He'd rather hear it from Jeff, didn't want to go through it all over again. He studied Raúl's face as Jeff recounted everything, saw anger narrowing his eyes, balling his hands into fists. In the end he rubbed his face with his hands and said just one word.

"*Joder.*"

Yeah. That he understood, had been saying it a lot lately. *Fuck*, and also *shit*, and *damn it all to hell*. And it didn't make it any better, the rage deep inside.

They were silent for a time till Raúl asked, "Why were you alone?"

"What do you mean alone?"

"That ceremony."

"The sweat lodge?"

Raúl nodded. "Isn't it a communal thing?"

Jeff shifted uncomfortably in his seat. "Not always. Depends on the end purpose."

"What was the purpose then?"

Jeff exchanged an almost panicked look with Sean. "We wanted…" he stammered. "We thought the atmosphere would help Daniel relax, let go a bit."

Raúl's eyes narrowed. "Was he stressed for some reason?"

"Uh, not exactly. We wanted him to feel comfortable enough to talk," Jeff said haltingly.

Raúl looked overtly suspicious now, so Sean thought they'd better put the truth out front. "We discovered by accident that he couldn't stand being restrained, but he wouldn't tell us why, so we figured there was a story there, and not a nice one by the look of it."

Raúl was angry now. "So you caused all this mess because you were fucking curious? Is that how it went?"

Sean felt heat suffusing him and his voice rose dangerously. "We didn't cause anything. It was Billy who—"

"Gentlemen, please, remember this is a hospital."

The three of them jerked their heads up. Shit. He was so furious he hadn't even heard the nurse approach. Raúl stood eagerly, making the woman crane her neck to keep looking at him.

"May I see Daniel now?"

"Are you family?"

Raúl hesitated, and Sean felt a wicked satisfaction. *Serves you right*, he thought, still outraged by the Spaniard's earlier suggestion.

"Brother," Jeff put in. "He's come all the way from Spain."

The grateful look in Raúl's eyes made Sean feel ashamed. He cast his eyes down as the nurse showed the tall foreigner the way and didn't look back up, even when he couldn't hear their footsteps anymore. Shit. What was he thinking? He couldn't resent Daniel's friend for acting protective. He didn't know them, had no reason to trust two strangers, and the circumstances kept everyone's nerves on edge.

"He's right," Jeff mumbled.

Sean looked up at him, anger rising to the bait. "No, he's not. It was Billy who 'caused this mess', and, whatever we did, you know we didn't do it out of curiosity."

Jeff gave him a skeptical look before his face closed into the expressionless mask Sean hated. "I need some coffee," he said as he rose from his chair without looking at Sean.

"Jeff...."

"Want some?"

"Jeff. We couldn't possibly have foreseen what happened." The Apache kept still, his back to Sean, his shoulders rigid. "Even if we had skipped the lodge, Billy might have found other ways to harm Daniel. It's not our fault and you know it." He could almost feel the tension coming in waves off Jeff's stiff back.

"I'll get the damned coffee."

Fuck. He would have followed Jeff down the hall and given him a piece of his mind, but he knew it was useless. Right now they were all angry and frustrated, or rather, scared to death, which made them angry and frustrated. They could, of course, vent it on each other, but that was not exactly the healthiest way to go about it.

Sean bent forward, elbows on his knees, and rested his head on his open hands. The floor swirled dangerously and he groaned, lifting his head back up in slow motion till it rested against the wall behind him. Lord. He wanted to yell so badly he seriously considered going outside to find a place where he could let out all his pent-up rage in one single, glass-shattering bellow. But he couldn't bear to leave Daniel's proximity. He might wake up while Sean was outside shouting his head off. Or he might.... Sean closed his eyes, refusing to go there. He took long, deep breaths to calm himself. He'd never been good at waiting. He solved problems, doing whatever it took, but never even considered waiting them out as an acceptable choice. And now, it was all he could do.

"You all right?" He opened his eyes to find Raúl looking down at him. He was back already? Did it mean...? Raúl must have sensed his apprehension for he hurried to explain. "Doctors came to see Daniel and threw me out."

"Did they tell you anything?"

Raúl shrugged. "That they are doing their best and all that."

Yeah, he was sick of them doing their best. Wondered what would happen if they didn't.

"I suppose it is good that Dani is a doctor."

Sean cocked his head to look at Raúl. Dani? Never heard it said that way, with an open A like the ones in "America." Sounded good, pretty much like Raúl: strong, open, and affectionate. "Yeah. It's become kind of personal for them now. Guess it'd look bad if they couldn't help one of their own."

Raúl nodded and held his gaze. "Sean, I am sorry about—"

Sean raised his hand to stop him. "No, it's all right, I understand. Not being able to do anything for Daniel is hard on the nerves. We all want to find someone to blame, and the fact that Billy was not in his right mind doesn't make things better."

"I blame myself too."

Sean gave him a wide-eyed stare. And then… "Why on earth should you blame yourself? You weren't even in this country."

Sean almost jumped out of his seat as a new voice interrupted them. The concussion must have affected his hearing because people kept startling him. Jeff was there, right in front of them, holding two cups in his hands, and Sean hadn't even heard him approach. He sounded pissed-off, as if Raúl had no right to feel guilty. Yeah, he felt entitled to the exclusive on guilt, the stubborn, pea-brained son of a bitch.

"I told him to come."

Sean turned his attention to Raúl. "You told Daniel to come back?"

"Not now, the first time."

"You mean the first summer he was here?"

Raúl nodded.

"Why?"

"He always goes to places with wars and epi…."

"Epidemics?"

"Yes, but that time I didn't want it. Daniel was not well and I was worried."

"He was ill?"

Raúl snorted and let out a string of angry words. "When *la tía asquerosa* left him for a *cirujano plástico*, Daniel didn't eat, didn't sleep, worked too much. I was worried something would happen to him, and I thought this country would be good, that he could rest, like a vacation, you know?"

Raúl had said it all so fast that Sean couldn't decide what to ask him first. "La tia what?" he said just as he heard Jeff ask: "A plastic surgeon?"

Raúl looked from one to the other. "Daniel didn't tell you about Estela." It wasn't even a question, and the name sounded like a sour piece of spoiled food in his mouth. Sean wished he knew enough Spanish to understand what Raúl had called her before.

"He told us that Estela and he had been together since medical school, but they'd discovered they wanted different things out of life and had had to part ways."

Raúl shook his head. "Of course they wanted different things. Daniel wanted a family and that bi—Estela, all she ever wants is money."

"When you say a family, you mean kids?"

"Daniel loves children, yes. That is why he is a… how do you say it, a child doctor?"

Sean had to summon all his willpower to keep a straight face. Jeff showed a sudden interest in the wall to his right, head turning sharply away.

"Pediatrician," Sean offered.

Raúl nodded and Sean could almost see his mind working as a smile curved his lips. "So, a child doctor is a boy with a big white coat, no?"

Sean had to chuckle as Jeff smiled openly. It was good to see him relax the tight control he had been forcing on himself since it all started.

"You can laugh, I know I speak funny. When I am angry, I forget all the English I learned."

"No, Raúl, we're most grateful that you speak English, and very well, at that. Jeff and I could barely make a full Spanish sentence out of the bits and pieces we know."

Raúl made a dismissive gesture. "We can't all be like Daniel."

"Like Daniel?"

"He is like a sponge for languages."

Sean exchanged one look with Jeff. "How many does he speak?"

"Let's see," Raúl answered, spreading his fingers as he went. "Spanish, Basque, English, French, and Japanese."

He whistled. "Did you say Japanese?"

"Yes. When he was in England, his roommate was a Japanese boy, so he 'sponged' the language."

Sean would have laughed at Raúl's choice of words if Jeff's expression hadn't given him pause. There was anger in those dark eyes, anger and something else Sean couldn't quite name. Raúl followed his gaze and studied Jeff for a moment. Then he nodded his understanding. "I suppose there are a lot of things Daniel never told you."

Jeff glared at him. "Why? He thought he might overwhelm the poor ignorant Americans? Did he expect us to feel more comfortable if he downgraded himself?"

Raúl glared right back. "No. He believes there is nothing to downgrade, you jerk."

Jeff's eyes went wide and Sean saw all his anger deflate and turn into shame.

"I thought you would have seen it by now."

Sean answered Raúl, keeping his eyes on Jeff as he spoke. "Oh, we have. We know with Daniel it's much more complicated than just not wanting to show off. We know. But it still hurts, feels like there's a reason why we shouldn't be trusted."

The Spaniard looked at them and then away. "He trusts you," he let out almost reluctantly.

They turned eager eyes on him. "He told you that?" Sean asked.

"No, but it shows. He has never...."

This time Sean did hear the nurse approach and he cursed inwardly. The damn woman had to choose that particular moment. Not that he was ever glad to see her, especially when she brandished a finger at him like she was doing now, her free hand going to her hip in a classic reprimanding mother figure.

"Now, Sheriff, you of all people should show some responsibility and go rest in a proper bed. Concussions are not to be taken lightly."

"I appreciate your concern, but I'm fine. Could we see Daniel now?"

She rolled her eyes. "Come on, stop worrying about Dr. Ugarte. The whole staff is keeping an eye on him." She winked. "You know every single nurse in this building has got a crush on that cutie pie."

In spite of the obvious joke, Sean couldn't help the tinge of jealousy that made him want to bring her statement down. "Every single nurse? You mean even that burly ER nurse who looks like a pro wrestler?"

"That big guy? He's the doctor's number-one fan." She lowered her voice to a conspiratorial whisper. "He's got a thing for sweet, small men, and Doctor Ugarte, he can be sweet as molasses, that one can. Am I wrong here?"

"No, ma'am, you sure ain't wrong at that," Jeff answered, dead serious.

The nurse glared at him. "Now don't you ma'am me, mister. Name is Sally, and I'd appreciate it if you'd let me do my work and went home to get some rest. Sheriff here needs his beauty sleep, and you can't stay if you're not family."

"We *are* family, Sally," Jeff said.

The nurse raised an eyebrow and looked pointedly from one to the other.

"Adopted," said Raúl, and Sean barely managed to keep a straight face till the nurse rolled her eyes and walked away, shaking her head.

"You know," she said, turning, "if my parents had adopted three guys like you, I'd be all for incest."

When the nurse finally disappeared around the corner, they burst out laughing, Sean holding his bandaged head with his hands, unable to stop in spite of the pain his movements brought. He knew it was useless, trying to convince them to leave: none of them would be able to rest till Daniel was out of danger. And that, if no other thing, was what made them family.

Chapter 18

JEFF closed the door behind him and took a deep breath. It was the third night, and still there was no change. Soon it would be too late. Christ, Daniel, why did you have to come to this godforsaken corner of the world? Ironically enough, Daniel had never been wounded before, even though he'd spent most of his summers in war-ridden countries. He had come to rest, to find some distraction; he'd just broken up with the woman who'd been his girlfriend for six years. Six whole years. Jeff couldn't begin to imagine what it would be like to be with someone that long, how it would feel to be left behind after all that time. Of course, knowing Daniel, he was most likely blaming himself, even though, according to Raúl, she had been cheating on him. Daniel must have been feeling hurt, lonely, and inadequate.

Jeff cursed aloud in the empty hallway. How could they have been so blind, so insensitive, forcing themselves on Daniel, shoving him around, giving him new insecurities? They had been more than a little patronizing, thinking they knew what was best for the man without taking the time to really hear him out. They had been outright arrogant.

He started walking down the hall, his mind back in that bed where Daniel seemed to sleep placidly. Yeah. With Daniel, everything seemed nice and easy, when nothing ever was. And they'd fallen for it, hook, line, and sinker, the blind fools that they were.

As he turned the corner, he saw the other fool, sprawled on the hard hospital chair, head resting uncomfortably against the wall, eyes closed. Jeff's chest grew tight as he took in the bandage, the ashen hue to his complexion, the dark circles around his eyes. Then he felt angry all over again. The big lug should know better than to add to their worries. What did he think he was doing? Well, Jeff knew what he was doing, knew the fear that was eating at him. Jeff's shoulders sagged. He also knew he shouldn't care about the stubborn Irishman, but he couldn't help it, and it made him feel hopeless.

"Hey, babe."

And damn if the way that scruffy face lit up at seeing him wasn't drilling a hole in his sternum.

"How's Daniel?" Jeff shook his head and heard Sean sigh. "I take it Raúl is with him now."

Jeff just nodded, afraid of the emotions his voice might betray if he spoke. Sean patted the empty chair by his side, and Jeff hesitated. "C'mere." Sean's eyes were warm, and Jeff almost surrendered to their plea, till the big man added, "I need you."

Oh no, he wasn't having any of that bullshit. "Let's come clean on this once and for all. I know it's not me you need, so drop the act already," Jeff spat through clenched teeth.

Sean eyes widened and then narrowed in anger, making the sheriff look like a startled owl. Jeff wasn't in the mood to find it funny, though, just irritating as all hell.

"Drop the act yourself, you arrogant prick."

Jeff snorted. "Now I'm arrogant?"

"No, not now. You've always been an arrogant son of a bitch, but you'd never been a liar before."

Jeff took a step forward, feeling as if he could punch the stupid fucker, never mind the bandage on his head. Sean stood to meet him halfway, blue eyes sparking with anger till they suddenly shut, the big man swaying in front of him. Jeff's arms reached out on their own, Sean leaning heavily on them, letting Jeff steer him back and help him sit.

"God, I hate this fucking concussion."

"Yeah, well, life sucks."

Sean tilted his head carefully to study him. Jeff didn't even try to look away. He couldn't care less; he was so tired all he wanted was to put an end to everything, whatever that meant. He didn't know anymore.

"Jeff—"

"Guys!"

They turned to see Raúl hurrying to them, his face a poem of nervous exhilaration. Jeff's breath caught and his knees threatened to give way under him.

"He opened his eyes!"

"Daniel's awake?"

Raúl shook his head, smiling to beat the band. "*Ya no*, I mean, he went back to sleep, but he is all right now, *sí*?"

Jeff sat down heavily, his eyes going shut. He stopped listening to the others' agitated voices. He didn't expect relief to feel this painful. Of course he felt glad that it was finally over, but he knew it to be over in other ways as well, knew the worst was yet to come. *Shit.* He wanted to slap himself. How could he be so selfish? The worst would have been to lose Daniel, *you damned coward*. Yeah, it would be tough from now on, tough to look again into those green eyes and know he had to sever all the ties. It would be tough, but he only had himself to blame. It was time to bear up.

HE FELT tired and sore all over. What had he been doing? Working overnight again? Daniel tried to shift to his side, but the pain coming from his shoulder was so unbearable he froze where he was, a loud moan escaping his lips.

"… ni."

Someone was trying to speak to him, but he couldn't place the voice. Didn't even remember where he was, but his lids felt too heavy to lift.

"Dani."

He smiled, or at least his lips twitched. Only Raúl called him that, so it was obvious where he was: back home in Spain, where there were no sheriffs, or Indians, or guns… *oh God.* Daniel's eyes fluttered open, bright lights blinding him for a moment.

"Dani, ¿me oyes?" As his eyes focused, Raúl's smiling face appeared in front of him. "Si vuelves a darme otro susto como este, te juro que te mato con mis propias manos."

And sure enough, those hands Raúl threatened to kill him with if he ever gave him another fright like that cupped his face gently as Raúl bent to kiss his forehead. Daniel closed his eyes, smiling broadly till he remembered and opened them wide.

"Sean? Jeff?"

"Right here, Daniel."

He turned to see them standing a little apart, Jeff looking tired, his throat marked by a ring of bruises, right hand sporting a bandage, and Sean beside him, his head all wrapped up in his own bandage.

"You okay?" Daniel managed to croak, his voice dry and hoarse.

"We're fine, don't you go worrying over us."

Daniel opened his mouth but Jeff cut his efforts short. "Uncle Charlie is fine, too. Even Billy is fine, should you want to know."

Jeff sounded strange, angry almost, but maybe it was just the gruffness still left in his voice. Daniel's smile came easier now, and his eyes roamed from one to the other of the male faces surrounding him. There they were, the most important people in his life, together around his bed. He blinked uncertainly as his addled brain processed that realization. How could those two men have become as important to him as Raúl was? He thought he knew how, but he pushed the knowledge to the farthest recesses of his mind.

"Daniel?"

He must have closed his eyes, judging by the concerned looks on their faces. He smiled at the different ways in which they expressed their worry. Raúl's hands were on him in a heartbeat, touching his arm, his shoulder, his hair, as if he needed to make sure he was still there.

Sean looked positively frightened and somehow frustrated, both his hands squeezing the sheets so close to Daniel's leg that it felt as if it was his flesh the big man was digging his fingers into. And Jeff, well... Jeff was scowling like an ancient picture of an Apache chief.

"What's so funny?" he barked in his raspy voice, and Daniel couldn't contain the mirth that escaped his throat in a sort of undignified giggle. "Shut up, you crazy Spaniard." Jeff was trying so hard to keep any trace of a smile from his lips that he ended up pouting like a ten-year-old.

"Who are you calling a crazy Spaniard, you famished *americano*?" Raúl threw back at Jeff, arms crossing in front of him as he stared the Apache down.

Daniel's bed shook with his laughter as he looked from one to the other of the growling men and then back to Sean's amused stare. He laughed so hard it turned into a coughing fit, the wound on his shoulder sending out sharp signals of distress. Three pairs of eyes zeroed in on him, and Daniel felt like a child caught with his hand in the cookie jar.

"Sorry," he mumbled, feeling himself blush.

Raúl grunted and pulled him from the bed into a bear hug, not giving a damn about the mess of wires and tubes coming in and out of his body. Not that he cared much himself; he could only focus on the warmth around him, the deep voice whispering Spanish words, the familiar scent of Raúl's cologne. He had crossed an ocean to be there for him, literally, and Daniel wondered for the hundredth time what he had done to deserve such a friend.

"Hey! Don't hog Daniel! You've had him for enough years already."

Raúl snorted and moved slightly away, one arm holding Daniel upright till Sean bent and wrapped his own arms around him, pulling Daniel to his chest with infinite care, as if he was a fragile, irreplaceable antique. *Christ.* If he kept that up, Daniel was going to embarrass himself and cry like a baby.

"Why are you standing there like a totem pole?" Sean's voice traveled through Daniel's body, making him shiver. "C'mere and help me keep him warm."

Daniel looked over Sean's shoulder at Jeff. It was obvious he couldn't decide what to do, his face showing so many conflicting emotions at the same time that it made Daniel dizzy. The moment he closed his eyes, though, the mattress dipped and two firm hands caught his and held tight. His eyes fluttered open and he met dark brown eyes, one single emotion now dilating those pupils till he couldn't tell where the irises began. He smiled and relaxed into Sean's embrace. As his lids grew heavy, he felt his hand still in Jeff's, Sean's arms still wrapped around him as if they couldn't let go of him. And how he wished they never would let him go.

Chapter 19

SEAN was restless. It was taking ages for Raúl and Daniel to come out of that fucking room. And Jeff was nowhere to be seen. Small wonder, that. He was on his best sneaky Indian behavior, had been since they'd crossed the hospital doors for the first time. With only one notable exception: the day Daniel recovered consciousness. That day, Jeff had allowed himself to show some feeling, and Sean could still see the smile on Daniel's face as he drifted off to sleep in his arms. He shook his head. Daniel had felt so thin, so worn out, and yet so at ease with their displays of affection that Sean wished he could have stopped time right that moment. Forever. But just as soon as that moment passed, everyone was back to their usual quirks.

Daniel was trying to disguise his pain under an artificial buoyancy that fooled no one; Raúl was growly in two languages, making Sean think Irish and Spaniards might have picked their stubbornness from the same source; and Jeff… Jeff was a different story. Every time Sean thought about Jeff's behavior, he felt like breaking something. The asshole. What did he think he was accomplishing? As soon as Daniel was out of danger, the bastard had started drifting away, till whole days went by without him stepping into the hospital. The second day he hadn't shown, Daniel had stopped asking after him, but the hurt was plain in his eyes. Those green marvels had gone dull, subdued, and Daniel had tried to convince Sean to do the same as Jeff. Without much success, that went without saying.

For once, Sean had been able to use a medical leave for something good. When it was obvious that they had to count Jeff out, he and Raúl had organized themselves to stick to Daniel's side, so that there was always one, most often two, of them in the room with him, day and night, for as long as it took. Not that Daniel hadn't tried to shoo them away every five minutes, but the most he got was the turns they had set up to sleep at Sean's place.

"What are you doing out here?"

He almost jumped out of his skin and then, almost jumped at Jeff in anger. "I'm waiting for Raúl to help Daniel get dressed. What are *you* doing here?"

Jeff had the decency to blush, or at least to change color a little, but before he could say anything, the sound of a wheelchair being pushed down the aisle made them both look away.

There Daniel was, looking a tad pale, a lot embarrassed, beaming uncertainly at them from the chair. God. If he kept up the lost puppy act, Sean was going to forget they were in public and do something outrageous.

"They wouldn't let me walk," Daniel said apologetically.

Raúl rolled his eyes. "Be thankful they even let you out, *cabeza de chorlito.*"

Sean cracked up. He couldn't help himself around Raúl's colorful invectives. He had learned a few over the days, but Raúl still managed to come up with new, delirious combinations. And whenever Daniel retaliated, Sean had to hold his head to avoid the last remnants of his concussion from showing up with his laughter.

"Stop laughing, you overgrown teddy bear."

"What did you call me?" he glared at Daniel, his hands on his hips, as Raúl chuckled. Daniel turned a smiling face to Sean's side.

"Sorry, Jeff."

"Don't apologize to me."

Oh shit. Jeff's tone cut through their mood like a knife. He saw the smile die on Daniel's lips.

Raúl made a point of ignoring the bastard. "Lead us to your car,

Sean."

Sean nodded and strode away without looking at Jeff. He didn't want to see him right now, didn't even care if he followed. As he helped a quiet Daniel into the back seat of his SUV, he wondered where to take the two Spaniards. He'd always assumed they'd go to Jeff's place, the four of them, but now he wasn't so sure. He couldn't anticipate Jeff's reactions anymore.

"Don't go anywhere, Doc, be right back."

Daniel nodded distractedly. No witty comeback, not even a roll of his eyes. Sean was going to kill Jeff, right after having this conversation he didn't want Daniel to hear. Just in case. He walked to where the Apache was standing, conveniently away from the SUV, just as Raúl came out of the hospital doors after giving back the wheelchair. Sean prayed that Jeff had a little dignity left.

"Raúl, we can't take Daniel to the health center. It's in no shape for him to rest there. I'll take you both to my place."

This is your cue, Injun, don't disappoint me now. And sure enough, Jeff spoke, his tone still curt, his face blank.

"Your place is too small. I'll give you the keys to my place."

He was about to smile when he realized what Jeff had just said. "The keys?"

"I'll stay with Uncle Charlie, so you can have the house."

What the fuck? He couldn't seem to find the right words to throw at the asshole's head, so he just stood there fuming till Raúl started to walk away.

"Take us to a hotel."

Sean turned to answer him when he saw Daniel standing by the SUV door. Oh shit. He couldn't have heard them, could he? The grim expression on his face told Sean he probably had. Shit. He was going to kill Jeff, slowly, painfully, and he was going to enjoy every second of it. But that would have to wait; there were open wounds he had to nurse right now.

"¡Dani! ¿Qué coño haces ahí de pie?"

"Joder, Raúl, deja de tratarme como a un inválido."

Wow. Daniel sounded even angrier in Spanish, his narrowed eyes letting out toxic green flames. "Who are you and what have you done with Daniel?"

That's right, smile for me, Doc.

"Sean...." He sounded defeated, and Sean fought the urge to clench his fists. Damn Indian. "Take us to that hotel by the town hall. We'll be fine there."

"No way. You're not going to a hotel."

"Your place is a matchbox, we can't stay there."

"Why not? You're already thin as a match; you'll fit in just fine."

Daniel gave him a tired smile. "You've already done enough, Sean. You need to rest, and for that you need your own space."

That sounded too much like good-bye for his comfort. He was going to kill that Apache. Well, he'd already established that. Now he had to do something about Daniel.

"If you won't drive us there, we'll take a taxi. Your choice."

Shit. Trust Spaniards to have even more pride than Jicarilla Apaches. They were driving him nuts, the whole lot of them. "Okay, okay. Get into the car, I'll take you there." Daniel hesitated. "To the hotel, Daniel, I'll drive you to the hotel. Now be a good boy and jump in."

"I'm not a dog, you know," he retorted even as he ducked his head to get into the back seat.

"You sure know how to bark your way around," Sean murmured.

"I can still hear you, Sheriff," came the voice from inside.

He grinned as he turned to Raúl. "Don't even try," the tall Spaniard warned and Sean had to chuckle as he moved to the driver's seat.

He drove the car out of the parking lot with not so much as a glance in Jeff's general direction. He didn't want to fill his mind with images of knives, guns, or rat poisons. He did look into the rearview mirror, though, watching as Raúl manhandled Daniel till he was more or less stretched on the back seat, with his head on the tall guy's lap.

Sean took his eyes back to the road and loosened the death grip on the steering wheel. He had to be calm now. That hotel was the nicest in town. They'd be all right while he did what he had to do. Yeah. If everything went as he planned, they wouldn't be there for more than a week.

Chapter 20

JEFF found himself at the door to the guest bedroom for the sixth time that evening. Nine days since Daniel had left the hospital. Nine days with their long, sleepless nights. If he closed his tired eyes he could still see the hurt in Daniel's eyes, the anger in Sean's. He rubbed his hand over his face. He had been so naïve. He'd thought he could simply drift apart, harmlessly evaporate like an early morning mist. He snorted. He was too thick in the head for any kind of mist. Why hadn't he anticipated it would be this painful? Some pain he did expect and welcome. He deserved some punishment, but he hadn't expected open-heart surgery without anesthesia.

He pushed himself off the door frame and into the room. It would all eventually fade away, just like the already faint scent in that piece of cloth he treasured. It was a stupid thing to do, stupid and immature, but he wasn't heeding his own professional advice. He was still wallowing in self-pity, and he still kept the pajamas Daniel wore when he'd spent that night in his guest bed. Shit. He would have kept Sean's, too, if the big man had ever slept in anything but his own skin.

He rested his hands on the chest of drawers as he closed his eyes. He could see Sean's naked body, all that glorious expanse of muscle rippling for him, wrapping him in an embrace that could be both hard and gentle, just like the big man's loving was: rough, possessive, and yet tender in its own unique way.

He took a deep breath. He was getting all excited just thinking about Sean. He let out a derisive chuckle. Wasn't that the point, blowing off some steam so he could go to bed and actually sleep?

He crouched to open the bottom drawer. There they were, the pajamas he'd lent Daniel. He sat on the floor and reached for them. Flashes from that night came rushing through his mind: Daniel shivering in Sean's arms as he carried him into the house, his own hands undressing Daniel and helping him don those same pajamas Jeff now held, that first rough kiss between Sean and him, that first tender kiss between him and Daniel, those tear-filled green eyes looking at him in surprise and finally surrendering to the wave of desire that glued the three of them together.

Jeff found himself clutching at the flannel in his hands and made a conscious effort at letting go. He then brought it to his face and let the soft fabric caress his skin. He sniffed carefully and closed his eyes as he detected the vague hint of a familiar scent. Yeah. That was the way Daniel smelled, just like freshly cut green grass. As his cock kept filling with the images that scent brought to his mind, Jeff felt a disquieting oppression in his chest. He tried to concentrate on the most sensual visions he could evoke, but the more his arousal grew, the more it hurt, till he watched in astonishment as a fat droplet fell on his thigh. He couldn't believe it. He was excited *and* crying?

"Jeff?"

He jumped so fast that his shoulder hit the chest of drawers and had him cursing aloud.

"You all right there?"

He jerked his head to the door and his eyes went wide as he took in the strong legs, the broad chest, the concerned blue eyes. Those eyes, roaming over Jeff's half-naked body as if looking for wounds. Jeff was suddenly too aware of the pajamas in his hand and, worse still, the wetness on his cheeks. And then he felt angry, unbearably angry. He sprung to his feet and let the words come out like a hiss through clenched teeth. "What the fuck are you doing in my house?"

Sean's expression hardened and he studied Jeff's eyes for a moment before looking down to the pajamas in his hand. Jeff barely contained the growl forming deep in his chest as he threw the cursed pajamas as far from him as he could manage: he would have burned them if he had been able to. Fucking white men. "Get out of here!" he shouted at the top of his lungs.

"No."

Just that. Just one word, and Jeff thought he was having a stroke, he was shaking so hard. "If you don't leave my property as of now," he snarled, "I'm having one of your deputies arrest you for trespassing."

The dumb bastard actually took a step toward him. "Stop it, Jeff."

"No, you stop it, motherfucker. You have no right to walk into my home as if you owned it and you sure—"

"You never answered the door."

"What?"

"I rang the bell. Four times."

Jeff looked at him, stunned. Had he been that absorbed in his thoughts?

"I need your help."

Jeff snickered. Now that was funny. "You need my Apache skills to track down some criminal? Need me to perform some ritual for you? No, wait, those always end up with you in a hospital bed."

Sean ignored his ranting and went on in the same even voice. "Daniel is leaving."

Jeff sobered, his heart beating so fast he felt a little light-headed. Daniel was leaving? He swallowed hard, lost for a moment in the middle of his own house. And then rage suffused him once more. Yeah. Of course he was leaving. This had always been just a passing phase for him, an adventure, an experiment. Someone like him would never invest more than a few months in such an unrewarding project with such worthless people.

"So what? He was leaving in two months anyway."

He saw Sean's countenance change, a menacing glint appearing in his eyes. "You cowardly little shit."

The big man strode angrily toward him and Jeff fought the urge to retreat. "Don't come any closer, Sean, I warn you."

Sean snorted as he took one more step forward. "You warn me? And what are you gonna do, you chicken, scream for help?"

"Stop or I swear I'll—"

Two hands landed flatly on his chest and shoved him hard. He took two unstable steps backwards as Sean kept growling and moving forward. "You swear you'll what? You'll go running to your uncle? Have him curse my soul?"

Jeff took an angry step toward the sneering man in front of him and opened his mouth to yell some obscenity when a hard mouth came crashing down on his. Jeff's whole body tensed to repel the hands grabbing him, the tongue ravishing his lips, but then, just as if his body had its own memory imprinted deep inside, it surged forward to meet the assault, his tongue pushing into the encroaching mouth, his fingers digging into hard muscle, his hips pushing to seek friction. Sean's thigh came between his legs and Jeff spread them unconsciously to let the strong thigh press against his aching groin.

The moment the jolt of pleasure ran up his spine to his brain, his mind seemed to dislodge and watch the action from afar. He saw his smaller body easily manhandled by the big man, submitting to him willingly, eagerly even, rubbing against him as if he couldn't get enough of the man he had wanted out of his house only a moment before. He felt the nausea rising inside as he finally saw what he really was: a shameless dog doing just about anything for a caress from his master. He growled into Sean's mouth as disgust rushed through his veins and shoved him with all his might. Sean let go momentarily and stood there panting in front of him, studying him like a predator would study his already secure prey. When Sean reached out to grab him again, Jeff couldn't take it anymore and his fist simply flew of its own accord, connecting with satisfactory precision.

Sean stumbled backward but never fell. He looked up at Jeff, his eyes wide, blood coming out of his parted lips. He stood there for a moment, looking lost, but then his expression changed into one of defeat. "So that's how it is, huh?"

Jeff blinked in confusion.

"You never believed a single word I told you," Sean whispered and then chuckled without humor. "Or rather, you believed everything.

I'm not sure which way it went."

Jeff shifted uncomfortably. He expected anger, even scorn, but not that hopeless grief.

"Oh, but I understand," Sean went on. "I know what you were doing. Yeah. It's easy to see it now. You were leaving me before I left you. Nice strategy, that. Strike before the enemy even thinks of attacking."

Jeff realized his throat was so dry he could hardly swallow. He tried to look away, to say something to stop those words from leaving Sean's lips, but he was frozen in place, his will held by a single thread dangling from Sean's fingers.

"You know?" the big man said now, almost conversationally. "When I called you a coward earlier, I was just trying to get a reaction. It never occurred to me that I could be right. All this time I'd been thinking that you wanted to protect Daniel, do what was best for him even when it meant sacrificing your feelings." He snorted. "Truth is you were protecting yourself, pushing Daniel away before he had a chance to reject you. And I, the big fool that I am, just went and told you that I loved you. Yeah. That must have made you piss your pants." Sean breathed audibly, blue eyes softening as he spoke. "I'm sorry, Jeff, for everything. I won't bother you anymore."

He gave Jeff a sad smile and walked out of the door. Jeff stood motionless till he heard the front door close and, a few moments after that, a car engine running and slowly fading into the distance. Then the thread that had sustained him snapped and his legs gave way under him. He fell to his side and when his head hit the floor, he caught sight of the flannel pajamas, lying in a crumpled heap on the rug by the bed. He stretched his fingers to reach the garment, but it was always some inches too far, no matter what he did. Of course he could reach it if he crawled forward... but that was the only thing he wouldn't do.

He had what he'd wished for: all the things he craved were now just out of reach, unless he crawled to beg for forgiveness, and that was something his pride would never allow. He'd finally made it, won the battle. He just never thought winning would feel so much like dying.

Chapter 21

HE KNOCKED on the door to room 408. Nice number, that, and nice room too. The whole building was an example of quiet elegance, sober and dignified, but Sean wasn't in the mood to appreciate the details that made it so.

For the first time in his life he was scared, really scared. He had thought he'd never find a companion, a partner, a lover; what with being gay and in the police force, it would make such things nearly impossible. But still, he'd kept hoping. Till now. He'd been stupid enough to imagine that, having found not only one but two Mr. Rights, the easiest part would be to keep them by his side. Boy, had he been wrong.

He'd already lost Jeff, and if he didn't play his cards well, Daniel would be leaving in a week. A week. He couldn't believe it. Daniel was quitting, leaving well before his due time. He said he was too exhausted to be of any use, and if he'd been someone else, anyone else, Sean would have understood. He looked spent, thinner than ever, the circles under his eyes so obvious on his pale skin that he was the walking image of a vampire fledgling, as beautiful and sad as those creatures appeared in the best gothic fiction. And that was exactly the problem: he looked not so much exhausted as sad. It gave Sean every reason to think being shot had nothing to do with his leaving.

"Hello, Sean," Raúl greeted, but instead of letting him in, he walked out of the room and all but closed the door behind him. Sean felt so paranoid; he thought Daniel wouldn't see him anymore.

"He is sleeping," Raúl added in a low voice, nodding toward the door. Sean breathed at that, till he remembered it was rather early to be already in bed.

"Is he all right?"

"Headache."

Shit. He always felt sure you couldn't have two different kinds of pain at the same time, but Daniel had proved him wrong by having a migraine *while* he recovered from a bullet wound. Well, if he couldn't see Daniel, he would have to use another tactic. "Could I have a word with you, Raúl?"

The Spaniard studied him for a moment and then nodded. "Wait a second."

He went into the room—to leave a note for Daniel, Sean assumed—and closed the door carefully after him when he came back out. He hadn't retrieved his jacket, so Sean supposed they wouldn't be leaving the building. Figured. Raúl wanted to stay as close to Daniel as he could, exactly what Sean would do if Daniel only let him.

They walked into the hotel bar as if they'd previously agreed on their destination and took a quiet table by the window. They had a view of the coquettish little courtyard, but Sean didn't even spare it a glance. As soon as the waitress brought their two tonics, he went straight for it.

"Why does Daniel want to leave now?"

Raúl made a face that meant the reason was anybody's guess.

"Yeah, I know he's been shot and he was leaving pretty soon anyway, but the Daniel I know would stay attached to his health center like a limpet to the last possible minute, bullet wound be damned."

Raúl sighed. "I insisted."

Sean stared in disbelief. "You pressed him to leave?"

When Raúl nodded, Sean couldn't keep the anger from his voice. "Why on earth would you do that?"

"Why?" Raúl sounded angry too. "What about not wanting my best friend to die?"

"That's bullshit. You know as soon as he recovers he'll be volunteering to some war-ravaged corner of the Third World, so don't tell me you're trying to keep him from danger."

"Yes, I am. But not that kind of danger."

"What are you talking about?"

Raúl lifted both his hands as if to imply Sean was dense. "I don't want to nurse him through heartbreak again."

Sean just looked at him, dumbfounded. "Has Daniel said...?"

Raúl snorted. "Daniel? You are joking, no?"

Sean had to smile at that. "No, I suppose he hasn't. God. Has he always been like this, keeping it all to himself?"

"Only when he is ashamed, or thinks that I will worry, or thinks that he will be a burden, or..." he shrugged, "you know."

"Yeah, I get the picture."

They sipped their drinks in silence.

"Raúl...." The Spaniard looked up at him. "I know Daniel was happy working with the reservation people, I could see how he enjoyed every minute of it. But that's not the only reason I want him to stay." He paused to gather the courage to say it aloud. "I'm in love with him."

Raúl didn't even bat an eye. "That much I guessed."

Sean let his temper flare, not caring who might hear. "So why in all hell are you making him leave? Running away from the people who love him doesn't strike me as the most intelligent way to prevent a heartbreak. And don't you dare tell me this is all because Daniel's not gay. I know perfectly well how his body responds to a man's touch."

Raúl narrowed his eyes and his voice came out dangerously low. "You are a selfish *hijo de puta*."

When those four words made his ire overflow all the restraining dams he'd built in the last few desperate days, Sean's training kicked in, and he moved as slowly as he could manage. He stood, took out his wallet, left a few bills on the table, put the wallet back in his pocket, and let the words come out evenly.

"Follow me."

"No." Only then did he look straight into Raúl's eyes. "I am not leaving Daniel alone."

Sean didn't even blink, his whole body frozen in an artificial calm that made his voice sound neutral, almost friendly. "If you don't come out with me right now, I'm going to arrest you and have this conversation behind bars."

He held Raúl's fiery glare till the Spaniard pushed his chair back and stood. Then he turned and walked all the way out of the building and into the parking lot. When he opened the passenger door of his SUV, Raúl climbed in without a word, and neither of them spoke until they were well out of town and on a deserted side road. No sooner had the engine died than Raúl was out of the car and striding round to the driver's side. Sean met him halfway, and so did his fist, landing squarely on Raúl's clenched jaw and sending him sprawling to the ground.

"Cabrón egoísta."

Sean took a step forward. If Raúl kept calling him selfish, he was going to hurt him really bad. "Get up, you stubborn prick."

There was no need to spur Raúl, though. He was already on his feet and trying to land one punch after another, till Sean was actually forced to put his five senses into the fight. Yeah, the man knew how to use his fists, Sean had to give him that. He even managed to slide past his defenses and draw blood from the cut left by Jeff's fist not that long before. He wiped his mouth with the back of his hand. This was probably the worst day in his whole life, and Sean found he had no idea how to go on with it.

"Why are you really doing this?"

Raúl must have heard the note of defeat in his voice because he dropped his hands and shook his head wordlessly.

"You know Daniel can be happy here," Sean pleaded. "He loves his job, and the people on the reservation adore him. You saw them flock to visit him, saw how that made Daniel feel. I'm not just being selfish, Raúl. I want him to be happy, want to give him all the love and care he deserves. I understand how you'd be wary after what happened with Estela, but I'm not like her. I was willing to let Daniel go when I thought he'd be better off back in Spain, but now that I'm sure he belongs here, I'll do whatever it takes."

"And what about Jeff? How does he fit into all that?"

Sean's words came out harsher than he intended. "He doesn't. He's out of the picture now."

"I am sorry, Sean, but I don't believe you. I have seen the way you look at each other. There is too much feeling there, and I will not risk Daniel getting between you two."

"He's always been between us, but not in the way you think. Daniel is our center, we're both drawn to him and that brought us together, not the other way around. It was never a question of choosing, but sharing."

"Sharing?" Raúl snorted derisively. "And what were you going to do, tear Daniel in two so you both could have your share of him?"

"No, give him twice the love one of us could give him."

Raúl closed his eyes in an obvious effort to calm down. "Jeff is not acting like he loves Daniel."

"Yeah, he's being a fucking idiot, but that's only because he's scared."

"*Jeff* is scared? Do you even imagine how Daniel is feeling?"

Sean lowered his head, chastised. "I suppose we've been giving him confusing signals."

"No, Sean, you have been hurting him."

"I've never—"

Raúl lifted a placating hand. "I know you have good intentions, but you don't understand Daniel. He has very little self-confidence and what has happened doesn't help."

"You mean the way his girlfriend dumped him?"

"No, I mean here, now. You and Jeff have been acting guilty. I am sure Dani thinks that you are by his side only because you feel you have failed him, that you did not stop him from getting hurt, and Jeff is leaving for the same reason. The result is that he is the reason you two are having problems, maybe even breaking up, because of him—and not because you love him. That hasn't even crossed his mind."

"Shit." Raúl only nodded and Sean felt angry, confused, and, most of all, frustrated. He ran a hand through his hair and let his back slide against the SUV till he was sitting in the dirt.

"I don't get it. Why should Daniel think he doesn't deserve anything? He's a successful professional, he's smart, funny, sweet, sexy and… well, to cut a long story short, simply drop-dead gorgeous. What is there to be insecure about?"

Raúl gave him a knowing look but didn't say a word.

"It goes way back, doesn't it?"

The Spaniard didn't answer. He moved closer to the SUV and sat, mimicking Sean's posture.

"What did his father do to him?"

"Let it rest, Sean, it is not your business anymore."

"You're taking him back to Spain no matter what I do or say."

Raúl sighed. "I am sorry, Sean, but I don't think you know how you feel. I don't want Daniel to think he is a poor substitute for all you could not have with Jeff. And I don't want Daniel to be there when you start missing Jeff and resent Daniel for driving him away."

"That will never happen."

"No, because Daniel will not be here."

"Don't do this, Raúl. I'm begging you."

Raúl didn't say a word, didn't even look at him, and Sean knew he had lost the battle. There was no way he could convince Raúl of the true extent of his feelings, and the worst of it all was that, deep inside, he understood. As his brother, Raúl was only protecting Daniel from what was obviously hurting him. He would have done the same. Damn. From the outside, it just looked like Jeff and him had been fooling around with Daniel, shoving him this way or that at their convenience. Sean closed his eyes. In the end, he supposed he even had to be grateful that Raúl didn't think they'd been experimenting with Daniel, luring him into their sex games just for fun.

Silence stretched heavily between them and Sean took in the

desolate landscape for the first time. It seemed quite fitting, being stranded in the middle of nowhere, feeling like the bulky slopes around them, just about to crumble into dust and be scattered about by the wind. Yeah. His heart was on its way to become a desert, too, but just like the landscape of that inhospitable corner of the world, it had first to break, little cracks appearing every day, every night, till all that was left was a sterile, flat extension of sand. Yet if everything was lost, he might as well start breaking a little right then.

"What did his father do to him?"

He felt Raúl's eyes, searching, but he didn't open his.

"Why does he panic when he's restrained?"

Sean waited so long that he thought Raúl was not going to answer him. When he began talking, though, Sean wished he hadn't asked. Then the tears started falling down his cheeks, and he hurt like he'd never hurt before, because for the first time in his life, there was nothing he could do about it, no cure, no solution, not even a simple explanation as to why things had to be the way they were. For the first time in his life, Sean felt useless, and he simply couldn't cope.

Chapter 22

AS HE'D been doing every single evening for the last month, the first thing Jeff did when he arrived home was turn on the television. Background noise. He had been needing it desperately, to drown out his thoughts, his memories, the itch in his too-taut skin, the ache in the center of his chest. Didn't they say hearts couldn't possibly produce pain? Maybe not, but then his sternum must be hurting enough to make up for it.

Jeff had expected a month would suffice to give him a little numbness, but he still took a long detour to avoid the health center, still kept the TV on to avoid hearing Sean's voice in the silence of his house. And why on earth had it never felt so empty before, his place? How had his sanctuary turned into a dry, menacing void? He'd never felt his ancestors' presence as anything but a comforting remembrance of who he was. Now he felt judged and found lacking, every step he took.

He went into the kitchen and splashed water on his face in the sink. He had to get his bearings. He was working late every day, even weekends, to spend as little time as he could in his own house. Which didn't feel like his own anymore. And if all the rooms felt somehow wrong, his bedroom was the most alien of them all. He only went to bed when he was completely exhausted, but even if he managed to fall sleep as soon as his head hit the pillow, he still dreamed. And when he didn't fall asleep, it was ten times worse. He had often made the mistake of touching himself to try to relax, but his body had an even stronger memory than he did. And God, how it hurt to remember. Even the less sentient of his body parts kept traces of fingers other than his, echoes of voices, lingering scents that his skin seemed to have absorbed in spite of all the soap he'd used in a month of showers. Lonely showers.

He let out a humorless laugh. How could one feel lonely in the shower, of all places? Individual acts of hygiene shouldn't be any more than that, but when you had an appreciative lover, the simple gestures of everyday became something else, those dreary routines were instantly enhanced, brought out of context by a look, a touch, a word, that changed them into an excitingly new experience. And once you'd had it, doing without it felt like deprivation.

Jeff forced himself to open the fridge and go through the motions of fixing something that could pass for supper. He wasn't hungry these days, but he knew he needed the energy, especially since he was working more hours than ever before. It kept his mind busy, away from… all that he wouldn't even mention in the hopes of making it, them, whatever, disappear.

He sat in front of the TV and ate, trying to just concentrate in what they were saying, those voices he didn't know.

"…the perpetrator's car went off the bridge and the driver was killed instantly. Two members of the local police continue to be in critical condition as we speak."

Jeff sat up straight, waiting for an indication that allowed him to put a place tag to the events and telling himself that "local police" didn't necessarily mean *their* local police, since the station covered a wide range of police jurisdictions. It could have happened anywhere, it could be anyone. And yet, when the images finally came, he didn't even stop to consider what he should do. He just moved on autopilot, his hands reaching for his cell phone and speed dialing without wondering why Sean's number was still programmed in the first place. When he got voice mail, he called first the hospital and then the sheriff's office, getting busy signals every time he tried. Then he didn't even pause to turn the TV off, he just grabbed his keys and went, his mind a solid block of fear with no space left for anything else. If someone had asked him his name then, he would have stared blankly and babbled some incoherent nonsense along the lines of "have to find Sean" or "Sean is in critical condition" or even "Sean is dying without me" as if that was the ultimate injustice.

He made it to town in record time, his foot glued to the pedal till he reached the sheriff's office and then just let go of it, not taking the time to get into any of the parking spaces, just climbing out of his pickup right where it had stopped and rushing into the building like a madman.

He ran into a deputy he didn't recognize and blurted out the word "sheriff" as if it meant everything he needed to convey. The young man didn't even stop on his way out.

"Hospital," he said without turning to meet Jeff's stricken face.

He stood there, frozen, trying to make his mind keep working enough to control the panic that seized him, when a hand touched his shoulder.

"Jeff?"

He spun around and thanked God for a familiar face. "Is he wounded?"

Alexa's dark eyes gave him a sad look. "No. He's still on sick leave, and I for one am happy he doesn't even have a TV at old Johnson's place, or he'd be all over here, vertigo or no."

He opened his mouth to ask a thousand questions, but Alexa kept talking.

"Please don't tell him Stevens is still at risk. He's been frustrated enough as it is."

With that she patted Jeff's shoulder and moved on out to the patrol cars waiting outside. At least Sean wasn't injured, that much he understood, but he didn't know what to make of the rest. Sick leave? Vertigo? And the bit about old Johnson's place and a TV was the most confusing of all. Why should there be a TV in an abandoned farmhouse? And what had it got to do with Sean?

Jeff walked back to his pickup in a daze. He felt somehow relieved, but his mind was still in turmoil. He knew worry would keep gnawing a hole in the pit of his stomach if he didn't get some answers, but he wasn't sure he had a right to them anymore.

He drove out of town till he reached the crossroads. If he turned right, he'd be back home in less than twenty minutes; if he turned left, he'd be in trouble in half the time. When he stepped on the gas, the wheels screeched loudly on the tarmac.

"Yeah, I know," he said to the empty road. "I'm screwed."

But then again, he'd been screwed for over a month. It wouldn't hurt to add another mistake to the pile. He might even reach his pain threshold and stop feeling for good.

It didn't take long before he caught a glimpse of the farmhouse through the sparse trees. Same old two-storied building, with its broken window and its… new roof?

"Holy shit."

As he drove up, he took in all the significant changes, from the new front door to the saplings barely throwing any shade over Sean's SUV. He parked beside it and stood gaping through the windshield. That close, he could see the cracked paint had been scrubbed in preparation for a new coat and all the window frames looked refurbished. He could almost smell the freshly cut wood, hear the tapping sound of nails being hammered. Yet, when he finally got out of his truck, he could only hear the light slap of the plastic sheets that covered most of the windows.

He climbed the brand new steps onto the front porch and rapped on the door. There was no answer, so Jeff took a deep breath and pushed the door open.

"Here we go," he mumbled under his breath.

He stepped into one of those nightmarish quarantine areas from movies about lethal viruses. The big, empty walls were painted stark white, and huge plastic sheets covered whole areas of what Jeff assumed was work in progress. Not at this time of day, though; now the house was deserted except for one very conspicuous occupant.

Sean sat sprawled on the few floorboards still extant, his back against the wall, the look in his eyes unfocused, as if he hadn't seen or heard anyone enter. Jeff ran his gaze over him in shock. He looked awful: gaunt, disheveled, with a vacant stare that was making the hair on Jeff's arms stand on end.

"Are you all right?" he blurted out.

Sean didn't even look up. "No. I'm seeing ghosts," he slurred, and Jeff felt so many emotions rushing through him he wasn't sure which one would surface till he said the words.

"You're drunk." He heard the disappointment in his own voice and wished he could erase it. He had no right to expect anything from the man in front of him, not anymore.

Sean was huffing now. "Got myself a clever ghost. Cool."

Jeff fought the urge to roll his eyes. "Sean."

"Oh. A true miracle. He even remembers my name."

"Sean, please."

The Irishman finally looked up at him. He was pale, his hair longer than usual, two days worth of stubble giving him the weird appearance of a bum. He had lost a lot of weight and the sparkling life in his blue eyes seemed to have gone with it. Now he stared at Jeff with something akin to detachment, the alcohol in his system making his lids move heavily, as if he was about to fall asleep.

"Sean." Jeff felt all the pain of the last month oozing out of him in that single word, making it sound like a lost cause.

"What, Jeff? What do you want from me now?"

He looked away from the anger in those hollow eyes. He knew he shouldn't be there. Sean had all the right in the world to be angry, and he was just intruding on a very private moment of... yeah, pure, thick despair. He knew he should leave, but he lowered himself onto the floor and hugged his knees.

"You bought old Johnson's place?"

Sean looked at him as if he couldn't believe Jeff was trying his hand at small talk. "No. I'm learning a new trade. Might come in handy when they throw me out of the police force."

Jeff tensed. "Throw you out? Are you getting drunk often?" He couldn't help it. Alcohol was an issue to him, and he guessed he was entitled to be a little harsh about it. The damn thing had brought him one disgrace after another and he hadn't ever tasted it in his whole life.

Sean gave him a murderous glance. "How many other times have you seen me drunk? How much liquor have you seen around my place? How many beers have you spotted in my fridge?"

He'd done it again. Offended Sean. He seemed to excel in that area of expertise. Jeff lowered his head to his propped-up knees and closed his eyes. He didn't want this. Didn't want to hurt Sean, though he guessed it was a little too late for that now.

"Don't know why I bother talking to a ghost."

Yeah. Maybe that was exactly what he was: a see-through, vengeful spirit, unable to grab at the good things life had to offer, just haunting other people's lives till he ruined them. He felt the familiar ache in his chest, right there in his breastbone, like a hand squeezing his entrails, making him want to cry out, beg for it to stop.

"Jeff?"

He looked up earnestly, hating himself for the mad hope that rushed through him at hearing his name in that voice he'd missed so much.

"What are you doing here?"

Sean didn't even sound angry, just vaguely curious, and Jeff felt the words clog his throat.

"I…." He swallowed. He had to be able to do this. He owed Sean the truth. "I was scared."

Sean made a rude noise. "Guess that's the story of your life."

The words stung so much, Jeff had to make a conscious effort to keep still. And he didn't even try to find a reason why they hurt, for he suspected only the truth could be that painful.

"I don't get it, though. You usually run when you're scared."

He looked into Sean's eyes and saw no anger there, not even a little resentment and, surprisingly enough, *that* made him furious. "Yeah, I'm a coward. So what? Doesn't look like being brave ol' sheriff McCallum got you anywhere with Daniel."

Sean let out a drunken laugh. "Wow. An angry ghost. Should've known tequila would mess with the fucking concussion."

Jeff's eyes went wide. "Sean! You're still getting trouble from that concussion?"

Sean waved his hand dismissively. "Nah. Just have 'recurrent bouts of vertigo,' as the doctor sweetly called them." And then he giggled, of all things. "Wouldn't believe how funny it is, carrying your own personal roller coaster wherever you go. It rocks, dude."

Jeff couldn't believe his ears. If Sean hadn't been drunk, he would have slapped his face hard enough to give him another concussion. But, of course, if Sean hadn't been drunk, he wouldn't be laughing at the cause of his medical leave; he would be drinking to forget it.

"You're thin as a ghost." Sean said it so seriously that Jeff's heart skipped a beat. Then he burst out laughing like a ten-year-old, and Jeff couldn't help shaking his head, a smile tugging at the corner of his lips.

"You're one to speak."

"Yeah. It's catching. You wouldn't believe how thin Daniel was when he left. Must be something in the water."

"Yep. One of those flesh-eating bacteria."

"Right. Bacteria."

They looked at each other, nodding sagely like two old men, and let the smiles finally creep onto their tired expressions.

"We're pathetic."

"No shit."

They kept like that for a while, sitting silently on the floor, watching each other as if they needed to build some solid memories they could feed from when they parted ways again.

"What happened, Sean?" He knew he didn't even have to mention Daniel. That was all they thought about those days.

Sean shrugged. "You didn't have the guts and I didn't have the stomach. That's what happened."

Jeff frowned. "What do you mean you 'didn't have the

stomach'?"

Sean sighed tiredly and Jeff thought he wasn't going to answer, the way he closed his eyes and let his head rest back against the wall. But then his voice dropped into an almost whisper, the words shuffling about them like the only true ghosts in the house.

"I thought I would do anything short of murder to keep Daniel from leaving." He snorted. "And it almost got to that when Raúl said I was being a selfish bastard. But then he told me about Daniel and I knew he was right." Sean didn't look at Jeff when he asked, "Remember us thinking Daniel had gone through some kind of abuse?"

Jeff nodded uselessly, hugging his knees tighter as if to shield himself from what he knew was coming.

"Turns out we underestimated the situation, like we did with everything else about Daniel."

Jeff started rocking back and forth, not wanting to think, not even wanting to listen but knowing there was no way out of it now.

"Daniel's father's one of those army men who keep a collection of weapons in display cases and see children as vertically challenged recruits."

Sean's drunken humor grated on Jeff's nerves, every slurred word a knife the big man kept twisting to cause even more damage in the wounds Jeff had been trying his best to ignore.

"Imagine what a disappointment it was to have a son who looked like a pretty girl, cried over dead fish, and whined every time he had a headache. That wouldn't do. He might not become a leader of men as his big brother seemed well on his way to be, but the colonel sure would make a man out of him. And you know how he went about it?"

Jeff didn't answer, didn't move, didn't even breathe.

"He thought he could kill two birds with one stone and train his eldest while he disciplined Daniel, so he made the little kid strip and had his brother hold his wrists while the colonel used a riding crop on him. It was masterly devised, you see. The youngest would be humiliated enough to be naked and punished in front of his brother, so he would be forced not to add more humiliation by crying out with every blow, while the eldest would strengthen his character by having to watch his brother being disciplined and actually keeping him in place so that every blow found its mark. Oh, and you're gonna love the final touch. You know people have to reflect on their punishment before it sinks in. It's just human nature, and no one knew human nature better than the good old colonel. That's why he kept a medieval relic among his treasured weapons: a pair of iron manacles, complete with ankle restraints, conveniently set on the attic wall so that he could chain his son, turn the lights off, and leave him there to reflect on his sins without fearing he could hurt himself or—God forbid—damage his collection. Don't you find it endearing?"

Jeff was on his feet and out of the door in two seconds. He barely made it outside before he was emptying his stomach in the dirt. There wasn't much in him anyway, so he mostly retched and dry-heaved till he thought he was going to break into two separate entities, the swirling nightmare of images his mind kept throwing at him and the searing pain his body had been reduced to.

When he finally lifted his head, he threw a quick glance in the direction of his pickup. All he wanted to do was jump into the driver's seat and fly so far away that people wouldn't even speak his language. He only hesitated for two heartbeats, though. He knew, maybe for the first time, that it would be useless, running away. Those images would be forever carved into his brain; that little boy chained to a wall would always stare back at him with Daniel's eyes, no matter where he chose to hide.

He forced himself to stand and took one wobbly step after another till he was in front of Sean once again. "Stand up," he said in a raspy voice. Sean looked dumbly at him, managing not to move any muscle from his neck down. "I said stand up, you stupid piece of Irish shit!"

He got a drunken guffaw for his trouble. "Wow. The vengeful ghost is back. My brother Timmy is gonna flip when I tell him I got myself a haunted house."

"And why on earth did you buy this monster of a house, huh?"

"Oh, I thought I could refurbish it and sell it at three times the price it cost me. You know, just a little investment."

"Bullshit."

Sean snorted. "Yeah, well, a big investment if you want, but you know what they say about thinking big."

"Bullshit! You bought it because you wanted to offer Daniel a good home, because you wanted to share your life with him." Sean just looked at him, blinking slowly, his glazed eyes hard to read. "You put yourself in a debt I cannot begin to imagine, spent your off time working to bring this old house into shape, begged me for help even though it was hard on your pride, punched the lights out of Raúl even though he's the closest Daniel has to family, and then simply let Raúl take him away from you? All he had to do was tell you a little sob story and you crumbled to the ground?"

"Well, you just threw up over that *little sob story*...."

Jeff glared at him. "Yeah. I'm a coward. We've already established that. Let's just concentrate on you for a moment there. Why in all hell did you let him go?"

Sean sighed audibly. "I thought Raúl was right. I was being selfish, never stopped to think what I was throwing on Daniel."

"Great. So you underestimated him all over again."

"I didn't want to hurt him on top of... everything else."

"And how were you going to hurt him? By loving him to death?"

Sean sat up straight. "Have you forgotten how many times you and I reached the same conclusion? It didn't feel right to keep him here, away from his country, his career, his friends.... Shit. We didn't even know for sure whether he was gay or not."

"Don't give that crap, Sean. He was happy here, you know that, and he never gave a damn about his career. His friends could visit and he might not be gay, but he sure is bi, the way he obviously enjoyed making out with *two* guys. No, that's not why you did it. Raúl told you about Daniel's childhood and you were scared. Admit it. You thought after all Daniel had gone through, he deserved to be real happy, and you were scared you wouldn't be man enough to make up for all of it."

"Shut up."

"You don't like hearing the truth, huh? When it was a question of doing things, you were all ready and eager. You would have built this house with your own hands if that was what it took. But when there was nothing to be done, when you couldn't change the past, you got lost."

"Shut up!" Sean yelled. He then lowered his voice and said without looking at him, "You don't know the half of it."

"I don't? Then be so kind as to enlighten this poor, ignorant Injun."

Sean glared at him again. At least it was better than his previous alcohol-induced indifference.

"I will, smartass. You know what Daniel thought?" Sean didn't wait for his answer. "He thought he was the cause of our breakup. He believed we felt guilty for not being able to protect him from Billy when he'd already cautioned us about him. He thought that put a strain on our relationship we couldn't get over."

Jeff felt his cheeks heat. Daniel had definitely been on the right track, at least concerning his own reasons for walking out of door.

"Sound familiar?"

"It's not exactly true."

Sean smirked. "Oh, *not exactly*. How subtle. You know what isn't exactly true either? That, even if Daniel had stayed with me, I wouldn't have missed you and resented him for it."

"You would never."

Sean narrowed his eyes. "You think I would never miss you? Is that what you're saying?"

"No. I *know* you would never resent Daniel, even if you happened to miss me. Some time."

Sean scoffed. "You don't know shit about me."

"That's a whole load of crap, buddy. You're not that complicated, so stop searching for more anal-retentive motives and admit you were simply scared. Just say it aloud. It can be liberating."

"Yeah, right, *my name is Sean and I am a scared piece of white shit*. And then what? Will you shake my hand and welcome me to Chickens Anonymous?"

There was an awkward silence and then Jeff said, "Man, that just sounds like one of McDonald's suppliers."

They looked at each other for two seconds before cracking up. When their laughter died down, Jeff didn't know what to say. A moment before, he had been ready to punch Sean into acting right, but the moment had passed and he didn't know what was right anymore.

Sean looked at him and patted the floorboards beside him. "C'mere."

Jeff stopped thinking and allowed himself to let go and oblige. He sat down inches away from the big man, not daring to touch till Sean's arm settled on his shoulders and pulled him to his side. Then he just closed his eyes, the emotions rising inside him so strong he feared he would start shaking.

Sean smelled like tequila, but under it Jeff could catch the scent that was only his: freshly cut wood with a touch of lemon from the soap he favored. It was strong enough to make him feel giddy till he realized the smell of wood was so strong because they were in the middle of a construction site full of lumber. He chuckled.

"What's so funny?"

"Nothing. I'm just stupid, that's all."

"Yeah, but I've missed you anyway."

Shit. The silly man had to use the past tense, as if just being there now had ended all their problems, no apologies needed, no reparation to be negotiated, no atonement, no suffering. Jeff felt both relieved and cheated: all his high motives to stay away, all his noble wallowing in self-pity would go unaccounted for?

He pulled himself a little apart to look at Sean's expression. Damn. Those blue eyes were so full of affection he would have choked if he hadn't been in dire need of that same affection he'd been trying to do without. It made him mad and made him want to cry all at once, and of course that only made him mad all over again. "Why on earth would you miss someone like me?"

Sean studied him seriously, as if he was about to let out some pearl of ancient wisdom. "Beats me," he finally said, and Jeff had to whack his shoulder.

"You crazy white man." But he knew Sean could hear the smile in his voice. Warm fingers traced a line from his cheek to his jaw.

"I would kiss you if I was sure which of the two Apaches is you."

"The dumbest of the two, that's which," he said as he cupped Sean's head and got himself a mouthful of white man. Two arms immediately snaked around him and lifted him till he was straddling the big man's lap, the taste of alcohol and Sean never leaving his busy lips. He was so starved he didn't mind the tequila flavor to their kisses, the hard floor against his knees, the way Sean's stubble chafed his skin. He couldn't get enough. His hands traveled all over Sean, clothes or no; his whole body pushed against the man beneath him, desperate for contact, friction, anything. His mouth latched onto Sean's as if he needed reanimation, which he probably did, the way he'd been dying for more than a month now. And if the big man moved a little more slowly, it was just because he was drunk, or at least had been a moment before. Jeff couldn't tell now, couldn't find it in him to care one way or the other; he just wanted that man, white skin and all, like he'd never wanted anything in his whole life... except, of course, for that other white man he couldn't get out of his system no matter how he tried, as if he was permanently drunk on him, on the memory of him.

He heard the animal noises he was making with detachment. That was simply how things were. He was in heat for this man and could be no more ashamed of it than a dog would be of rubbing against his mate. Such was life, and he'd better start accepting it, his role in it.

Sean's hands found their way under Jeff's loose jeans and grabbed his ass, pushing him even closer into the warm body beneath him, making him feel so desperately needed that all his pent-up desire poured out of him as he jerked astride Sean, the noise he let out guttural and harsh, hot seed soaking his underwear. Just coming didn't fulfill his need, though, so even before he stopped shuddering, he slid down Sean's body till his head was level with the man's crotch and fumbled with button and zipper till he got what he wanted. Then he just couldn't wait to take Sean to the root and suck so hard that the big man's hips left the floor as he came down Jeff's throat with a cry. He swallowed eagerly, humming at the familiar taste. Yes, that was more like it, though it wasn't enough by far.

Sean pulled him up for a kiss and he let himself be handled, enjoying the strength of those arms that now held him close, as if the Irishman really believed he was a ghost about to vanish into thin air.

They were in no hurry now, tasting, licking, laving every patch of skin they could find. It was amazing, recovering all those sensations he thought he'd never feel again, but it was unleashing something inside him he'd always fought to control and, with the dams broken, he found he didn't care which way the flood would go. He felt stupid all of a sudden. What had he been so afraid of? Pain? Of course it hurt, hunger always did, and he knew now there was no way he'd ever get enough of this man to ever be sated. Yeah, hunger was a bitch, but then again, only living things felt it. Want was life-generating; fear, the great destroyer of logic, freedom, and, ultimately, life itself.

Sean nuzzled his neck and started sucking up a mark, slowly, painstakingly, as if he was tattooing his name on Jeff's skin. Yeah, it was frightening, Sean's need to claim him, and more so because he'd never felt really wanted in all his years of existence. He always felt kind of handed down, always someone ready to give him up, no matter how much they said it cost them. Yet this man he'd pushed away still wanted him, had never in fact stopped wanting him, the need for him so strong it had been eating away at him till he was only a resemblance of his big, old powerful self.

"Sean...." The pleading note to his voice didn't surprise him, though he wasn't sure what he was begging for. Blue eyes met his, searching.

"What is it, babe? What do you need?"

Oh God. He needed everything, but how could he even begin to ask for it, after all he had done? He only whimpered, unable to speak, and Sean's hand held his head still to look into his eyes.

"Talk to me, Jeff. Let me hear your voice."

Jeff rolled his hips forward, trying to convey the heap of words he had been piling up on his chest till his breastbone was about to be crushed.

"No, babe, not this time." Sean's fingers dug into his scalp and he moaned in pain, in need, in fear, in agony. "Your body has always known what it needs, but your mind is living in its own dimension, and I won't put up with one half of you anymore. You're always trying to please someone: your family, your ancestors, your people. There's a whole crowd traveling with you, making you toe the line, and I've never been good on the sharing. So tell me what you want, Redbear, or this ends right this moment. Just say it aloud. It can be liberating, you know."

Jeff saw the smirk on those lips he had just kissed swollen and felt panic change into a brutal need to strike and draw blood. "You motherfucking son of a filthy whore!"

Sean gave him a sad smile. "See? Wasn't that difficult, saying what you really think about me."

As soon as those strong fingers started moving away from him, Jeff knew what true fear was, and his hands darted out to grab Sean's wrists. "No. That's not what I think of you."

Drunken exhaustion was back in Sean's eyes, and Jeff hated it, hated how easy it was to hurt the man, because he cared too much, because everything Jeff said mattered to him, because he believed every word that came out of his treacherous mouth.

"So? What other category of white trash do I fit into? Just tell me, I've probably been called it before, so go ahead and get it off your chest. It'll give me the perfect sense of closure. You owe me that at least."

Jeff didn't know why he felt so angry... or he did, but knowing there was no way out only made it worse, so he just shook Sean's wrists and yelled at him for all he was worth. "Are you blind on top of everything else? Can't you see I have to think the worst of you so I can not be in love with you?"

Sean blinked in confusion. "Care to repeat that so I can get it straight?"

"There's no way you can get it straight. It's so fucked up you'd have to be on something far stronger than tequila before it even sounded like English to you."

"Oh, you'd be surprised at how many brain cells tequila can leave you without. See if I'm any close here: are you saying that you hate my guts because you've fallen for me, or is it that you have to hate me to avoid getting there in the first place?"

"I'm well past the point of no return. And I hate it."

"And you hate me."

"Yeah, you most of all."

"Uh huh." Sean gave him a thoughtful look. "Why again?"

Jeff shook Sean's wrists in frustration. "Because you had to go and love some piece of Indian shit like me, you stupid white man."

Sean's eyes went wide. "Jeff! You've never been ashamed of what you are!"

"No, but I've never been loved for what I am either."

"I don't get it."

"Of course you don't. I already told you."

He got a growl in return. "Then explain it to me, damn it!"

He hissed. "I've always been the proud Apache, yes, I've been so proud and faithful to my roots that I've become the perfect picture to be framed and left hanging. But you know what sucks about roots? They're buried deep underground, and people just go on about their lives without minding them till they're close to being buried themselves. So I've been always alone with my fucking pride, because nobody else gave a damn about me or my roots. Except you. You and Daniel had to come and show me how bright glass beads were. And how could I put up with the old muddy pottery when there was shiny glass to be had? Problem was, one day the native would stop being exotic, would have nothing left to offer you, and when you'd go, I'd be left with nothing, not even my pride—especially not my pride. And that's all I have, Sean."

A big, gentle hand stroked his cheek. "Sometimes I wonder what you have your brilliant mind for." Jeff tried to feel insulted, but Sean's voice, his touch, didn't carry an ounce of offense in them. "Daniel and I were smitten with you from day one, and not because you appeared *exotic* to us. You're an amazing man, Indian or not. Of course you wouldn't be yourself if you weren't an Apache, but it's you we've always been attracted to, not the perfect museum display you threw at us sometimes, mostly to push us away." Jeff frowned. "Don't give me that look. You know as well as I that you gave us the hostile native act when you wanted to discourage us—especially Daniel, whenever he risked affecting your calm, which I'd bet was most of the time."

Jeff looked down now, unable to meet Sean's eyes. So the big man had known from the beginning. It was probably Daniel who didn't have a clue, Daniel who'd left thinking he hadn't caused them anything but trouble.

There were now two hands framing his face and Jeff just wanted them to stay there. Forever.

"This has to end here, Jeff."

He felt all the air in his lungs leaving him, as if he'd been punched. He kept his eyes tightly shut, fearing he'd cry if he caught only one glimpse of those blue eyes he'd never see again. He surely deserved it; had, in fact, brought it on himself, wanted it even. But God, how it hurt. Sean went on in the same gentle tone, and it was ten times worse that way. If he had been shouting, at least Jeff could have felt angry, but all he could do now was keep very still to fight back tears.

"I can't take it anymore. I know it's only been one month, but seems one month of hell is all I can put up with."

Jeff didn't answer, couldn't possibly have pulled one single word out of his constricted throat.

"I need to go on with my life, and to do so I need to be sure which direction I shall take next. So tell me what it's gonna be, Jeff."

His eyes flicked open in panic. "What?" he croaked, not sure he understood anything at all.

Sean gave him a level look. "Tell me what you want, Jeff. Let me know where I stand, where Daniel stands."

"You mean…?"

"Yeah, I mean you have to say the words, or not, depending on what you want from me. Just say it once, Jeff. Tell me to go fuck myself if you want, but tell me. I need to be sure."

Jeff took a shaky breath. The time had finally come to take the plunge. Or to stay forever watching the tide retreat from a safe, dry place.

"I… I love you, Sean."

Sean's face didn't move, didn't show any emotion, and for a moment Jeff thought he hadn't said the words aloud.

"Daniel?"

So the interrogation wasn't over yet. He thought his heart was going to explode, but he trudged on. The die was cast, as they said.

"I love Daniel too."

"How far are you ready to go for that love?"

That was the crux of it all, he realized now. The rest didn't matter, never had. His feelings had been there all the time, but without his will to do anything about them, it would all burn down to dead ashes.

He closed his eyes and started to shake as fear gripped his entrails. He thought it was the most difficult decision he'd ever made till he really considered what each side of the scales held. Then it was the easiest thing to just let the tears fall down as the words left his mouth. "I would give my life to have you back, to have Daniel back."

Two strong arms pulled him down and wrapped him while he cried like a baby with his face buried in Sean's warm chest. "That's it. Let it out, babe. I've got you now, and I swear I'll never let go of you again, no matter how many hissy fits you throw from now on."

Jeff looked up at him through his tears. "I don't throw hissy fits."

Sean gave him an amused but oh-so-loving look, and Jeff melted against him.

"Temper tantrums, then?"

He punched the solid chest. "Shut up, you grouchy bear," but if he smiled any wider his face would split in two, happy-to-death halves.

Sean just laughed and hugged him, like a true bear would.

Chapter 23

DANIEL closed the door behind him, thinking it felt heavier today, like everything else did. A month had already gone by since he'd left the reservation and, though he usually made it through his shift with not so much trouble, today he seemed to be dragging the whole month behind him, each and all of the thirty days weighing him down and making his every move slow and painful. And to tell the truth, that was exactly how his heart felt: achingly morose. Even his blood pressure was low these days, so low it gave him an air of unearthly calm in the hectic scenery of the emergency room. *Just like a Zen master in a multiple-car crash*, a fellow doctor had joked, but he felt very far from the inner peace that image suggested. The problem was, his mind wasn't attuned to the complete detachment his body enjoyed. He kept thinking, day and night. And then he dreamed, ugly little nightmares creeping into his fitful sleep to leave him drained and sore, as if he'd been running the darkened streets around his apartment.

He shook off his coat and let it crumple in a heap on the floor. He couldn't make himself care. In fact, as soon as he was barefoot and had taken two steps forward, he seemed to forget where he should be headed and simply sat down on the living room carpet, waiting for it to carry him … anywhere, he guessed. So when the phone rang, he just reached out and picked it up from the coffee table, his voice sounding as dull and empty as he felt.

"Diga."

"Daniel?"

His heart took up such a thunderous rhythm he thought he would be sick. Then that voice he knew so well came like a whisper, as if spoken far from the receiver.

"Think I got the wrong number."

He should have said something, but his throat was closed, his mouth dry, his eyes blinking hard.

"Excuse me. I'm trying to reach Dr. Ugarte, Daniel Ugarte."

He took a deep breath and managed to croak a single word. "Jeff."

"Daniel? Is that you? Are you all right?"

The concern in Jeff's voice made him regain his bearings. When he spoke next, it came out curt, almost angry to his ears. "Yes, it's me. I'm fine."

There. Jeff was probably calling over some bureaucratic loose end or other, no point in getting all worked up. No point in *showing* how worked up he was, anyway.

"Daniel, I'm sorry to bother you, but I need to have a word with you."

Right on the mark: there would be some silly form Jeff had to fill out, and the call didn't mean anything else beyond that. Anything at all. Yet Daniel couldn't explain for the life of him why it made him so disappointed and, yes, so angry. He could almost see the wire cringing from the edge in his voice. "Don't worry, Jeff, it's all right. I've nothing better to do."

For a moment there was only a charged silence filling the air like some heavy-handed static. Then a muffled curse sounded in the distance, followed by the clatter of the receiver banging against something.

"Hey there, handsome. Sorry about that, but you know how clumsy these Injuns can be."

Sean. It was Sean. And he was there, with Jeff. That was what the call was about. Daniel felt the anger disappear, leaving only pain in its wake. He supposed he should be glad they were back together. In fact, he *knew* he would be glad for them, in a day or two maybe, in a year or three most probably, but he would. Right now, he just felt left out, betrayed, if that made any sense.

He could hear them arguing on the other end and found he couldn't take it, especially not the way their tones showed all the intimacy their impatient words seemed to mask. It wasn't his responsibility anymore, so he just reached out with trembling fingers and hung up.

When the phone started ringing immediately, he laughed out loud. That had been a childish reflex, thinking he could get away by just closing the door on the landslide coming onto him. Of course he could always disconnect the phone, but that would only gain him some precarious time. The end result would be the same, so he might as well get it over with.

"Sorry about that." He wasn't going to explain what got into him. "How are you guys?"

"We're okay, Daniel, but… well, you know, it's been a hard month."

He almost snorted into the receiver. *They'd* had a hard month? Then he thought Jeff might not be speaking about them and froze. Was that why they were calling? Had anything happened?

"Is everything all right on the reservation?"

"Oh, yeah, don't worry. Everything's fine. That's not why I… why we…."

He let out a relieved sigh. And then anger was back, directing his words in a straight, sharp line. "So what's this all about, Jeff?"

"Don't be mad, Daniel. He'll get to it. Eventually. Just be patient, huh?"

That was Sean again. Daniel could imagine them, leaning close to each other so they could hold the receiver between them. And he couldn't help feeling a little envious, a little annoyed, a little embarrassed.

"Okay. Here I go." Jeff took a deep breath. "First, I want to apologize for being an asshole to you half the time."

He heard his thoughts in Sean's voice. "Half the time?"

"All right. *Most* of the time. I'm very sorry, Daniel. You didn't deserve it. You came here to help and you did a lot for my people, you—"

"Don't even go there, Jeff. I'm not in this for the praises, so just skip it. I accept your apologies, if that's what you wanted to hear."

"No. I mean… Damn! I could use some help here, Sheriff."

"Oh, no, you're not getting away from this. You're gonna say it even if I have to tie you to the phone."

Daniel was losing his patience. He didn't want to hear anything about the reservation or them. It was hard enough trying to forget it all without them popping up like inexhaustible jack-in-the-boxes.

"If you're trying to tell me that you're back together, don't bother. It's more than obvious. I'm happy about you and wish you the best of luck." He knew he sounded a little too final, but he didn't care. It was them who had let him go without seeing him to the airport, Raúl and him sneaking out of the country like another pair of unwanted immigrants.

"Yes, we're together, but that's not why I'm calling."

"Then what is it?" He couldn't control the irritation in his voice. "What do you want from me?"

"I just want it all, Daniel."

"What the fuck…?"

"I love you. Have been in love with you from the very beginning."

Daniel tried to count to ten with his eyes tightly shut. When he managed to control the urge to bang the receiver against the wall, he spoke as calmly as he could. "If you think that was funny…"

"No, no, Daniel, please, I wouldn't joke about something like that. I know you're mad at me and you have every right to be. I cannot apologize enough for the way I behaved the last weeks you were here. But even that I did because I love you. I thought you'd be better without me. I wanted to sever all the ties drastically, so that it'd be easier to let you go."

"Easier? You thought making me feel like shit would ease my way out? That's some fucked-up logic you got there, buddy."

"I'm sorry, Daniel, I really am. I've been all kinds of stupid, but I've finally understood pushing you away only makes it worse. I've been missing you every single minute of every single day, and I can't go on like this. I need you."

Daniel shook his head, trying to put some order into the torrent of thoughts cascading over his stricken brain. He grabbed the first piece of logic he could find. "What about Sean? You just told me you're back together."

"Yes. We're together in loving you."

Now he did snort. "Right. And he's been in love with me from the very beginning."

"Yes, I have, Daniel." Sean's serious voice answered him. "We both fell for you. That was the only thing Jeff and I had in common, and it was that which brought us together in the first place."

Daniel closed his eyes again. He felt as if a hand was squeezing his guts and he knew he was about to be sick. His voice came out thin, strained. "I've no time for this right now. I'm really glad you patched up things between you, but please don't try to... whatever you're trying. Leave me out of this. Jeff, I promise I'll keep the lines open between my hospital and the reservation health center, so that help will keep coming, but, please, just let me be. Don't call me again."

"Don't hang up, Daniel. I beg you."

Jeff sounded so desperate that Daniel found it difficult to breathe. He couldn't name his feelings, didn't know if it was anger, or fear, or pain that tore at his lungs, but he knew hanging up was beyond his physical capabilities right then.

"Please listen to us. Let us explain. You don't have to say anything, just listen. Please, Daniel."

As if he could say anything. Daniel just sat there with the receiver plastered to his ear, the sound of two different voices alternating to fill his head with dread or pain or whatever it was that made his body start to shake as those two men retold the story of the last months in such a different light that he might as well have been dreaming if it wasn't for the solid presence of the floor under him. He was still shaking when Jeff concluded.

"So I never set out to hurt you, Daniel, but I wasn't ready to suddenly find the love of my life in two men."

"Two white men. Just say it all, Jeff," Sean said.

There was a pause and then Jeff's voice came back softly. "More like a grizzly and its fiery cub, the way I feared you'd rip out my heart and eat it alive."

"We already did, babe," Sean said.

"Yeah, I suppose you did at that."

In the silence that followed, Daniel could hear his own shallow breathing against the carpet. Sometime during the conversation he had lowered himself onto the floor, not caring where his head landed as long as he had something solid to stop his free fall. He didn't know what to think, what to feel. His whole being was suspended in one of those self-repeating loops in which nothing moved forward or backward, time frozen in the same, blank second for a whole eternity of unchanged motion.

"You think you can begin to forgive us, Daniel?"

"Daniel?"

He tried to force a word, any word, out of himself, but found he couldn't.

"You all right there?"

"Daniel, please, say something."

The deeply felt concern in those voices he'd missed so much made Daniel shudder and that, on top of his shaking on the living room carpet, just tore a laugh out of him. Problem was, once it left his throat, it sounded much more like a sob.

"Christ, Daniel. I wish I could be there right now, to look into those amazing eyes of yours and know what you're feeling."

"Wish you could," he managed to whisper into the phone. There was a gasp on the other end and then Sean's voice came back to him, sounding a little hoarse, a little shaky too.

"Do you think you could ever feel something for us? Would you consider giving it a try, giving us a chance?"

"I…." He couldn't go on, the anticipation in Sean's voice derailing any logical train of thought.

"It's okay, Daniel. I know this is all too sudden, too new for you. Just think about it, please. Take your time. We will be waiting for you when you're ready to answer."

"Yeah, Sean's right, and I suppose it's already late over there, so we'll let you rest now, call you in a few days. If you still want to hear from us, that is."

"No."

"You don't want us to call back." Jeff's voice was drained of all hope, so much so that he didn't even make it a question.

"No!" Daniel almost shouted into the receiver, "I don't want you to hang up, *atontado*!"

Sean laughed heartily, the sound familiar, comforting.

"What did he just call me?"

"Sounded like a cross between dummy and asshole, but could be worse for all I know."

"Yeah, God knows he has the right to call me anything from filthy Injun to chicken shit."

"Me too."

"Well, not really. He couldn't call you *Injun*, could he now?"

"Maybe not that, but *puto gringo* he could for sure, and perhaps—"

"Shut up already, you fucking crazy *americanos*."

There was an amused silence on the other end that eased Daniel's shaking more than any word could have. "Go and learn some Spanish if you want me to even consider talking to you again. And here is your first lesson, for free: *gringo* is a Mexican word. We Spaniards call you a whole lot of different things, but not that. Got it?"

"Yes, sir."

"Fine."

"Okay."

"Good." Daniel shifted from the fetal position he had unconsciously curled into and stretched his legs all the way.

"Daniel?"

"Mm?"

"What's that rustling? Where are you?"

"I'm on the f—" He closed his mouth abruptly. He couldn't well tell them where he was. "On the couch, I'm on the couch. Was trying to find a comfortable position."

"You tired? Had a tough day at work?"

"Not exactly. I just haven't been at my best lately."

"Sorry, Daniel."

"It's not your fault; I should have forgotten everything and…."

"I'm glad you haven't—forgotten us, I mean."

"Sean…."

"All right. I won't tell you again how much I love you."

"I won't repeat how much I love you, either," Jeff said.

He groaned. "Guys, please. Give me some breathing space here. I still don't know whether I should stop being angry at you or not, can't even think further than that."

"Fair enough, Daniel."

He took a deep breath and felt the tension in his muscles ease a little. "Where are you calling from?"

"The kitchen."

He chuckled. "I meant whose place."

"Mine. Sean's is too small for strategic planning."

"Oh, so you thought you needed a plan to win me over?"

"More like a twelve-step program."

"Yeah, since we're addicted to you."

"Come on…."

"Not joking here, green eyes."

Daniel couldn't help shuddering again. Nobody had given him a pet name before, not even something as obvious as that. He realized now that even the obvious needed some caring, and only Raúl had cared enough to shorten his name affectionately. Until now.

"You're living together?"

"Not yet."

"Why not?" There was some sort of uncomfortable silence and Daniel frowned.

"Uh…we have to settle some things first."

"Set a dish-washing schedule and other important things like that."

"Yeah, sweeping the floor is important. And nobody wants to do it."

"You know it."

Daniel shook his head. He hadn't smiled so easily in what seemed like ages now. "I've missed you," he said softly, his fingers squeezing the receiver as he would the hands holding the other receiver… Sean's big, strong fingers, Jeff's thin, nimble ones.

Two male voices answered at the same time. "I've missed you too."

He closed his eyes, emotion threatening to fill them. Could it be possible? Could those two men…? "Do you really…?" He heard himself babble. "I mean, you both…?"

"Yeah, Daniel, we both love you, really."

"But—"

"No buts. There's nothing to be surprised about. You're smart, handsome, funny…."

"Don't forget sexy."

"What?" Daniel asked.

"Yeah, you're utterly edible, pretty boy."

He felt his cheeks heat. "I'm not…"

"Yes, you are, and edible too."

He chuckled. Sean knew him well enough to anticipate his denying the pretty-boy thing first. Then he frowned. "What if…?" Daniel paused, swallowed. "Let's assume I take your word at face value and accept that you love me."

"Yes, please, let's assume that you do."

"Let me finish," he chided, "I'm theorizing here."

"Okay, theorize away."

"Let's assume that you love me and that I feel something for you in return. That would mean I'd have to move there."

"I thought that was what you wanted, even with us out of the picture."

"Yeah, that's not the problem."

"Then what…?"

"Will you please let me finish? This is rather embarrassing."

"Sorry."

"What if, once I'm there, with you, we find out that I'm not… that we are not… uh… compatible?"

"Oh, come on, we've been together long enough, of course we're compatible, we get along perfectly fine."

"Uh, I think he's talking about sex, Jeff."

"Oh."

Sean had the nerve to laugh.

"It's not funny. I don't suppose you'll put up with holding hands and *getting along*," Daniel said waspishly.

"No, we won't, and no, it's not funny. But you don't have to worry. We are compatible all right."

"How can you know that?"

"We've already… had sex, and I can tell you there was nothing wrong with it."

"Definitely nothing wrong there," Jeff agreed, and Daniel had to roll his eyes.

"Maybe not, but you have to admit the circumstances were pretty special."

"They only made it happen; they didn't change us into different people."

"Still, I've never—"

"Daniel, stop. Don't fret about that. Just take my word. You're everything we want, and if you're inexperienced, that'll only give us an added thrill. Just imagining we'd get to be your first in many things makes my mouth dry."

Daniel felt his own mouth go dry as he pictured strong male hands traveling over his body, undressing him, tongues licking his fevered skin, lips closing on his. And he guessed he wasn't the only one imagining, for there was something close to a whimper coming from the other end. He felt his cock twitch and his mind did a double take. Wasn't he supposed to be angry? Had he not only forgiven them but decided then and there that he was ready to have sex with them? On the phone? After a month of frustration, or rather, outright despair? He rose so quickly that he banged his elbow against the coffee table with a loud crash.

"¡*La leche*!" he cursed.

"Daniel? What happened? You all right?"

He didn't know why, but hearing Jeff sound so concerned made his stomach feel funny. Maybe he wasn't used to the stoic Apache showing any emotion. Toward him, at least.

"I'm fine. I just hit the table."

"You fell forward?"

"Forward? No, I got up too fast."

"From the couch?"

Shit. Trust a cop to remember every word he'd said. "Uh, no. I was on the floor, on the carpet."

"And what on earth were you doing on the floor?"

Oh yeah, there it was again: anger, deep, red-hot, and ready to explode.

"What was I doing? The same thing I've been doing for a month: working my ass off so I wouldn't think about the way I had to leave the reservation, with a project unfinished, people who trusted me left unattended, a bullet wound in my shoulder, and the two people I came to consider my friends avoiding me as if I had the plague. So every time I come home I make sure it's late enough and I'm exhausted enough that I don't have a single thought. Just sometimes I do it so well that I don't have the energy to reach the bed and just sink to the floor as soon as I arrive. And be happy this time I made it to the living room, 'cause you wouldn't be speaking with me otherwise."

There was an awkward silence over the line, and then Jeff's voice came back, hushed. "We really did hurt you."

"Yes, you did, Jeff. And I really, really hope you didn't realize that just now."

"No, but I've been enough of a coward to hope you didn't care much, that you'd only be angry for some little time."

"Yeah, well, think twice."

"I'm sorry, Daniel. You can't begin to imagine how sorry I am."

"Don't tell me what I can or cannot begin to do."

Sean cracked up. "That's my fiery cub."

"You shut up and wait your turn. I'm not done with Redcoyote yet."

"Christ. I've missed hearing you call me that."

Daniel sobered at the longing in Jeff's voice. He took a deep breath to steady his own voice. "What does Sean call you?" He didn't know why he'd asked that but found that he really wanted to hear the answer, wanted to sense a little bit of what they were sharing.

"I mostly call him babe, but sometimes he just looks to me like one of those slick, wild cats, all contained danger ready to spring on you."

Daniel closed his eyes and imagined Jeff's hard features, his long limbs, the way he moved about, silent and graceful like a big predator.

"Guess some people would call me racist for comparing him to a wild beast, but I can't help it. He's beautiful that way."

He heard some rustling and then a soft, wet sound. They were kissing, and Daniel tried to visualize Sean's hand on Jeff's luscious hair, their lips touching gently, parting to let their tongues play catch. The moan that came from the receiver could have been his for all he knew.

"I need to touch you."

"Don't mind me," Daniel heard himself say, surprised at the annoyance in his voice. "Go on and touch him."

"Uh… he's already touching me, Doc. He means he needs to touch *you*."

Daniel was glad he was already on the floor: when all the blood left his addled brain to travel south, he just had to lower himself back onto the carpet and take big gulps of air.

"You okay, Daniel?"

He made a noncommittal sound. He didn't think he could manage words right now.

"Guess we're overwhelming you. We'd better say our good-byes for today and—"

"No!" he squeaked into the phone. Then he made a conscious effort to control his panic and be reasonable, though he knew his voice was trembling. "I'm sorry. I suppose you got things to do. I just…."

"It's all right, Daniel. There's nothing we'd rather be doing— except kissing you out of breath, that is, but you have to rest. We'll call you tomorrow."

"You promise?" He knew it was childish, but that was how he felt, like a child afraid to go to sleep for fear of finding his parents gone when he opened his eyes again.

"You have our word, Daniel."

"Yeah, don't worry about that. We're not making the same mistake twice; we're not letting go of you, not this time, pretty cub, not ever again."

"Okay."

"Fine. Now get that tight little ass off the floor and go to bed."

"Sean!"

"What? You know he has a fine ass by all standards…."

"Of course I know. But you know how that white boy can blush, so don't go embarrassing him, at least not till we can enjoy seeing him go all red and cute."

"Hey! I'm still here!" But Daniel bet they could hear the smile in his voice. Just as well they couldn't see the flush that had spread up to the tips of his ears.

"And what are you doing still there? It's time for little cubs to be in bed."

"We'll call you tomorrow."

"I'll be waiting by the phone."

"Fine, but not on the floor, okay?"

He chuckled. "Okay. No floor for me."

"Yeah. You have to start taking better care of yourself. And don't work overtime."

"And eat."

"That, too, and rest a lot."

"And eat."

God, how he loved those two men. It took him a moment to realize what he'd just thought and then he couldn't find it in him to be shocked. Maybe it was that easy after all.

"Little cub? You fallen asleep on us?"

"No, I just…." Maybe feeling it was easy enough, but saying it out loud would take some time, a lot of courage.

"It's all right, Doc, don't worry about anything. Just go to bed. We'll be here tomorrow, and the day after tomorrow, and every day after that."

"Okay. Good night, then, Jeff, Sean."

"Good night, Daniel, sleep well."

"Good night, pretty cub."

Daniel replaced the receiver slowly and rested his head back on the carpet. He was so relaxed, so melted and tired to the bone that he just couldn't gather enough energy to get up. It was all right. This kind of exhaustion he could take any day, because it carried its own hope with it. He curled into a ball and closed his eyes. He'd move in a minute. He'd just go over the conversation once or twice, replaying it quietly in his head till he convinced himself it had really happened.

He was asleep in the next second, curled like a cat on the living room carpet, with a catlike smile on his lips.

Chapter 24

SEAN closed the door to his office and smiled. He smiled a lot these days. And people were noticing. Just that morning, Judge Brenner had told him over a cup of coffee, *Son, you should stop grinning like that. Every time you enter the court room I have to run through the calendar, check if Santa is early this year.* Yeah. Felt like Christmas all the time for him—a warm, bright Christmas after the worst season in his whole life. And the biggest present was still to be opened.

He drove out of town with the smile plastered on his face, remembering the latest long-distance calls they'd been making. Damn. He never imagined people who already knew each other so well could talk so much. They had covered every single topic known to man, from tortillas to their blood test results, which of course would come in handy when they had to share food and other spicy things. They already knew they could do both without curry and condoms.

It didn't really matter what they talked about. They just needed to hear that sweet voice on the other end, had to make sure every day that someone like Daniel really existed and, miracle of miracles, would be interested in them.

It had taken some planning, some negotiating, but they'd finally agreed to some kind of test drive. Daniel would come back, seemingly to finish his open lines of work in the reservation health center, but mostly to make up his mind about what he wanted to do in the immediate future.

Sean wasn't worried about that. He knew as soon as Daniel was there, they wouldn't let him go. But Jeff wasn't so confident, and he understood why. The man had been ready to push both of them away for fear of having to go through rejection. And he knew the Apache couldn't help expecting Daniel to come back and see how little they had to offer. Sean couldn't blame him. Jeff had a history of abandonment that made him sure nothing he could do would ever be enough, that he would never be worth the trouble of staying by his side, for him, because of him. Well, only time could cure him of that fear, and Sean was already doing his best to show him that he, for one, would not leave. Not that he had to force it, but he tried not to suppress it either, the possessive streak he knew he'd always had. He liked to mark his lover, show him as much as tell him who he belonged to. It wasn't a one-sided thing, or a display of power: he didn't want submission or dependence, but he sure liked their bonds to hold them tight. And when Jeff dared to let himself go, he was more than a touch possessive himself. He just had learned the hard way not to get too attached to things that could and *would* be taken from him.

Sean killed the engine and smiled. Enough of that already. He was just a small-town sheriff, not an FBI profiler. It didn't take an analyst to know what he and his men needed, and it wasn't exactly deep thoughts and big words. Well, just one or two big words, like *mine* and *love*. The rest didn't even have to be recognized as English.

He grabbed the bag of takeout and got out of the car. He marched to the front door with something close to nerves making his stomach flutter. God. It was just like dating, as exciting and nerve-racking as dating.

They had decided to wait till the big house was ready and, most importantly, Daniel was there to stay, before they made any change in their living arrangements. So Sean still lived in the tiny apartment downtown, though he didn't really spend many nights there. It felt like getting to know each other all over again, running over their schedules and arranging time together every day. It kept him all excited, like a kid on Christmas morning, and there it was—one of his two favorite presents, ready for him to unwrap.

"Hey, babe."

Jeff took in his face-splitting grin, his hungry eyes, the way he was almost bouncing on the front step. "Damn crazy Irish folk," he mumbled as he turned to get back inside. Sean laughed and reached out to grab a feel of that wondrous retreating ass. Jeff swatted his hand away as he looked over the other man's shoulder. Oh, yeah, the door. The house was the only one in miles, but still Jeff worried about someone seeing them. Sean didn't mind; he was territorial, he liked showing his mate off, but he respected the Apache's need for privacy, though it had taken him some time to discover just how audience-shy Jeff could get to be. In many ways he was worse than Daniel. The Spaniard would blush for nothing, but he was more open, emotions showing easily on his face, his entire body language an invitation for contact. Jeff was the perfect picture of the aloof native—till you closed the door, that is. So Sean hurried to comply and, sure enough, met big, black eyes devouring him as soon as he turned around.

"Mm. Love the way you look at me."

"And how's that?" Jeff's voice was already as dark as his eyes and Sean felt a tinge of anticipation traveling down his spine.

"Just like a hunter measuring up his prey." Sean took a step forward, set a hand on the slim waist and waited, his eyes holding Jeff's hungry gaze.

"Measuring, uh? Seeing if the bear rug would fit between the fireplace and the coffee table?"

Sean chuckled, still not moving. "Oh, I guess the bedroom would be better for this particular bear skin."

Jeff inched forward, getting closer but still not close enough for their bodies to touch. "You think?" the Apache almost whispered, eyes dancing. "I don't know. It wouldn't make a good match, wall colors and all."

Sean let his fingers slide farther down, feeling taut muscle under the worn fabric. "Don't you worry about that. White goes well with everything."

Jeff managed to move even closer without touching him, and Sean forgot what the conversation had been all about.

"Yeah, white is good." Didn't seem Jeff was any more coherent, but still he kept his distance as they panted and ogled each other. The man was truly competitive: every little game became a battle for him, and Sean just loved it.

"Yeah, white, bedroom. Good." He made no sense, but he guessed the general bedroom intention was clear. If they kept at this for a second longer, the bulges in the front of their pants would cover the distance for them.

Jeff moved impossibly closer, but kept his hip tilted backwards to avoid contact. The bastard.

"Tease."

Jeff gave him a smug smile. "I'm not the one with his hand on someone else's butt."

"You mean this hand?" He did his best to appear innocent, moving said hand lightly to rub across Jeff's crack. And sure enough, the smaller man's hip bucked at the touch, crushing their erections together.

"Shit."

"Fuck."

It was just like throwing a hair dryer into a full bathtub: there was no way to stop the electric shock, and so they kept shuddering and hissing until they started laughing and falling to the floor in a heap of tangled limbs.

"Hey, what's that noise you just made?"

"Oh shit. That was our dinner."

"Chinese?"

"You wish. No containers, just smashed tamales."

"Rosita's tamales?"

Sean nodded ruefully.

"Shit. They're the best."

"I know. Maybe we can salvage some."

He opened the bag and a tasty smell wafted to his nose, making his stomach grumble. He picked up the best-looking morsel and brought it to Jeff's lips. His mouth opened to take both food and fingers in, a wet tongue swirling playfully around Sean's flesh, lips sucking the fingers clean before they let them go.

"Sexy bastard."

Jeff gave him a lopsided grin, chewing contentedly.

"Share a taste?"

He didn't have to ask twice. Jeff moved forward until their lips met and opened for him easily, letting Sean taste a spicy mixture.

"Hmm. Jicarilla-Mex, my favorite."

Jeff snorted. "Shut up and give me more."

"Bossy."

Jeff tilted his head to study him with mock seriousness. "Having authority issues now, Sheriff?"

He offered another bite. "Nope. No issues here. You can boss me around as much as you want."

The Apache gave him a devilish grin, ignoring the food presented to him. "You sure about that?"

"Yes, sir, completely sure."

He saw Jeff's eyes grow darker when he gave him the "sir" treatment. Oh, yeah. Time for a little game. The Apache took the piece of tamal from Sean's fingers and stood up, keeping his hand high enough that Sean would have to kneel if he wanted to reach the food.

"Come get it, boy."

He felt like barking, but he knew Jeff would enjoy the words more, and damn if his own cock didn't enjoy the way he had to look up into those smoldering eyes and say "Yes, sir" as he moved to obey. He was sure the fact that he was still in his uniform was an added turn-on for Jeff. Shit, he was sure it was many men's secret fantasy, having the sheriff kneel before them, but there was only one man who'd get to fulfill his dream… or probably two. Sean almost laughed, imagining the way even Daniel's nails would blush if Sean were to go down on his knees for him. Then his position brought his eyes level with Jeff's groin, and his mind went instantly blank. He might even have let his tongue come lolling out of his mouth at the sight of Jeff's erection beautifully outlined in the enclosure of his jeans.

"Here, boy. Eat."

The tasty morsel was shaken tauntingly in front of his eyes, the smell making his nostrils flare. He barely hesitated before he went for the food he was hungry for.

"Shit." Jeff shuddered from head to toe when Sean's tongue traced the length of his cock over the soft fabric covering it. The Apache looked down at him, eyes slightly wide, pupils dilated, his voice coarse now.

"Bad boy."

Sean waited with his heart pounding away in his chest. Was this getting into the punish-the-bad-boy game? Not that he minded. With Jeff, he was more than ready to experience anything.

"You have to unwrap the food before licking at it."

Oh. Teaching the boy good manners. Even better.

"I'm sorry, sir."

"That's okay. Just go at it properly now."

He pushed a little further. "Yes, sir. Shall I use my hands, sir?"

God, the look those eyes had for him. It almost made him come in his pants, his uniform pants. Maybe this was many sheriffs' secret fantasy too.

"No. You don't touch food with your dirty hands. Use your mouth."

Oh yeah. "Yes, sir."

He clasped his hands firmly behind his back to avoid the temptation to use them and went at it eagerly, though the one button turned out to be a tricky business for his mouth. The way Jeff kept shivering and biting his lip as he watched was worth it, the more so when he finally got to a patch of bare skin and discovered Jeff had gone commando.

His tongue darted forward to taste that salty skin and the Apache moaned. He looked up at that incredible face... black eyes looking at him over high cheekbones, desire darkening the smooth complexion, parting, full lips, a string of brilliant, blue-black hair escaping the ponytail and falling forward, taunting Sean, making him crave the use of his hands to latch onto it.

"The fly," Jeff croaked, and Sean let out an eager "yes, sir" before lunging forward to grab the zipper with his teeth. He brought it down slowly, delighting in the small encouraging noises Jeff kept making.

Now more than ever Sean appreciated the kind of loose-fitting jeans the Apache favored, for, as soon as the fly was open, they slid a good distance down, hanging precariously from the slim hips, revealing the only patch of curly hair Jeff had on his whole body. His engorged cock proved a far better obstacle, and Sean heard a frustrated curse before long fingers pushed at the fabric impatiently. He couldn't help smiling at the way Jeff only used one hand, the other still holding the bit of Mexican delicacy. His wild lover was really prim when it came to throwing food around.

He didn't care anymore when that single hand managed to free a darkly flushed, beautiful, dripping cock that stood, untended, in front of his eager mouth. Sean looked up, silently asking for permission. This was all about Jeff holding the reins, and he wouldn't do anything to spoil the pleasure for him, even if his own cock was throbbing for release, his hands twitching to reach out and touch the flesh displayed in front of him, his mouth salivating in anticipation.

Jeff held his gaze for a moment, and Sean noticed for the first time that his Apache was trembling. He swallowed hard. It was the most desperately erotic moment he had ever experienced, time stretched thin over their pulling desire, blood ticking away in their veins, pooling up like sand inside an hourglass, with nowhere to go till a hand reached out and turned the world upside down.

"Suck me."

Or powerful words made the glass explode in brilliant shards of light.

"Yes, sir."

He managed to make it sound more like devotion than obedience, restraining his urge to devour and going at it with the delicacy and thoroughness of proper worship. He first licked and laved, running his tongue along the shaft, coating the head with a generous amount of his saliva, humming at the taste of pre-come in his avid mouth, wrapping his lips around each ball in turn and working them gently. The effort at control was making him sweat, but the way Jeff was writhing and moaning and cursing was worth the torment.

"Sean!"

He looked up. Sweet Jesus. Jeff was panting hard, his eyes wide and begging, looking at him as if he was the only person in his whole world who could give him what Jeff needed, all that he needed, exactly what he needed. Nobody had ever looked at Sean that way, and he felt his chest grow tight even as the wet spot on his shorts front spread.

"Yes, sir," he mumbled at the unspoken request, and it sounded so much like "I'm yours to do with as you like" that he saw Jeff's eyes go even wider before Sean opened his mouth and took him to the root.

His beautiful Apache cried out, slender fingers grabbing a fistful of blond hair and tugging painfully. He moaned around the hot flesh sliding on his tongue, deep-throating as best he could, offering a steady suction, working hard and fast, for he sensed Jeff's release was close and wanted to make the most of the few seconds left.

When he swirled his tongue around the retreating head, Jeff's hips bucked wildly and he cried out Sean's name, his come filling the mouth that kept working gently around his shaft. Sean looked up in time to see Jeff's eyes roll in his head, the control over his closed features finally slipping to show ecstasy, pleasure so intense that his moans sounded almost plaintive now. As soon as he stopped shaking, those hot eyes zeroed in on him, so full of emotion that Sean felt his balls draw up. And then his Apache was out of his mouth and all over him, kissing him as if it was the end of the world, one hand fumbling with Sean's zipper to pull out his leaking cock.

Sean felt like laughing when he noticed Jeff's other hand was still holding a piece of the food Sean had brought for him, but instead he found it so endearing that he whimpered like a lost puppy till Jeff tugged at his cock firmly just once and made him see stars. Then he simply collapsed into Jeff's open arms and let his lover hold and rock him like a child.

They stayed like that for a long time, the slowing sound of Jeff's heartbeat lulling Sean into a state of Zen-like peace—or not exactly that, for this peace was the opposite of emptiness, and if it was his inner self communing with something, that something was quite limited to a single other presence.

"Didn't know I had it in me."

Sean looked up. He knew his Apache well enough to distinguish when he was blushing, though nobody else might have noticed; in fact, Sean was sure he had gotten away with it until now.

"What? You didn't know you were bossy?" He gave Jeff a skeptical look.

"Not bossy. Kinky."

Sean struggled to hide a smirk.

"Go on, laugh at me."

He did laugh then but quickly pressed a kiss to the pouting Apache's forehead.

"You have a lot of things in you, Jeff Redbear." Now it was Jeff's turn to look skeptical. "Yessir, you do, and I will bring them out one by one."

"Is that a promise?"

Sean met Jeff's serious eyes and sobered. "It is a promise."

He offered his hand for a formal closure of the deal, and Jeff moved to take it with equal formality, till his hand proved to be improperly full of tamales. They looked at their hands and then at each other, and laughed so hard they knew they would never manage to stand up again. And it didn't really matter, as long as they were sharing the same patch of hard wood floor.

Chapter 25

IT WAS so dark, and yet he could clearly see Alonso's eyes looking right into him. His brother wasn't a kid anymore; in fact, he was in full uniform, white and starchy from head to toe, all those prim clothes making Daniel's own nakedness even more humiliating. He tried to break away, but Alonso tsked, his big hands holding Daniel's wrists down against the oak table, its wood sinking deep into his exposed belly. He was sweaty all over, his body sore from the whipping, his head about to explode. He felt dirty and small and helpless, his brother looking down at him just as if he knew exactly how he felt. Those thin lips even lifted into a smirk, white teeth showing as he bent to whisper in Daniel's ear.

"As soon as Father chains you to the wall, I'm gonna shove the crop handle up your pretty ass and fuck you with it till you beg for more. 'Cause that's what you'll do, you little faggot, beg for a real man to fuck you. And then you'll moan for me like a whore, beg me to fuck your pretty mouth, too, and come inside you again, and again, and again."

He struggled to get free and was slammed against the wall, heavy shackles closing around his ankles and wrists. It was his father who now stood facing him, his expression disgusted as he spoke.

"God knows I've tried everything with you, Daniel, but your nature is flawed and you do nothing to improve it. You're weak and lazy and never willing to learn. You make me feel so ashamed to have sired someone like you. But not anymore, you're not making me feel guilty ever again; I've put up long enough with you. From now on you're gonna stay here, where nobody else sees you, where you can't disgrace your family anymore."

As tears streamed down his cheeks, there was Alonso again, his face inches from Daniel's, mouthing "crybaby" before the lights went out and he lost it, screaming, shaking, pulling at his restraints savagely.

Daniel jerked awake, breath coming out ragged, fingers fumbling for the light. He blinked at the sudden brightness, not knowing where he was till he saw the framed photo hanging from the wall. Raúl's guest bedroom. He felt both relieved and disappointed, and he almost laughed at himself for feeling so. He was safe from the greasy tendrils of the nightmare, but he wasn't home.

He rubbed his hands over his face. He was tired. Every day was a frantic succession of errands, and every night the dreams came back to haunt him, to wake him in the early hours of the following day, his head throbbing with all kinds of aches, from the light, tension headaches to the full-fledged migraines. He was tired, and confused, and insecure, and he missed his men something fierce. His men. Sounded weird on his lips. And not only to him, by the look on his closest friends' faces. Even the gay ones, the same ones who had teased him if he ever commented on another guy's graces, had gone suddenly silent, all their sassiness deserting them, replaced by utterly dumbfounded expressions. Sometimes he'd even got brief flashes of disapproval before they were carefully hidden behind strained smiles. He guessed everyone fantasized about threesomes, but actually living in one seemed impossible. In spite of all their professed open-mindedness, they still thought you couldn't love more than one guy at a time; every other combination must be only about sex, the more the merrier, but still not love. He didn't really care what his friends thought—or wouldn't have if he'd felt sure of what he was doing—but he was afraid, afraid of losing what he could feel in Sean and Jeff's voices every time he talked to them and terrified he would only break a relationship that would have worked perfectly without him.

The first time he told Raúl, his brother had been mad at him for being so easily led, mad at them for leading him on, mad at the world for not moving forward and allowing Daniel to forget and heal, which were one and the same in Raúl's mind. They hadn't exchanged a single word in four days, a record in their friendship, and then Raúl had come to his place one night and hugged him so tightly that, if the relief Daniel felt hadn't already been choking him, Raúl's squeezing arms would have anyway. He found himself with no air left in his lungs to articulate any coherent word. Raúl hadn't spoken either, he'd just nodded, a whole encyclopedia of meaning in that small gesture. From then on, he had been helping him as best he could, accepting Daniel's decision to go for a drastic change in his life no matter what the result of his trip to the States would be. That was why he was sleeping in Raúl's spare bedroom now, because he'd left his own apartment, sold or given away all the things he didn't need, and kept only the contents of a few boxes piled up against one wall. Just the basics to start a new life, be it in another country or, if he were to come back, in whatever place offered him the kind of job he'd been longing for. It was time to stop treading ahead mindlessly, time to take the reins of his life and choose consciously which road to take. If he was to have company on that road, he'd be more than happy, but he would accept it either way.

He reached out for the glass of water on the nightstand. His throat was dry, he must have been screaming in his nightmare. Good thing Raúl was out for the night. He hated worrying him.

He finished the water in the tumbler, wishing he could get drunk on it. He chuckled humorlessly. He couldn't even get drunk on alcohol, two sips and his head would start the fireworks. Wonderful. And that was what he was taking back to Sean and Jeff, nights full of horrid dreams, days busy with migraines and that constant certainty nudging at the edge of his conscience, that voice that kept whispering how weak he was, how defective, unwholesome.

He set the glass down, almost knocking the cordless phone Raúl had placed on his nightstand. *When you start doubting, call your men*, he'd said with a wink. Daniel smiled. He'd said *when*, not *if*, knowing full well he'd go over his decision again and again, even when he already had the plane ticket in that drawer.

He checked his watch. It'd be late in the afternoon back home. He chuckled. When he wasn't thinking things through, his mind had no doubt where home was. He should probably trust his instincts and stop worrying. Probably.

He hit the numbers and waited. It was Sunday, they should be both home, enjoying the last lazy hours of their day off. The phone rang three times before he started thinking he shouldn't intrude, worry them. He was about to hang up when Jeff's voice came through, the sound making his stomach flutter.

"Yeah."

"Hi Jeff."

"Daniel! Hey, how are you?" He sounded so pleased, utterly happy to hear him.

Daniel had to clear his voice, emotion constricting his throat. "Fine, just missing you." He hadn't intended to say that, but it kind of slipped out. He hurried to add, "How are things over there?"

"Would be fine if you were here. To say we miss you is the understatement of the century."

Daniel closed his eyes. His mind was a whirlpool of conflicting emotions, words stuck on the roof of his mouth like a bite of something too sour to swallow, too big to spit. Then he heard Jeff's voice become muffled, as if he spoke away from the receiver.

"Move your ass over here, Sheriff, our little cub is on the phone."

God. The names they gave him. Those men just couldn't stop calling him sweet, silly things that felt like warm touches even through the phone, especially through the phone, where only their voices could reach him.

"Hey, sweet prince, how you doing?"

Damn. He was about to cry. "Hey, Sean. I'm fine."

"You don't sound fine."

"What! He's got migraine or something?"

"You heard Jeff?"

"Yeah. And no, my head is fine. I'm just...."

"Wishing you were already here?"

"Yeah, I keep looking at the drawer where the plane ticket is, just hoping it would teleport me by sheer concentration."

That got him two chuckles and Daniel could almost see them, bodies leaning into each other, the receiver held between them so that they could both hear him and talk to him without passing it back and forth.

"Are you in bed?"

"Yeah, Raúl left the cordless phone on my nightstand."

"Good man."

"I know. I'm lucky."

"No. You deserve it. Tell him we said hello."

"He's not home today, had to leave Madrid for some days."

"Oh, so you're on your own, is that why you're calling so late? It must be what, two or three in the morning there?"

"Yeah, half past three."

"Don't tell me you've been working all that time."

"No, no, I just woke from a…." Shit but he was stupid.

"A nightmare?"

Fucking stupid.

"Yeah. A silly thing, really."

"Want to tell us about it?"

"No." He sounded brusque even to his own ears. "Sorry, I just…."

"It's okay, you don't have to. Sometimes talking doesn't help."

"Sorry."

"So now you're too riled up to go back to sleep, aren't you?"

Daniel hesitated, didn't know what Sean was up to. "Yeah, guess you could say that."

"Okay, that's good."

"Good?"

"Yeah, good. Are you wearing those silk pajamas that look so cool on you?"

"Yeah."

"What color?"

"Black."

"Great. That would make your skin look even whiter, porcelain-smooth to the touch."

What on earth was Sean…? "Start unbuttoning your top."

"*What?*"

"You heard me, little cub, get your top open but don't take it off, just bare your front, give us some skin, and I'll get Jeff all naked for you."

Oh Lord. How did Sean manage to do that? A few simple words and he was all excited, his cock already bulging in his pants.

"Come on, pretty boy, I'm four buttons ahead of you and Jeff is getting impatient 'cause I'm not letting him help. He can't touch himself if you don't, and I can tell you, he's hungry."

Daniel groaned into the phone and fumbled with his buttons.

"That's right. Now expose your chest."

He did, just opening his pajamas, his arms still inside the black sleeves.

"Beautiful. All that white skin, those pink nubs hard, begging for attention."

That was… how did he know his nipples were hard? His hand started to reach out to them when the voice came back.

"No touching till I say so, little cub. Wait for Jeff. He's behaving wonderfully, arms stretched to hold the phone for me, his tanned skin displayed for us, his nipples erect, craving your touch."

Daniel heard a moan the moment he started moaning himself.

"Hmm. That's sweet. Love hearing your sexy voices. Now, my prince, put those beautiful, long fingers inside your waistband and slide your pants down, ever so slowly."

He obeyed, pushing the elastic band down his hips.

"Slowly. Shift your tight little ass and bring them down slowly, very slowly."

He dug his heels into the mattress and lifted his butt, the silk sliding easily down, the movement stretching the elastic band over his cock and along his shaft. He gasped.

"Hmm. It's reached your pretty cock. Let it stay there, feel it trapping your erection, keeping you hard."

Daniel heard a whimper on the other end.

"Yeah, our wild cat is impatient. Wants to show you his need. It's okay, babe, I'm gonna free you right now, let Daniel see all of you, see how hot you are for him."

He moaned low, let his buttocks land back on the mattress with a thud.

"Don't move now, little cub, feel that pressure on your cock, imagine it's my fingers closing on your shaft, making a cock ring for you, not allowing you to climax till your whole body is shaking with need, begging for us to take you."

He grunted, the voice on the other end getting huskier by the moment, coaxing and seductive, making him eager to please it, to get the rewards it promised him if he obeyed.

"I'm unfastening Jeff's pants now. He's wearing no underwear 'cause he likes the rough fabric rubbing on his sensitive cock, likes being reminded he's hard for you all day long, unable to come if he can't touch you, see you, hear your voice."

Daniel babbled something, didn't know what, didn't care what, his chest aching deep inside, matching the slow burn in his trapped shaft, the light pull on his balls.

"That's right, pretty cub, make sweet noises for us. Jeff is aching now, so I'm gonna wrench his jeans down, hard and fast, making him feel the burn of the fabric, making him as hot as you are now, my sweet, sexy prince."

Daniel heard a rustle and a sharp cry, and almost came, imagining Jeff there, completely naked, clutching the phone as if for dear life, his legs, his cock all flushed dark by the sudden friction of the jeans Sean had dragged over his skin.

"Wish you could see our bobcat right now. He's so wanton, so graceful, his proud cock leaking for you, his nipples hard as steel, his eyes glazed, big pupils dilated, drugged on you, on the smell of your arousal."

Daniel shuddered, fighting the urge to remove his pants and take his cock in his hand. He clenched his fingers on the sheets, squeezing so hard it hurt.

"You are so beautiful, the two of you. You make me ache."

Daniel hummed, wiggled a little to try to shift the pressure on his shaft.

"I want to mark you both, let the world know you're mine," Sean said.

He heard Jeff moan. God. Didn't think he could hold it anymore, not if that voice went on, not if Jeff made those sexy noises again.

"I want you to help me, little cub. I'm gonna sink my teeth in Jeff's shoulder, and I want you to mark yourself for me."

Oh, oh. That was simply too much. He keened, his fists clenching on the sheets even tighter.

"Shhh, my sweet cub, do it for me. Focus now. Remember, Jeff is waiting on you, holding back for us, controlling his need for you. I'm gonna mark him now, my pretty, and I want you to bring your hand to your left shoulder, find the tight muscle there, dig your fingers into it, hard, bruising yourself for me."

Daniel stopped thinking and simply obeyed, fingers digging in, nails first. His cry was matched by Jeff's, and he almost felt Sean's teeth on him, claiming them both at the same time.

"Mmm. My brave little cub. It's gonna bruise nicely for me. You'll wear my mark like this beautiful cat here, both mine for everyone to see."

Daniel moaned, started shaking at the pride in that voice. It was addictive, the wet spot on his pants spreading further. He heard Jeff now, a coarse, needy whisper.

"Please...."

Just that whimpered word and Daniel's back arched off the

mattress, his balls going so tight he knew he couldn't last much longer.

"You heard that, pretty cub? He's begging for you, trembling for you. Will you release this beautiful, wild creature?"

Daniel hissed through his teeth, eager, desperate now. "Yessss."

But the voice kept on torturing him, driving him crazy. "Will you reward him for being so good?"

"Yes…." It sounded much like a whine to him, but he couldn't care less. He was hurting now.

"Will you come with him, at my word?"

Oh God, yes, please. "Please…."

"Hmm. So sexy, my little cub."

Daniel keened desperately, shaking so hard the headboard rattled gently against the wall.

"Shhh, one more little step, my pretty. Push your pants down, show us how much you need."

He heard a low grunt from Jeff and almost lost it, his fingers fumbling to comply, the elastic band slapping against his thighs as his cock sprang free. He hissed as cold air touched his heated skin, his ass leaving the mattress as he strove to control his urgency, sweat trickling down his chest, his shaft slick with pre-come.

"Give it all for me now, my lovers," Sean growled.

Daniel cried out, another sharp cry echoing his own on the other end of the line, his hips bucking wildly as his seed splashed over his belly, his chest, aftershocks shaking his whole frame for so long, he thought he was never going to stop coming for his men. His men. The ones he trusted so much as to abandon himself completely, in a way he never had before, because he now knew he would be exposed and yet safe, vulnerable and yet shielded, open and yet out of harm's way.

He let out a sob, the phone finally falling from the tight grip on his shoulder. His name came from the receiver, and he fumbled to pick it up and hold it against his already flaming ear. He tried to control his voice before he spoke.

"Daniel?"

"Sorry, I dropped the phone."

Twin chuckles answered him. Now it was Jeff who spoke, his voice a little hoarse. "Not surprised you dropped it, little cub. You put on an amazing show for us."

"Oh, now, look who's talking."

Jeff laughed. "Yeah, well, but I've got some training. You, my boy, are a natural."

"Jeff's right. You make it all so intense, so exciting. It's like a first time all over again."

"Could it be because *it is* my first time? Maybe?"

He could almost hear them smile. "That could help, yeah, but it's not all. You give yourself completely, Daniel, make everything special."

"That's because you make me feel special."

"No, that's because *you are* special."

"Yes, you are."

Daniel bit his lower lip. They sounded so serious now.

"You are our pretty little cub."

"Maybe," Daniel allowed.

"Maybe?"

He grinned into the phone. "You know, I've been wondering, how come a bear and a bobcat can produce cubs together?"

"Crap. I told you he'd work it out. Our cub is bright."

"Yeah, he is. Should have told him before he left."

"Told me what?"

"We didn't want to give you a trauma or anything, but…."

"But?"

"You're adopted, my pretty."

He fought back laughter, covering his mouth with his palm.

"You know we love you as if you were our own."

Daniel sobered, trying hard to convey his feelings in spite of the distance, the impossibility of looking into their eyes. "I am your own."

Jeff moaned, Sean answering for him. "You sure are, our pretty little cub, and don't you go forgetting it."

"I won't."

"Good. Now close those beautiful eyes and sleep. We won't let any nightmare get to you," Sean said.

"No. I'll make a dreamcatcher with your name on it. You'll only have sweet dreams from now on," Jeff added.

"Thank you."

"Don't thank me. We Apaches protect our own."

"Yeah, we Irish protect our own too."

Daniel smiled. "Okay. I'm not strong enough to protect you, but I'll be there to heal you whenever you need me."

"Mmm. That's sweet, pretty cub, but don't go saying you're not strong 'cause that'd be lying."

"And we didn't raise you to be a liar."

He chuckled. "I'll be a good cub, I promise I won't lie."

"You better. Now go to sleep, it's too late for cubs to be up."

"Okay. Good night, then."

"Good night, sweet prince."

He heard Jeff snort.

"What? Aren't cops allowed to read Shakespeare? If you cut us, do we not bleed?"

"Oh, shut up, you crazy Irishman."

"No, you shut up, you ignorant Injun."

Daniel smiled so hard he thought his lips would start bleeding. He was simply happy, boneless, warm, and happy all over. He drifted into sleep even before his men stopped bantering, their familiar voices lulling him into a dreamless, replenishing sort of coma.

Chapter 26

JEFF was so mad he could bite. Everything was so screwed up, from the most trivial stuff—like Sean's SUV, forcing him to go to town to pick him up—to the big, important things, like the damn family meeting he'd just had. Shit. And it was taking Daniel forever to come back. He had things to settle, papers to sign, stuff to pack, but Jeff couldn't help being anxious about it. Of course he missed him every minute of every day, but he was also frightened. The longer Daniel stayed away, the more he fretted, knowing doubts would start creeping back into Daniel's mind, making him think once again it was in their best interest if he just disappeared from their lives. And there were so many things they should have done differently.

It was a powerful enemy they were fighting, one that'd had the field for ages. Daniel had managed to do much more than merely survive on his own, but still he was scarred, still there was that voice in the back of his mind never allowing him to forget how worthless he was. They had years of abuse to make up for, so even if they'd told Daniel how extraordinary he was four times a day for the rest of their lives, they'd still be decades short.

Jeff banged his hand against the steering wheel. Fuck. He was mad at his own stupidity. Just calling Daniel sweet names when they had phone sex was less than enough; he might think they were just passion-fueled pleasantries. He was straight, for Christ's sake, had been living with that damn woman for years, wanting to marry her, have kids with her, never once having reason to doubt his own sexuality. And now he was coming back to be with not only one but two men. That would make even the strongest of personalities shake to their core. It wasn't easy to admit you were suddenly on the wrong side of everyone's perception. Being exclusively gay was enough in itself, but discovering you were equally attracted to both sexes could be just as mind-boggling. So many people thought bisexuality was a myth that you found yourself doubting every step of the way; whatever you chose always made to believe you were betraying your true self. Jeff had experienced it firsthand but well, being an Apache had already turned him into an outcast, so it didn't quite matter, adding insult to injury and swinging both ways. But Daniel didn't have that background. He was one of the privileged few: white, handsome, professionally successful, straight. Every mother would want Daniel to marry their daughter. And yet he had only resisted the advances of two men because he didn't think he was good enough for them. He, the perfect matrimonial prospect for high society girls, not good enough for a small-town cop and an Indian.

Jeff forced his hands to loosen their grip on the wheel. He knew it was useless to go over all the things he should have told Daniel, but he couldn't help it. He should make a list and carry it everywhere so that he wouldn't forget next time. If there was a next time, if Daniel didn't decide he was better in his own country, or worse still, that *they* would be better that way. Maybe next time Daniel called he should start telling him, one call, one line on his list, pick up the phone and simply say, "Hey, Daniel, I miss you because you are brave; I love you because you are strong; I need you because you are sweet; I want you because you are smart, kind, sexy, funny, amazing, gorgeous, mine." Damn. The list was so long he should have started months ago. But no, he had been too busy resenting Daniel for every single thing on that list.

Jeff smiled grimly to himself. He still remembered his reaction when Daniel had first remarked on his name. Yeah. The man was bright, it took him no time to discover "Redbear" didn't sound much the Jicarilla name, that it sounded all the way the made-up thing it was. Daniel had been very careful wording his doubts, but Jeff... oh, well, he'd been simply an asshole. It would have been easy to explain it was a nickname the soldiers gave one of his ancestors, a name he proudly embraced since it was uttered in fear of his unusual size and his prowess in battle. It would have been easy but for his own damn pride. How on earth would he admit to a white man his own name came from another white man? No. He'd rather do what he had done, pull on his sarcastic mask and let Daniel know what he thought of his sudden expertise on Jicarilla naming traditions. Daniel had simply changed the topic to work-related matters, but Jeff could still see the hurt in those lake-green eyes.

That stupid pride of his had almost made him drive away the love of his life. And if Sean was still with him, it was simply because the man could be stubborn as a mule, not because Jeff hadn't tried to ignore or resist his own feelings for yet another obnoxious white man. And now his pride had forced him to make that stupid move he was still seething from.

He couldn't have approached the members of his family separately, used his people skills to broach the subject in a gradual manner they wouldn't find menacing, dropped casual suggestions so that they could get used to the fact that he had his own family now and was going to move in with them as soon as Daniel was there. Shit. He was trained to handle that kind of situation. But no, his pride was at stake here, so he'd gathered the whole bunch of his relatives and force-fed them the notion that there were suddenly two new additions to the clan. Two white new additions. And that even before Daniel had set foot in the country, even before they were sure it would work, even before... yeah. He knew leaving his place wouldn't go unnoticed, and he truly wanted the house to stay in the family, but he could have used some harmless lie and waited till everything was really settled, if it ever got settled, anyway. He supposed he'd simply done it out of fear, thinking that if everybody knew, there would be no way to prevent it from happening. But damn if he hadn't been arrogant, stupid, and generally out of his mind to do such a thing. And of course, his Uncle Jack had bolted. He wasn't famous for his lack of prejudice to begin with, but, above all, he had one hundred times the pride Jeff flaunted, so he had stood to the challenge and blurted out a never-ending string of perfect, textbook examples of homophobic opinions at the top of his lungs.

It hadn't been pretty. And it would have been even uglier if Aunt

Helena hadn't dragged him out of the house. One more word from that foul mouth and Jeff would have punched the lights out of the head of the Redbear clan. He wasn't sure it *wouldn't* still come to blows the next time he met his uncle anyway, but a strategic retreat had been the most reasonable option then, especially considering it had all sprouted from his own lack of finesse in dealing with the problem. Right now, though, he couldn't care less about reasonable. He desperately needed to dispense righteous violence, and having to drive to town and put on an agreeable mask for Sean's deputies' sake wasn't helping his mood. In fact he was very much tempted to drive his pickup into one of the patrol cars and smash all its flashy lights. Instead, he made the pickup swerve away from its target and parked beside one of the cars, wheels screeching on the pavement. Then he stormed into the sheriff's office, a startled female deputy leaping from her seat to stand in his way.

"Sorry, Mr. Redbear, but you can't go in there."

"What?"

"Sheriff McCallum is holding a meeting right now."

Great. Just what he needed.

"Who's with him?" The deputy hesitated and Jeff glared at her. "Forget I asked. I understand national security depends greatly on what goes on in this town sheriff's headquarters."

The woman rolled her eyes. "Stop being a jerk, will you please? I don't even know who those dudes are. Boss just came in with them an hour ago, and they're still in there. Look like FBI to me, but I could be wrong."

Jeff blinked, took a calming, deep breath. "Sorry, Alexa, didn't mean to snap at you."

"Apologies accepted, Mr. Redbear."

"Oh, please, could you drop that already?"

"Don't seem I can. You know I was trained to get all polite with troublesome patrons. It's said to calm them."

"Well, it's making me rather mad, if you must know."

"Guess it doesn't work with troublesome Native American patrons."

He chuckled. "No, it doesn't work with annoying social workers; we know all the tricks of the trade."

Alexa smiled at last. "Why don't you wait in the meeting room? I'm sure it won't take much longer." Jeff raised an eyebrow at her. "Oh, call it female intuition or whatever, but I know."

"Hope you're right," he said as he walked into the empty room and sat. The moment he did, he recalled every single time they'd been there, the three of them, working together, and his mood instantly changed from anger to melancholy. God. How he missed that, being three again. It wasn't the same with just Sean and him. All they seemed to be doing was comforting each other in their shared loss. And what if that was the only thing they'd be doing for the rest of their lives? What if Daniel…? He slammed his open hand against the table in frustration. He couldn't go on like this, couldn't stand the amount of fear ensconced in the deepest recesses of his brain. It hurt.

Jeff stood and paced. If he could at least see Sean, discuss it with him, he would sure feel better. At least he could distract himself by cursing his uncle aloud. He glared at the wall. Sean was right there, behind that flimsy pile of… brick? He doubted it was that solid, but he couldn't hear any sound coming from the office next door, so maybe it was solidly built or at least well insulated. He shook his head, almost laughed aloud. When had he developed such an interest in construction materials? Well, it was either that or checking his watch every other second. He took a look at it now to see that only five minutes had gone by. Shit. What were they doing in there? Alexa said they'd been at it for an hour now; it was about time they finished. He needed the sheriff and Sean should know it. Jeff had only told him he was going to see his relatives, but he imagined Sean must have guessed what the reunion would be about. He was a fucking cop, wasn't he? Needn't be told every single detail to sort it out.

Jeff kicked the nearest chair. Truth was he hadn't told Sean because he had wanted to surprise him, come back home from his uncle's and tell his partner how he had made them see Daniel and him were now as much a part of the family as if they'd married into the clan. He'd even imagined the gratitude in Sean's eyes, the pride those blue irises would reflect. And now he couldn't even tell him how miserably he'd failed. Shit. He flung himself into the chair. At least

Daniel was thousands of miles away; otherwise he would have thought he was causing Jeff trouble and might have decided, yet again, they'd be better without him.

He looked at his watch. Fifteen more minutes. What on earth were those dudes about? He needed Sean, now! And the big man should know better than to keep him waiting. He damn well knew Jeff was coming to pick him up, the least he could do was call to warn him he'd be late. He had other things to do, important things to do, like wallow in self-pity, go over all the reasons Daniel might find to stay where he was, wonder at the stupidity of all the Native Americans who believed everything they deemed wrong came from the white man, never stopping to think they only thought it wrong because the white man had made them believe it was so. Yeah, he had important things to do, couldn't stay put like a limousine driver waiting on his employer. In fact, he didn't even have to. He could leave right that moment, let Sean take a patrol car home, or a taxi, or whatever. He couldn't care less. Foolish man should have remembered he was coming, taken the time to pick up the phone and call him. It wasn't that difficult, was it now?

Jeff took one more look at his watch. He had waited twenty fucking minutes. Guessed it was far more than enough. He was scramming, right now.

As Jeff started walking to the door it suddenly opened, Sean's head peering into the room. "Ah, there you are."

Jeff felt all the anger he'd been storing for the last few hours catch fire and explode inside him. "Of course I'm here, you dumbass," he yelled. "It was you who told me to pick you up, you who haven't had the decency to call me to cancel it when you'd be late. Where on earth did you think I'd be?" He shut his mouth, his jaw so tight his teeth ached. If Sean said just another stupid word, he was gonna let his fist fly.

Sean's face closed, his eyes narrowing as he crossed the space between them in two long strides, door slamming shut behind him. He stopped mere inches from Jeff, so close he could feel the heat radiating from Sean's body. Sean stared down at him, anger sparking in his blue eyes. Jeff thought he was going to hit him, but he didn't shrink away. Oh, no, he wasn't giving the big man the satisfaction of showing fear;

no, he would stand his ground, give back as much as he got. His fists were aching for a good fight, and if it couldn't be his Uncle Jack, he'd take Sean instead. Didn't matter as long as he could vent his frustration on someone who could defend themselves.

Sean moved fast, so fast Jeff didn't see his fingers moving until they grabbed a handful of his hair and pulled. His head was tilted forcefully, his mouth taken in a hard kiss that made their teeth clash. His whole body tensed, his tongue fighting Sean's, one arm moving up to shove him off. Sean's free hand caught his wrist, the big body pressing against his, a powerful thigh coming between Jeff's legs to push against his groin. He made a strange sound, part howl, part moan, anger and pain and desperation raging inside him, making him lunge against Sean's suddenly overwhelming weight. The grip on his hair disappeared and he almost gave a victory cry till he heard something click behind him. Just as Sean shifted and he tried to raise his hand another click resonated and he was unable to move his arms. It only took him two seconds to realize his wrists had been cuffed. Then his anger rose another notch and he bared his teeth at Sean.

"What do you think you're doing, you asshole!" he shouted, pulling at the cuffs. "Take these off right now or I swear I'm gonna—"

His words were cut short by Sean's hands grabbing his shirtfront and tearing it open in one swift movement, buttons flying about wildly, his medicine pouch bumping against his breastbone. His shirt was then pulled all the way back and down till it formed puddles on his bound wrists.

Jeff's eyes went wide with shock, goose bumps covering his flesh as his skin was suddenly exposed. He had trouble focusing on his anger again, especially since his cock seemed to find the situation interesting. And it was mostly that which made him mad all over again, the notion that he could find excitement in being controlled by another man. He yelled every insult he could think of, fear and anger so entwined he wasn't seeing clearly, wasn't even hearing right, or rather, couldn't pay attention to what he saw or heard, so that the sound of ripped fabric meant nothing to him till a coarse bundle of rags was shoved into his mouth. He groaned in frustration and pulled at the cuffs, hard metal chafing his skin till a strong hand stilled his movements. As the hand lifted, Jeff looked up, only to see a blur before everything went dark.

He froze. Sean had actually blindfolded him? Handcuffed, gagged, and blindfolded him? He didn't have time to ponder the implications of it all because right then agile fingers undid his pants and shoved them, with his underwear, right down to his ankles. He gasped, the gag drowning the sound.

He was suddenly aware of the silence around him, his own heartbeats the only loud thing in the seemingly empty room. He cocked his head, trying to locate Sean. He couldn't have left, even if he was mad at him he wouldn't leave him like that, naked and bound and... he swallowed, anger evaporating as fear started crawling up his spine. He tried to make a sound that could be heard through the gag, but thought better of it. It could be worse if someone heard him and came in to find him like that. Shame would surely kill him. God. *Sean, please, don't do this to me. Please.* His mind begged for all that his mouth couldn't, and, just as if he'd been heard, a hand landed on his ankle, resting there, letting him know he wasn't alone.

Relief flooded Jeff, his body suddenly relaxing from the tension he hadn't noticed stifling his muscles. He would have laughed at his childish fears, but he found he couldn't; he was so riled up the only noise he made came out as a sob, thankfully muffled by the gag.

The hand on his ankle moved, lifting his foot to take off everything he was still wearing. He didn't care. He wanted to be touched. Needed it. The emptiness around him, the silence, was driving him crazy; he didn't want to lose that contact, wanted more, much more, the fewer obstacles between his skin and that reassuring hand, the better.

His other foot was lifted, his pants, socks, and boots discarded somewhere he couldn't see. Then two hands settled on his ankles and he shuddered. Yes. That was it. The touch was so comforting he pushed into it, trying to get more pressure. The hands responded, fingers squeezing tightly, digging into his flesh, bruising. Yes! He cried into the gag, his cock filling as his whole body felt the burning mark of those hot fingers on his skin. He kept pushing into the painful grip and the hands raked nails up his legs, tracing a red hot line along the back of his knees, up his inner thighs and down again to his ankles, every inch of his naked flesh mauled, bruised, claimed.

By the time the hands settled Jeff was shaking, his cock fully erect, his knees about to give way under him. Only his legs seemed to exist now, only the parts of him that had been touched seemed alive to his altered perception, and he wanted more, wanted to feel alive all over, throw himself into that maddening touch. But the hands were still now, peacefully resting on his ankles. He just wished he could beg. He whimpered into the gag, the sound loud to his hyper-sensitized ears.

The hands rewarded him with a new, excruciating roam over his legs, not so thorough this time, but Jeff was okay with it, it gave him hope that they might proceed further up… as they now did, sinking into his hips and pressing so hard he lost his balance and stepped back till his butt slammed against something solid. He yelped, the gag making it sound like another desperate whimper.

The hands kept him pressed against what seemed to be a table, plywood etching its design into his exposed ass. He savored the different sensations the new contact provided, exploring the contrast between those two pressures, the blindfold magnifying every little detail his nerve endings seemed now to be shouting into his brain. Sean's fingers were hot on his skin, pliant, the hurting grip almost soft in the personal meaning they conveyed, whereas the hard wood was cold and mute, indifferent to him, to the pain and pleasure it might inflict on his helpless flesh. Jeff moaned. He wanted more of those fingers, wanted them all over him and, surprisingly enough, not on his already aching cock. He would relish that ache, let it last, but the rest of his body craved the bruising contact, needed to be awoken, branded all over by those burning fingers, needed to feel alive, cared for. Yes, care was the word. Those hands were working only for him, making the world disappear, showing him he was loved, worshiped, floating in a universe where only he existed, him and the hands that claimed him into that very existence.

He tried to move forward, away from the table and into the bruising fingers. He was pushed back hard and held there, trembling with need. He keened, his mind begging nonstop, the rational part of him that could analyze the whole situation and find it humiliating or insane, completely drowning in the darkness that surrounded him, his senses only open to the messages those hands decided to communicate. He tried to speak into the gag, beg words into the fabric, and was rewarded with a tiny motion of the hands up his waist. He moaned his relief, pleasure filling him when the hands petted his belly. As he relaxed, wet heat wrapped one of his nipples just a second before teeth closed on the already erect nub. He cried, hips bucking till the hands stilled him. God. That mouth tortured both his nipples, tongue soothing after hard teeth, again and again till he was shaking all over, pre-come trickling down his cock. One hand came down to squeeze at the base of his head, making the urge recede. Then that mouth closed on his throat and he made a strangled, surprised noise. A mark was sucked on his flesh and he arched his neck, baring more skin. The hands moved up his sides, lips and tongue traveling over his throat and jaw. He moaned loudly. His senses were overwhelmed, his cock dripping again, and he still wanted more, wanted all, not just hands and lips but everything behind them, all he was being kept from, made to crave, forced to earn.

He pushed into the mouth devouring him and cried his lover's name into the fabric of his own shirt. Then all contact ceased and he almost fell without the support of those big hands, his body slamming back against the table. No. Please. He shook as silence and darkness draped over him like a wet, suffocating cloth. Please. He couldn't even whimper, his throat suddenly dry. Please.

The gag was removed from his mouth and he panted, waiting. When no sound, no contact followed, he tried to find his voice.

"Sean?"

Nothing. He shut his eyes behind the blindfold. He needed to do this, couldn't take it anymore, would sink to his knees if that was what it took to bring the touch back. He gathered all his courage and spoke that single word, loud and clear.

"Please."

A hand cupped his cheek and he felt tears welling in his eyes.

"Shhh, I'm here, babe."

He let the tears fall, let his voice come out and beg even more. "Please, Sean."

Gentle hands stroked his hair, his face. "Yes, babe, tell me what you need, I'm here for you."

Jeff moaned. "I...."

"Come on, tell me. What is it that you need?"

"I need…" he inhaled deeply, "I need you, please, Sean."

Sean kissed his forehead softly, his hands still petting him. "I'm here for you, babe, just tell me how you want me." He let out a frustrated noise. Sean's husky voice whispered in his ear. "Just say it, babe. You know I'll give you anything you want, but you have to ask."

Jeff shuddered and moaned low, unable to wait a moment longer. "I want you in me, deep, hard, *now*. Please?"

Sean growled, the sound vibrating along Jeff's over-stimulated body, making him ache deep inside. Strong hands closed on him, turning him and bending him over the table. Then his legs were spread and Sean's cock pushed into him with no more delay, stretching him wide, his whole body screaming his hard-earned pleasure.

Sean kept still for a maddening second, waiting for Jeff's muscles to adjust to him, and all Jeff could do was shudder and whimper beneath him.

"Come on, babe, open for me, let me in."

Jeff took a deep breath, forced himself to relax.

"That's it, my beautiful babe, let me inside you."

He moaned and pushed back, Sean's cock sliding easily, his balls slamming hard against Jeff's ass. "Sean, please!"

"Yes, babe, I'm here, for you, in you. Gonna make you fly."

Sean pulled almost completely out of him and then thrust back in hard, the tip of his cock hitting his gland. Jeff cried, hips bucking uncontrollably.

"Oh God, do that again."

"Every time you need, babe."

Sean started a rhythm, thrusting hard into him, always true to his mark, making Jeff's eyes roll, his breath coming out in ragged pants, his voice hoarse from shouting. Sean bent over him, his hands never letting go of his hips, his cock slamming into him, his chest pressing over his bound arms as he breathed into his ear.

"Come on my cock now, babe. I wanna feel you."

Jeff cried out his name, his come splashing over his belly and the table, his body clamping down hard on Sean's cock, squeezing his orgasm out of him, his seed filling Jeff as they both shook for long, dazzling moments.

When Sean finally pulled out of him, Jeff's knees buckled, making him lean against the table until big hands lifted him and pressed him against Sean's body. Warm arms wrapped around him, and he was pulled down to sit on the floor, or rather in Sean's lap as the big man sprawled on the floor.

As soon as his hands were freed, Jeff closed them around the strong neck and curled right into Sean.

"That was amazing, babe."

"Hmm."

Sean chuckled. "You're beat, huh?" Jeff didn't answer, just nuzzled Sean's throat and nestled his head in the warm, cozy shoulder. "Don't get too comfortable, we still got to make it home."

Home? Oh, my. Jeff's body jerked up, moving away from Sean just as Sean pulled the blindfold from his eyes and held his head still.

"Easy now. Look at me."

Jeff blinked, tried to focus. There was too much light, too many things he didn't want to see.

"Don't close your eyes. Look at me."

He forced his eyes open and met dark blue orbs gazing intently at him. Had Sean's eyes always been that dark, almost navy blue? Had they always been so full of…?

"I love you, my beautiful, proud wildcat."

Jeff searched those eyes for any trace of hesitation or mockery and found none. He moaned, his heart pounding in his chest. "Sean."

"Yeah?"

His lover stroked his hair now, and he fought the urge to sink into his arms and forget everything else. He knew he had to say it, had the impression it was only Sean who said it all the time and it just wasn't fair.

"I love you, Sean."

Sean beamed at him, smug as you please. "I know."

Jeff punched his chest playfully. "Cocky bastard."

Sean laughed and pulled him into his arms, tender fingers caressing his back.

"Hmm. Don't want to move. Ever."

That got him a chuckle, a kiss to the top of his head. "I know, but we have to eat sometime, get a nice shower, make out on a warm, soft bed."

"Sounds good to me."

His lips were taken in a sweetly slow kiss. "Come on, let's get moving."

Jeff shifted, hands pressing Sean's shoulders to find leverage and rise. Sean seemed to follow his every move, hot eyes traveling over his body as it was displayed in front of him. Jeff almost closed his eyes, his cock twitching at the possessive lust in that stare.

"You're so sexy."

God. They were never going to make it to the car. Sean stood, looming over him. "I'd rather you never wore clothes anymore." Sean's hand reached out to pet him gently and Jeff leaned heavily into the touch. "But this view is for my eyes only."

"Yeah, just for you and…."

"And our little cub. He loves the way you look when you are like this."

"He does?"

"Oh, yeah, he does."

Jeff looked up into Sean's serious eyes. "But what if he—"

Sean pressed a finger to his lips, silencing him. "Won't happen this time. He'll come back even if we have to drag him all the way here."

Jeff nodded. Maybe he was being silly, but he found comfort in Sean's words, knew he believed them, believed they wouldn't let

Daniel keep any distance between them.

"Get dressed now. Let's go home."

Jeff obeyed reluctantly, put on jeans and boots and made a chagrined sound when he picked what was left of his shirt from the floor.

"Oh, Sean, how am I gonna…?"

Sean gave him a sheepish smile. "Sorry, babe, couldn't think of another way to…."

"Yeah, I know, I needed that." Sean's smile showed amused tenderness at his words. Jeff rolled his eyes. "What?"

"Nothing. I just never thought your pride would allow you to admit you'd be needing that kind of stuff."

Jeff felt his cheeks heat. Thank God for his kind of skin, never letting blushes show.

Sean's smile widened, though. "Don't be embarrassed. I love it that you can be honest with me."

Shit. There was no hiding from the man; he just seemed to see right through him. Jeff groaned. "How on earth do you do that?"

"Do what?"

"Always know what I need, when it hasn't even crossed my mind that it'd be exactly that I'd be wanting?"

"I know 'cause I see you." Jeff waited for Sean to elaborate. "I don't just look at you. I see you, learn you. You're mine, every little thing you do echoes in my mind, your need resonates in me, bringing over my own need to fit yours. We're not just you and me anymore, we've evolved into something different, more complex, something that is not just the sum of us, something that can affect everything we are, change us in a way we alone couldn't."

"Downward causation?"

Sean laughed. "Yeah… love's emergence."

Jeff cackled in turn. "You read too much for a cop."

"So I've been told."

Jeff tried to put on his shredded shirt and found there was no way to hide what had happened to it. "Now, Mr. Bookworm, just tell me how am I gonna leave this room looking like this."

"Don't worry, there's only Alexa out there."

Jeff shut his eyes. Damn. He'd forgotten. "You think she might have heard…?"

Sean shrugged, obviously fighting back a huge grin. "Well, you were rather vocal when I took the gag off."

Jeff cursed.

"Oh, come on." Sean threw an arm over his shoulders, smiling openly now. "She'll be just as embarrassed as you are."

Jeff groaned and snuggled close, wanting to disappear behind Sean's broad back. "Don't give it another thought, let's go now," Sean said, his hand already on the door knob. Jeff inhaled deeply.

"Okay, but don't let go of me."

Sean gave him an intense look. "I will never let go of you, babe. Don't you forget it."

Oh. Well. With that, he could face anything—shame and fear and hate, and everything else he couldn't control. He wasn't going to forget now, but he might still need to hear it a few more times, just to enjoy the thrill of it.

Chapter 27

SEAN rearranged the papers on his desk. For the third time. He couldn't concentrate. Jeff had told him about the family gathering, about his uncle Jack. He could quite picture the situation, that big bull of a man shouting his head off while Jeff stood his ground, seething with the urge to shut his uncle up in the worst possible way. Sean knew it had been hard on Jeff. It gave him a sense of failure. He, who was so good at family intermediation, had wreaked havoc in his own family, not even knowing how to mend the damage. But there was much more to it.

Jeff was a proud man, knew who he was, what he was, and that gave him the strength to ignore everybody's opinions or attitudes toward him. But that pride had always had the strong backup of the Redbear clan. Having lost both his parents through death or abandonment, he'd counted on the extended family, his aunts and uncles, forming a tight support network he could rely on. Jeff had always been their pride and joy, the first one of their clan to attend university, the first one that, having a career prospect opened for him out of the reservation, had chosen to come back and put his knowledge to work for the community. And he was good at what he did. People admired him, respected him. The whole reservation had been in awe at the way he'd managed to bring them a doctor to make their health center work. No less than a European specialist, first-class medical attention from a man who happened to treat their patients as if they truly were human beings, even if they were Apache. Daniel got to the heart of people in no time but after the episode with Billy, he was simply their hero. And Jeff, no matter what he himself thought, was seen as having played a crucial part in handling that serious predicament that had risked the lives of both the healers on the reservation. Hell, after Billy's rampage, even Sean was deemed worthy of respect.

So Jeff's association with those two white men was seen with good eyes, till it became more than teamwork. Jeff could surely put up with some misunderstanding, could even ignore certain looks, certain words that would settle hard on his stomach. That he would survive. But his own family? It hurt. Badly. The more so since Jeff had a deep seated sense of justice that made it ever so difficult for him to ignore anything that was clearly unfair. Pride and righteousness were the pillars of Jeff's strength, and they'd received a hard blow to their foundations, since it was his family Jeff's pride stemmed from.

Sean had sensed Jeff needed him badly, had seen the fear in those dark eyes. He was one of the strongest men Sean had ever met—both he *and* Daniel were—but maybe they were strong because of the things they'd overcome, the things that still lurked in the back of their minds, waiting for a moment of vulnerability to crawl out.

Jeff hid his fear well. He was an independent man, caring about everyone selflessly, apparently not needing to be cared for. Apparently. The way his mother chose his sister to take with her and left him behind set a sharp icicle in the center of his heart and every time someone came close enough to melt the ice, he pushed them away before they gave him a new wound. That's why Jeff had fought his feelings for Daniel, because he knew there was no way that awesome creature was not leaving his side. As for Sean, the harder Jeff shoved him, the harder Sean fought back, pushing Jeff beyond his very limits and being right there to hold him when he lost his feet.

And now Jeff was losing his family's support, one of the few unconditional things he'd always counted on. One more time he was being left behind by the ones who were supposed to love him even if nobody else did.

They had talked long into the night. Sean had tried to reassure him that most members of his family didn't think along the same lines as his Uncle Jack, and, even if they did, they would still support Jeff, never cast him out of the family.

Jeff had reluctantly agreed that the best he could do was let things settle, act normal, let his actions speak for him, and finally accept he might never be able to set things to rights as far as justice was concerned, but simply take what he could get from them if he intended to keep their bonds working.

It was somewhat easier for Sean. Not that he was estranged from his own family, but with so many of them there was always a chance to skip close supervision or judgment. And they lived really far away. His career election had made him leave the family home early and had taken him farther away with every new post he accepted. His lifestyle was something they didn't approve of, and the less they saw of it, the better. Sean wasn't hiding, either, but he didn't want any kind-hearted admonition, especially since his lack of stable relationships would confirm their idea of how unhappy his chosen life was making him.

Now things had changed completely. He *was* happy, he was proud of what he had, so much so that he wanted his family to see, to share his happiness. He wasn't ingenuous, though. It'd been hard enough for them to accept their son was gay. To now face the fact that, not only had he not straightened his ways but had sunk even further down by living in sin with *two* men: that would sure prove an ordeal to their Catholic minds.

It was about time he told them anyway, whatever the consequences. In fact, it was about time he simply called them. It had been months since his last call to any of them. He hadn't wanted them to worry, so he hadn't told them about the incident with Billy and, after that, well, there hadn't been much room left in him for anything that wasn't mourning the death of all his hopes first and then rekindling them all over again.

Sean took a deep breath. Maybe now was just the right moment, since he couldn't focus on his work. As he reached out for the receiver, the phone started ringing, making him jump. He sighed. So much for his good intentions.

"McCallum."

"I'm a McCallum, too, and I don't go flaunting it."

He laughed into the phone. "Timmy? Is that you?"

"Yeah, big brother, it's me. Glad you still remember how my voice sounds."

He smiled. Tim had four other big brothers, but still he only gave that title to Sean, and damn if it didn't make him feel ten feet tall.

"Sorry, kid, been really busy lately."

"Yeah, yeah, that must be in the McCallum's coat of arms. 'Semper ocupatus' or some other crap like that."

Sean cackled happily. He'd always got along well with his kid brother; he was a charming, humorous little man—little to McCallum's standards, that is.

"Stop bitching and tell me how things are going.   How is everyone back home?"

"Oh no, I'm the one asking questions here, Sheriff."

He chuckled. "All right. Shoot."

"Well, first of all, why is it that you're never home, no matter what time I call you? Is that town keeping you so busy you even spend the nights at work?"

Oh crap. He'd forgotten. "No, it's just that... well, I sort of moved."

"Great. Thank you for letting your family know."

"Sorry, Timmy, I simply—"

"Yeah, you simply forgot. There are so few of us it's easy to forget we exist."

His brother sounded real pissed and he had every right to be. "Timmy..."

"No, big brother, you do that a lot, keep us out of your life. I understand the whole McCallum bunch can be a little bit smothering but, damn, you could divide and conquer, talk to one at a time, talk to *me*, for Christ's sake."

"I'm sorry, Timmy, really sorry." And he was. Timmy stood as his favorite brother, and he hated hurting him.

"You used to tell me everything, Sean, even before the others knew. It made me feel… special."

"You *are* special."

"Yeah, sure."

"Yes, you are. You know, you're the only one who's called me, worried enough to wonder why I wasn't keeping in touch."

"None of the others called you?"

"No."

"Not even Viv?"

"No, not even Vivien. You always care about me, even when I'm being a jerk."

"Which you've been a lot lately, I must say."

"Yeah, maybe, but don't push your luck, I'm still bigger than you." He heard his brother laugh and breathed his relief.

"Well, I may be small, but I had a brother who taught me how to defend myself from big bullies, so don't get too careless around me."

"Okay, tough guy, I won't try to rough you up. And since you've been a good boy, I'm going to let you in on a secret nobody else knows, not even Viv."

"Oh yes, tell me, Sean, please, please, please."

He could almost see the spark in his brother's eyes. He was cute, his little brother. And maybe he could gauge his family's reaction by what Timmy had to say once he'd told him, since he'd always been the most understanding of the lot.

"Remember I told you about Jeff Redbear, the social worker I was working with?"

"Yeah, the Apache guy."

"Right. Well, it's his house I've more or less moved into." He didn't wait for his brother to process the information. "And remember the Spanish doctor?"

"Daniel, wasn't it? The nice guy?"

He smiled. "Yeah, you got that right. Well, he's going to move with us into a bigger place."

"You mean you're going to share a house with them?"

"No. I mean I'm going to share a bed with them."

"Oh." There was a silence on the other end of the line and then his brother asked, "You mean them as in *the two of them*?"

"Yeah, the three of us."

"Wow. Cool."

Sean's eyes went wide. He was glad he wasn't drinking his coffee for he would have spurted it all over his desk. "Cool?"

"Yeah, Sean, cool. You know I never imagined you to be chaste, so I already supposed you'd shared a bed with a few men, but you never seemed to actually want to share the house the bed was in with anyone before. Those guys must be something else."

Sean smiled, a warm feeling settling over him. "*You* are something else, Timmy."

"Don't flatter me, big brother. I grew up in a family of cops, I notice things."

"No, you care enough to notice."

His brother swallowed audibly, making Sean's smile widen.

"I love you, little brother."

"Shut up. Don't think buttering me up will get you forgiven. You shouldn't have waited for me to call. Shit. This family only remembers to pick up the phone when they land their ass in an emergency room."

Well, at least Sean had avoided that. "Why? Have they been visiting emergency rooms as of late?"

"No, and don't change the subject. I want to meet your... what's the right thing to say? Lovers, partners, mates?"

"Family. They are my family now, Timmy."

"Wow. You got it bad, big brother."

"Yeah, I'm afraid so."

"I'm happy for you."

"Thank you, kid, you're good to me."

"Yeah, I'm too nice for my own good."

Sean chuckled. "Well, this time, though, it might get you a trip to a real Jicarilla Apache reservation, food and lodgings included."

"Oh, wow, I'd love that. *Really* love that."

"The house is undergoing some reshaping right now, but it will be ready when Daniel gets back and will have a nice guest room by that time, so you are definitely invited."

"The doctor is not there with you now?

Ooops. He hadn't really told Timmy anything but, well, there'd be time, since he seemed genuinely eager to know. God, it was refreshing to have someone actually interested in the details of his new life.

"No, he's had to go back to Spain, to get everything ready to settle here."

"He's leaving his country behind for you?"

Sean couldn't deny that question made him a little anxious, but it also made his chest swell with pride, because he felt he already knew the answer. He said it aloud, as much a prayer as the certainty he felt it was. "Yeah, for me and Jeff, and his patients on the reservation."

"That's amazing. I can't wait to meet those guys."

Then Timmy seemed to realize something, and hesitate. Sean frowned.

"What is it, kid?"

"Will I…? I might be in the way. You might wanna be alone."

Sean smiled. "You won't be in the way. If we ever want to be alone, we'll throw you out into the wilderness. Our place is an old farmhouse."

"Oh, great, no neighbors, must be incredible."

"Yeah, will give us a lot of privacy."

"Don't even go there, big brother. I can imagine what three horny men might be up to in the middle of nowhere."

"Oh, no, you can't begin to imagine."

"Sean! I'm just a kid!"

"No, you might be my kid brother, but you're legal already, so I warn you, when you come visit, we're not cutting down on the PDA in our own house. We might moderate the howling, but nothing else."

Timmy giggled embarrassedly. "Well, thank you, you're very considerate."

"You're welcome."

"Okay."

"I mean it, in every sense."

"I know."

"Will you really come?"

"Of course I will! What are you, deaf?" Timmy asked.

"No, thankful."

"What for?"

"For you, Jeff, Daniel, this place, everything. You know, lately my life is so full of great things, I have the urge to check them from time to time, see that they're still there, that they're real."

"Of course they are real! And you more than deserve them. You've been fighting for them for a long time too," Timmy said.

"Have I?"

"Oh, don't play dumb with me. I still remember the years you spent in the LAPD. That city was trying to turn you into one of those stone-hearted, cynical cops, but you saw it coming and shook it off, took the risk, fought for your happiness, even if it seemed a drawback in your career. And now look at yourself: you're happy in your job, have built your own family. I'm very proud of you, big brother."

Sean just wanted to catch a plane and go embrace his favorite brother right then. "Thank you, Timmy. Really."

"You're welcome, Sean."

"Just wish the others would react half as well as you have."

"Oh, don't worry about it, they'll bitch for months, but they'll end up coming round to accept it. You know they always do in the end."

"I hope so."

"You know what's gonna happen the moment they meet your men. Pa and the brothers are gonna be impressed by your Apache when they find out he is more fiercely butch than them, and as for mum and Viv, I guess your doctor could charm them into anything."

It was Sean's time to be pleasantly surprised.

"Wow, Timmy, and you don't even know them."

"Well, I'm going to."

"Sure you are."

"Okay. I must go now. But don't wait so long before calling, you hear me?"

"Yes, sir, loud and clear."

"That's better. Well, bye for now, big brother."

"Bye, Timmy. Love you."

"Love you, too, though I might forget if you don't keep in touch."

Sean chuckled. "I will. I promise."

"Okay, then. Bye."

"Bye, Timmy."

He kept looking at the receiver, grinning like a fool. Some days were just great, or rather, some people were, and it made it easier going through the bad days because of them. That was really all they needed, Jeff and him. They were lucky enough to have people who supported them unconditionally, and that was all that mattered. They couldn't force the rest of the world to accept or even understand them. It was all right. They would more than manage to live without the rest of the world.

Chapter 28

JEFF raised his head to check the arrivals one more time.

"It won't change even if you keep looking at it, you know," Sean said.

"I'm nervous, okay?"

"I know, babe."

A big hand landed on the small of his back and he leaned into the contact. Yeah. Much better. "You think he'll like the house?"

"He'll love it."

"I'm not sure it's such a good idea to wait till tomorrow to show him. Can't we go today?"

"We talked it over, Jeff. He'll be too tired and we're more than a little anxious as it is. The last thing we all need are more surprises. Let's leave it for tomorrow as we decided."

"Okay."

The hand on his back moved a little, stroking, loving on him as much as they could allow themselves in the crowded airport. Daniel had chosen an early Sunday flight, knowing it was the only day they could be free. Problem was, the rest of the world had the day off, too, and they seemed to have all decided to spend the day sauntering about the airport. On a working day it might have been less busy, maybe even deserted enough they could have kissed, though it was probably better this way. He needed Daniel so much, he wouldn't have stopped at a kiss. Besides, on a working day, they probably wouldn't have made it, so Daniel would have had to rent a car and drive home after the long flight.

"You think he'll be all right?"

Sean shifted beside him to look into his eyes. "You worried the plane might give him one of his headaches?"

"Yeah. He didn't seem to be hurting the last time, but...."

"But he's good at pretending."

Jeff nodded. Sean's hand moved to settle on his nape, the pressure comforting, reassuring. "Don't worry. We're better at reading him now, we'll notice."

"Hmm."

Sean was right. They knew Daniel much better now, knew every expression on that beautiful face by heart. They wouldn't let him hide anymore.

The panel lights flicked and a gate number appeared beside Daniel's flight information. Sean gave his neck a last reassuring squeeze and started walking toward the gate.

"Let's get our cub back."

Jeff chuckled and followed the big man to the designated gate. By the time they arrived, though, he had managed to work himself into a bundle of fluttering nerves. What if Daniel regretted his decision to come back? What if abandoning his successful career for an underpaid post at an Indian reservation was beginning to look as foolish as it sounded? What if, after two months in his home country, he wasn't that much thrilled by the prospect of spending his days in a foreign, remote, English-speaking place? What if sharing the rest of his life with two guys felt too overwhelming for him? What if the moment he laid eyes on them he wondered what on earth had he ever found attractive in those two plain country bumpkins? He groaned aloud.

"Stop worrying, Jeff. You know it can be as infectious as yawning."

"Yawning?"

"Yeah. I even made a dog yawn once."

"You what?"

"There was this big mastiff in the house next door, and we kids were fascinated by him. Man, he was the only real imperturbable guy I'd ever met. You could even bite his ears and he'd look at you with those tired eyes that said, *Oh, come on, I've got fleas more threatening than you.*"

Jeff chuckled, Sean's deep voice slowly calming him, settling his nerves.

"So I told my brothers I would make the big beast obey my will if they'd mow the lawn in my place for a year."

"Hard bargain."

"Oh, not so much. I offered to clean the bathroom if I failed."

"For a year?"

"Yup."

"Well, that might have given you the right motivation, I suppose."

Sean smirked. "Yeah, exactly. Remember there were seven people and one single bathroom."

"That's a lot of traffic."

"Yep, so there was no way I was failing. I went on my hands and knees in front of the mutt and started yawning as if my life depended on it."

"And you made it? The dog actually yawned?"

"Yeah. Poor bastard was so bored of my antics that he finally opened his huge mouth in the biggest, jaw-cracking yawn I've ever seen."

Jeff had to laugh at the picture in his head: Sean as a kid, on all fours, facing the big mastiff, both yawning to beat the band. That must have been awfully cute.

Passengers started pouring out of the gate right then, and they both turned to face them, Jeff's heart about to come out of his mouth. He grabbed Sean's arm for support, squeezing hard.

He searched tired faces, somehow afraid he might miss Daniel in the constant flow of people. And then he saw him and almost laughed aloud. He had forgotten the way Daniel stood out in any crowd. All the faces around him seemed plain, all the clothes people wore drab and shapeless.

There he was, slender and beautiful, casual and imposing, just like a model stepping out of the pages of a fashion magazine. Jeff swallowed, almost wanting the moment to last, almost wishing Daniel's searching eyes wouldn't find them. Suddenly he was sure there was no way a man like that would want anything to do with them, with him. He moved even closer to Sean, wanting to hide behind him, to spare himself the disappointment in Daniel's eyes. Sean's arm went around him, pulling Jeff to his side and keeping him there, the message just as clear as if he'd said, *We're together in this, so hold your head high and bear it like a man.*

And so he did, eyes fixed on Daniel as if there was nobody else in the whole airport, anxiety leaving his insides in a knot, his knees weak, his breath short. Then Daniel saw them and his face lit up like a power plant. Oh, God, the smile on those sweet lips. Jeff felt his entrails slowly melting, his knees definitely buckling, only Sean's grip keeping him standing as Daniel crossed the distance between them.

He stopped a few feet away, big green eyes traveling from him to Sean and back again, just as if he needed to make sure they were real, as if he didn't know what to do with the emotions coloring his gaze. Jeff didn't know what to do either, what to say. Daniel looked so beautiful, so unattainable, and yet so close, so insecure, so open that he felt overwhelmed with the desire to both run away and right into those lean arms.

Finally Sean broke the spell and pulled Daniel into a bone-crushing hug. Daniel dropped his travel bag, arms closing around Sean's midsection, face hidden in the big man's chest.

Jeff's hands reached out on their own, desperately needing the contact. Daniel lifted his head and smiled at him, eyes bright with tears. It made Jeff's heart ache so sharply he had to fight back the urge to kiss Daniel's eyes dry and just stroke the slender back till Daniel's fingers came up and grazed his cheek, ever so lightly, the gesture so tender Jeff almost fell to the floor in a puddle of melted bones.

"Hey, strangers."

"Look who's talking."

They kept grinning like fools, never letting go of each other.

"You look great, both of you," Daniel said.

"You look thin."

Daniel pulled away from Sean and punched his shoulder. "You know I'll never be as big as you, so stop trying."

Jeff chuckled. "If you were as big as him, we'd need a galactic-emperor-size bed."

"Ha ha."

"Don't tease the man, Jeff, you know we both love the size he comes in." As soon as he uttered the words, Daniel seemed to realize the implications of what he'd just said and blushed. Sean and Jeff managed to keep straight faces for two heartbeats before doubling over with laughter, people turning to look at them.

Daniel rolled his eyes and moved away from them. As he bent to gather his travel bag, they got a close-up of that small, tight ass they hadn't seen in two months, the vision sobering them fast and good. Now Jeff was sure his eyes showed the same hungry look Sean's blue orbs sported. Shit. And they still had to take care of Daniel's cases, put them in the car, and drive home. He didn't think he could keep his hands to himself for so long. God, but he needed to touch that beautiful face, rip off the expensive clothes, and run his fingers all over that amazing body.

Daniel turned to them as he reached the cart with his luggage. Oh yeah. He had seen the look in their eyes, there was no mistaking the way he worried his lower lip with his teeth. The gesture was small but loud as a growl and ten times as sexy. Jeff was only glad he didn't favor tight clothes, because right then his cock was expanding alarmingly behind the zipper.

"Here they are." Daniel pointed to his cases, two hard, metallic boxes with black handles.

"Oh, you've brought the fancy ones."

"No, Jeff, all his cases are fancy. He just brought the time-travel ones."

Daniel ignored them, leaning forward to pick up the silver cases before Sean moved beside him and snatched them out of his reach.

"Hey! I'm not an invalid, I can carry my own cases."

"Come on, Daniel, indulge him," Jeff said. "You know how he likes to flaunt his strength."

Sean didn't stop to answer him, striding toward the nearest exit as if he had a plane to catch. Not that Jeff didn't understand what the hurry was all about, anyway. "Let's go, Daniel, it's not good to make the sheriff wait."

"You think he'll accept a tip?"

Jeff chuckled. "From you, that man would accept anything."

Daniel blinked at him, and Jeff was glad the flow of people forced them to move on without speaking till they finally reached the exit and found Sean's SUV already waiting for them, engine running. Daniel took the back seat and Jeff hesitated only half a second before following him and slamming the door shut. And then it was torture for miles and miles, the three of them jabbering away while only their eyes betrayed the undercurrent of emotion none dared to release just yet.

Jeff was so nervous he couldn't help fidgeting in his seat, nervous and excited, his eyes following the dance of Daniel's long fingers as he spoke, his tongue coming out to wet his lips, just dying to get close to that sexy mouth and kiss Daniel till he forgot his name. He was only glad they had decided to go to his place first, leave the new house, their house, for another, calmer day, because he couldn't face any more excitement right now, couldn't see anything that wasn't Daniel.

For miles of busy highway the fear of being seen from other cars kept Jeff in his corner, but when they hit a back road, it was another kind of fear that paralyzed him. It was as excruciating as a first date: he was afraid of overwhelming Daniel with the intensity of his need, afraid it might be too soon, afraid Daniel might freak out and push him away.

They drove in silence for some minutes, his eyes meeting Sean's in the rearview mirror and finding the same fear in them.

"Jeff?"

He turned to look at Daniel. He had scooted a little closer, a slender hand resting on the upholstery between them.

"Can I...." Daniel cleared his throat, his eyes closing for a second before he whispered, "Can I kiss you?"

Oh, my God. That was the sweetest, sexiest thing Jeff had ever heard, and Daniel's big eyes were searching his, pleading, his look that of an abandoned puppy begging for attention.

Jeff couldn't help himself. He pounced on Daniel like a wild beast, the lean back slamming against the car door as Jeff's mouth closed on his, Jeff's hands coming up to hold his head in place as he pressed his body against Daniel. When they both moaned at the same time, he felt Daniel smiling into the kiss, green eyes fluttering open to shine at him.

"Sorry to interrupt, but you're distracting the driver."

Jeff pulled a little away and searched Daniel's eyes. "You wanna stop?" Daniel shook his head, already unable to find his voice. Jeff pulled a little further away. "Even if we are distracting the—"

He couldn't finish the sentence, Daniel's arms closing around his neck and pulling him down for a scorching kiss. Jeff stopped pretending he even cared about their safety and focused on the sweet tongue chasing his, the heat from the body against his, the bulge tenting those soft, designer pants. His hands fumbled with Daniel's clothes, wanting to touch skin. Daniel whimpered, the awkward position hardly allowing any movement, their fingers colliding, Jeff's head hitting the roof as he tried to straddle the thin hips.

They maneuvered as best they could without breaking contact. Jeff was starved for that mouth, that pale skin that looked even whiter against his dark hands as he pushed rumpled clothes all the way they could go without wasting time on buttons and zippers. And Daniel seemed as hungry as he was, his already swollen lips desperately searching his, as if he couldn't breathe on his own, long fingers crawling under his shirt to explore his back, his ribs, his chest, every accessible part of him touched, caressed, learned. Daniel's lean form scooted down right beneath him on the backseat, his hands moving to

Jeff's hips to urge him forward and down against his inviting body.

Jeff moaned low, the sound primal, coming right from his gut, matched by a strained groan from Sean's deep voice. Yeah. He knew he was being selfish, feasting on Daniel all by himself, but he also knew he would die if he didn't touch that amazing creature beneath him, that sweet, wanton angel who right then was dragging his palms over his belly, up his chest, the pressure maddening and necessary, fingertips only grazing his eager nipples to move further up to his throat, a hungry mouth following them and closing on his pulse, sucking hard, as if Daniel needed to feed on him.

A shudder shook Jeff from head to toe. He pressed down to grind their erections together and heard Daniel hiss as rough denim rubbed over thin, silky pants. He tried to pull away, fearing he might burn that delicate skin, but eager hands clutched at his ass to keep the pressure going, and he just let go, unable to hold back any longer, unable to deny his precious lover anything he needed, whatever it was, whatever it took. And then that incredible man snaked his hands between them and shoved his pants down without even undoing them, his hips lifting immediately to press a beautiful dripping cock against Jeff's jeans, deft fingers finding their way under Jeff's waistband to cup his cheeks and urge him to move, to rub hard against him, as if Daniel craved the burn, desperately needing to be marked, reclaimed, reassured of where he stood in Jeff's heart.

Jeff growled like a wild beast, any rational thought deserting his short-circuited brain, his chest about to explode as he surged forward to sink hungry teeth into the exposed throat of his willing prey. Daniel's cry was sweet music to his ears and he never let go, delighted at his responsive lover's movements beneath him, that abused cock leaving wet trails on Jeff's zipper, hot hands held tight on his ass by the effectively restraining bond of his jeans.

He humped against Daniel hard and fast, his balls impossibly tight, his cock straining for release as Daniel keened and squirmed under his attack. The moment he felt his teeth break that soft skin and draw blood into his mouth, Daniel froze beneath him, and all it took was one last hard shove of his hips to bring a shattering orgasm to both of them, come spurting over and under his jeans as they shook, the scent of sweat and sex and Daniel as dizzying as their shared pleasure.

Jeff collapsed on Daniel, his lover's hands extricating themselves from under his jeans to wrap tightly around him in a sweet, protective, eager gesture.

"Damn."

That was Sean's voice, low and strained. Daniel whimpered against Jeff's neck and Jeff pulled just the tiniest possible distance away to look into his eyes.

"My precious little cub. You want the big bear, too, don't you?"

Daniel only moaned, his pupils huge in those bottomless wells of green desire. He heard Sean curse under his breath and nuzzled Daniel's throat, his tongue coming out to lick the small cuts his teeth had left on that immaculate skin. Daniel whimpered again, his arms tightening around Jeff.

"Shhh, be patient, my pretty. We're almost there, and Sean will be all yours to taste."

The sweet, hungry noise Daniel made was enough to make his sated cock start filling again, and he could only imagine what it did to the big man, driving now as if a pursuing party was hot on their heels.

Jeff kept showering lazy kisses all over Daniel's beautiful face, feeding him sweet nonsense that kept Daniel's need building steadily and slowly rubbing against him till the car stopped and Sean all but jumped out of it to tear the back door open.

Jeff pulled away reluctantly, but Sean didn't have any patience left in him and he just bent to put his hands under Daniel's arms and drag him forcefully out of the car and against his chest.

As Jeff rounded the trunk to get to them, they were already kissing like drowning men, Sean's fingers pushing Daniel's rumpled clothes further away, the small body almost naked now against his fully clothed lover. The image was so sexy Jeff's cock perked right up, the need not so demanding now but definitely there. It was time to give a little hand, to help Sean take the edge off before he exploded.

Jeff moved decidedly forward, unbuttoning the big man's clothes, pulling Daniel's all the way off while they never stopped kissing, rewarding him with encouraging, hungry noises. Then Daniel was completely naked, Sean's clothes all loose but still on and Jeff let it at that, finding the contrast perversely arousing: Daniel's body open to the demanding paws all over him, as if the smaller man was offering himself in sacrifice to the powerful beast devouring him. And just when Jeff moved back a little to simply enjoy the view of his lovers, Daniel did the most amazing thing: he disentangled himself from Sean's tight grip to go down on his knees in front of the big man. Jeff stood frozen in place, his eyes drinking in every move Daniel made as his hands closed on Sean's exposed erection and guided it to his mouth. Jesus fucking Christ. That was…. Jeff lifted his eyes to meet Sean's desperate look and would have no doubt creamed his pants if he hadn't just come. As things were, he had only time to step forward and take Sean's mouth in his before the big man started shaking and coming down Daniel's throat.

Jeff kept his legs gently pressed against Daniel's naked back as that sweet mouth went on sucking, pulling aftershocks from Sean till the Irishman leaned heavily on Jeff, foreheads bumping softly as their lips finally parted. And still Daniel kept on working Sean's cock, keeping it hard, making them both moan, till Sean couldn't take it anymore and pulled away all but growling in frustration, big arms reaching down to lift that amazing creature off the ground and carry him all the way home.

Jeff hurried to open the door for them, and as Sean crossed the threshold with Daniel's body curled into his broad chest, Jeff felt his own body ache all over with a sweet pain he'd never felt before. Those two men were ingrained into his system now: it would have taken more than a scalpel to extract them from his soul, and he couldn't understand how it had happened to him, the proud, aloof Apache that had never truly let anyone into his house, much less into his heart.

And yet those white men looked at him in a way that made him feel proud, looked at him the way they were doing right now in the front room of his own house, need so clear in their eyes Jeff could feel no doubt he was wanted just the way he was. Or rather, he was wanted for *all* that he was: it was finally him and not an image of what they thought he was that those incredible men cherished, loved.

Yeah, that was the crux of it all. Jeff simply couldn't doubt those men loved him. Whatever happened between them, it was there in their eyes. He didn't have to fight to earn that love, didn't have to prove anything. All he had to do was reach out and take all that was selflessly offered, no price tag attached, just free love his tired heart had no problem giving back in kind.

Sean tore his gaze from Jeff to look down at Daniel in his arms. "Wanna take a shower, pretty cub?"

"No, I...."

"What do you need? Tell me."

"I just...."

Jeff found himself frowning. He moved closer to them, wanting to see Daniel's face, see what he was hiding.

Sean exchanged a concerned look with him. "Are you in pain, angel?" Daniel hurried to shake his head. Maybe he'd hurried too much for their comfort. "Are you sure? You know you can tell us, whatever it is."

"Especially if you are hurting," Jeff added.

Daniel huffed in frustration, fighting to pull away from Sean's arms.

"Easy now, Doc. I won't let you go until you fess up."

"All right," Daniel growled. "I want no fucking shower because right now all I need is both your cocks inside me in whatever order you choose, and I don't think I can wait till we're all squeaky clean. Was that clear enough for you, you stubborn worrywarts?"

Jeff's eyes couldn't open any wider. He wasn't sure what surprised him more, Daniel's blunt language or what he thought he understood Daniel wanted from them. Sean phrased his confusion for him.

"Did you just say what I think you did?"

"Yeah, I did. What are you, deaf?"

"Maybe. Would you care to repeat it just in case?"

Daniel all but yelled. "I want you to fuck me, okay?"

"Oh. My. God."

"And no, I'm not your god, I'm just your little cub, remember?"

Jeff and Sean looked at each other and burst out laughing.

"Sure got us a fiery cub."

"Well, it sort of runs in the family, I guess."

Jeff reached out to stroke brown hair and met green, pleading eyes. He swallowed hard, his voice croaking as he asked Sean, "Bed?"

Sean just grunted and hurried down the hall to their bedroom with his precious load in his arms. Jeff followed close, shrugging off his clothes as he went. When he reached the bedroom, Sean had already deposited Daniel on the clean sheets and their beautiful lover opened his arms for Jeff, calling him with his whole body.

Jeff didn't hesitate. He flung himself into those slender arms, wrapping his own arms and legs around the lean body, lips pressed together as their tongues beckoned one another. Then the bed shifted, and Jeff opened his eyes to see Sean plaster himself against Daniel's back, the big body easily enveloping their smaller lover in a protective cocoon of muscle.

"Come here, sweet cub, make me remember what this beautiful skin of yours feels like," Sean said.

Daniel moaned into Jeff's mouth, his cock pressing hard against Jeff's belly. The big man's hand traveled all over Daniel's body, making him squirm and shift under his touch, his sensitive hands digging into Jeff's hair, tilting his head to deepen the kiss and drive Jeff crazy with anticipation.

"Now, my prince, will you let us get you all ready?"

"Hmm."

"Babe, let go of his mouth. I wanna hear that sweet voice."

Jeff took one more kiss before releasing him and Daniel whispered into his parting lips. "Yes, please, I want you."

"Okay, get the lube, babe, we're gonna get our little cub all wet and open for us."

Daniel bit his lower lip and Jeff almost cursed aloud. Damn Sean for making the simplest of things sound sexy as hell.

Jeff turned to search the nightstand for lube, feeling two sets of hungry eyes follow his every move. Damn. His hands were shaking as he handed the tube to Sean, his mind still shying away from the enormity of what was about to happen, still not quite believing Daniel would want it.

He got lost in big, slightly frightened green eyes till wet fingers closed around his. He yelped at the sudden cold contact as Sean pulled Jeff's hand over Daniel's hip to his tight little butt. Oh God. He was never going to be able to do it.

"Now, pretty cub, lie on your chest, let us explore."

Daniel obeyed, turning to lie flat on the mattress, his eyes going closed as his head rested on the pillow. Jeff swallowed. Daniel was so beautiful. That lean, white back, tapering down into a thin waist, tight ass curving softly, long legs covered in barely visible blond fuzz, tiny, perfect toes ending delicately boned feet.

Sean's left hand landed on Daniel's vulnerable nape, big fingers looking so strong and yet so gentle that Jeff couldn't help comparing it in his mind to the sloppy, tender touch big animals dispensed to their cubs. Yeah, Sean's intense blue eyes were full of tenderness, too, but there the likeness ended, since beside the desire to protect there was a strong undercurrent of another, much stronger desire to possess the sensual beauty so willingly offered. Jeff's need was equally made of the same amount of selfless care and the undeniable craving to own what was so tantalizingly exposed before him. Daniel's trusting abandon made the craving even sharper, in a way Jeff had never experienced before. Never before had he wanted to own another human being, much less be owned by one. If someone had even suggested such a thing, he would have thought them insane. Right now, though, he couldn't think in any other terms, and couldn't find it in him to judge it wrong. On the contrary, for the first time in his life, it just seemed the right thing to do, the right thing to want. The realization sobered him somehow, anxiety finally leaving him with a clear, sure path in front of him. It was time to show a little courage and shake off the last inherited notions of what was good or bad. He already knew what was good for him; all he had to do was be brave enough to take it. His men wouldn't expect less from him.

Sean's hand moved to Daniel's shoulder as blue eyes fixed Jeff with an expectant stare. Jeff understood, his hand immediately following Sean's lead to settle on Daniel's other shoulder. His fingers weren't shaking anymore and, when both their hands started massaging their way down Daniel's back, his touch was sure, so much in synch with Sean's that their hands seemed to belong to the same man. And there was such a proud look in Sean's eyes that Jeff's heart almost burst out of his chest.

Their fingers traveled slowly, working Daniel's tense muscles one by one, tearing pleased moans out of him. They kneaded Daniel's ass, both their hands moving to spread his cheeks, to get access to his puckered hole. Sean nodded to him and Jeff pressed a lube-covered finger against the tight entrance. Daniel gasped, his muscles clenching.

"Shhh, relax, my prince, just enjoy the sensations," Sean murmured.

Daniel slowly relaxed, Jeff's fingers gently teasing his opening before pushing just his first knuckle inside. Daniel tensed a little in response and Sean bent to nuzzle his neck.

"Hush, pretty cub, it's going to feel a little odd at first, but you know we would never hurt you."

"I know. I'm sorry."

"Shh. No apologies. Nothing you feel is wrong. Just trust us. And if it gets to be too much, tell us to stop, okay?"

"Okay."

"That's our cub. Now relax, let us in."

Jeff felt the tight muscles give way around him and pressed his finger all the way in. Daniel made a surprised little noise and Jeff smiled widely. It was so good, making Daniel experience completely new things, being there to guide him and feel it with him.

"Now Jeff is inside you, touching you where nobody else has ever touched you."

Shit. The things Sean could say. Daniel moaned and shifted a little, legs spreading wider.

"You want more, little cub? Want my finger inside you too?"

Daniel whimpered, his head nodding just once, eyes tightly shut, face flushed a rosy shade.

"Hmm. So sweet. I'm dying to touch you here," Sean said as his finger pressed against Daniel's entrance, "feel your body opening for me, letting me in."

Jeff pulled his finger almost all the way out and then plunged back in at the same time as Sean's thick finger breached Daniel's ring of muscle.

Daniel cried out, his body clenching around their fingers. He was so hot inside, so tight, it felt so good being trapped inside him with Sean that it was all Jeff could do not to come with just his one finger inside Daniel.

"So tight, my pretty angel, burning for us. You have no idea how good you feel."

Daniel's hips rolled a little, tentatively testing the sensations moving would bring him.

"You want us to move inside you, little cub, spread you wide for our cocks?"

"Mmm."

They set up a rhythm, moving in and out of him, careful to stroke his gland every time, making Daniel shudder and moan, one knee coming up to give them more access.

"So sexy, my pretty cub, so responsive. I wish you could see yourself know, so beautiful, our fingers inside you, touching you deep."

Sean pushed a third finger in, Daniel whimpering, shifting a little to accommodate the increased pressure. "That's our beautiful little cub; you take us so well, so ready for us now, so open."

It was Jeff's turn to moan now, pre-come dripping on the sheets, his chest aching as much as his cock at the view in front of him, at the heat radiating from Sean's body beside him, at the voice caressing his addled brain and the sexy noises escaping Daniel's throat, the shudders their fingers brought to that stunning body.

"Hmm. You're making us need badly, little cub. Wanna make us wait?" Daniel shook his head, unable to speak. "Think you can take Jeff's cock now? Want this beautiful bobcat inside you, fucking you wild?"

Daniel whimpered plaintively, their fingers never stopping their sweet torture on his hole. Sean's free hand gave Jeff the lube, passion-filled blue eyes lingering for a moment on his face, encouraging, wanting, needing him to be there as much as they both needed Daniel. There was no precedence in Sean's heart, both Daniel and Jeff belonged there in their own right, both held so tightly to the big man's soul there was no room left for anybody else... just him and Daniel, Daniel and him, the only gods in Sean's firmament, the only ones he would bow his head to.

Sean pressed a tender kiss to Jeff's trembling lips, reassuring him as they pulled their fingers free from Daniel's body's warm embrace. Daniel made a distressed noise at the sudden emptiness.

"Shhh, it's all right, little cub. Jeff's getting ready for you." Sean stroked Daniel's damp bangs out of his face. "Will you let me hold you while Jeff makes love to you, sweet prince, will you lie against me?"

Daniel turned a little, heavy-lidded eyes looking up at them. His burning gaze traveled all over Jeff's body, lingering on his hands as they coated his cock with lube. He bit his lower lip, hard, and Jeff moaned, his fingers squeezing the base of his shaft to make the urge recede. Then Daniel turned to look at Sean, Jeff's own gaze following his over the muscled body of their lover, taking in his powerful stance, strong thighs supporting a magnificent torso: ridged belly, wide pectorals, erect, rosy nipples, their color almost as flushed as the thick cock that stood at attention from a bush of blond curls, its shaft already slick with pre-come... all his body, his bright blue eyes, putting on an incredible display of control, the full intensity of his need reined in for them, waiting on them, reserving himself for his lovers, just waiting to give them all, waiting for them to be ready to receive him, be fully claimed by him.

Sean moved to rest his back against the headboard and then opened his arms for Daniel. "Come to me, little cub."

Daniel didn't hesitate. He sat up, taking Sean's hands, the big man pulling him to his chest with no apparent effort, manhandling the smaller body till Daniel lay between his legs, thick fingers pushing under Daniel's thighs and lifting the long legs to rest on Sean's slightly folded knees, effectively spreading him for Jeff.

"You're ready now, pretty cub?"

"Uh huh."

"Want Jeff?"

Dark, green eyes met Jeff's, the answer so clear in them that Jeff shuddered, unable to tear his gaze from that hypnotic need in Daniel's eyes.

"Come on, my prince, tell him, don't keep him waiting."

"Jeff, please." Daniel's arms reached out and Jeff could just have stayed there forever, his lovers so beautiful in front of him, so sexy together, their eyes hot on him, their need for him in plain sight. He could have stayed just feasting his eyes on them, but he wanted to be part of them, wanted to sink into those outstretched arms and lie there protected, needed, loved.

"Jeff...."

He moved between Daniel's legs, his eyes never leaving that gorgeous face as his cock pressed against the exposed hole, Daniel's hands closing on his arms and holding tight. As he pushed gently inside, Daniel's body tensed, his eyes closing in a painful gesture. God, he was so tight. Even with their ministrations, it was going to burn like hell.

"Relax, little cub. It's just a little discomfort till your body gets used to it." Sean's big hands stroked Daniel's sides, his legs, his belly, petting, soothing, his voice gentle and reassuring.

"Easy now, angel, just let go, breathe deeply and relax. Let Jeff make you fly."

Daniel took a deep breath, his eyes fluttering open, looking at Jeff pleadingly. "Kiss me?"

Oh God. So sweet, his pretty lover. Jeff surged forward to take those swollen lips in his, Daniel opening for him, his whole body relaxing as Jeff's tongue breached his mouth, Jeff's hips moving as soon as he felt the tight muscles giving way a little, his cock pushing past the first defenses to sink deep down into the burning furnace that was Daniel's body. Daniel cried into his mouth, and Jeff let go of his lips to look into his face.

"You all right, pretty one?"

Daniel gave him a wide-eyed, overwhelmed look, and Jeff almost pulled all the way out.

"Am I hurting you?"

Daniel opened his mouth and only a sob came out. Jeff's heart clenched in fear, his body retreating instinctively till Daniel's arms wrapped around him and pulled him to his chest.

"Jeff, please."

"Yeah, what is it, my love? What do you need?"

"Don't stop. Please?"

Damn. Damn. And damn.

He pulled a little away to kiss Daniel's forehead and saw Sean's feral smile.

"You're his first, babe, remember how that felt?"

Oh my. How could he be so stupid? No matter how many times Daniel had made love, he would never have been prepared for this, for what it felt to be touched so deep inside, filled by another man's cock. Jeff sensed a smile stretching his lips, and he knew he looked just as Sean did, civilized masks dropping to show the most primal, possessive satisfaction at being the first to claim virgin soil. It was lame, but Jeff couldn't care less. There had been no other man before them in Daniel's past and there would be no other in his future, just Sean and him. And damn if it didn't make him howl with pride.

"Jeff...."

He held Daniel's face in his hands and started thrusting slowly, watching Daniel's eyes as they glazed, listening to every little sound he made.

"My pretty little cub." Daniel whimpered as Sean's fingers found his nipples and tugged gently. "You like it, sweet angel, feeling Jeff moving inside you, claiming you?"

"Hmm...."

Sean's hand went down to cup Daniel's balls, and the thin body arched right into Jeff's forward thrust. Jeff let out a strangled cry and closed his mouth on Daniel's, his tongue pushing in deep, his movements frantic now, the need to devour that sweet, beautiful creature so intense there was no place for anything else in his mind, the grip of Daniel's fingers on his arms pleasantly painful, the noises that filled their kiss sharp, Sean voicing what their brains had no energy left to turn into words.

"So sexy, my men, so good together."

Jeff's teeth caught Daniel's lower lip and tugged a little at the soft, deep red flesh. Daniel moaned, his hips bucking to meet Jeff's thrusts. He shifted slightly, angling his cock to nail Daniel's gland. He was almost there, Daniel so tight and hot around him, so responsive, so trusting, he knew he wouldn't last much longer, and he wanted Daniel to come with him.

His next stroke made Daniel cry out sharply, his back arching beautifully, Sean's hands moving up to draw his ecstatic contours and coming back down to close on his dripping shaft. Daniel keened now, his back bowing even further, Jeff moving into him hard and fast, his aching balls slapping against Daniel's spread cheeks.

"That's it, pretty cub, offer yourself up, let that wild cat feed on you, tear you open and eat you alive."

"Jeff!"

His name was cried out in that sweet voice, and it was suddenly too much, the sensations burning in his body, the sight of his beautiful lover completely lost in the feelings they were pulling out of him, Sean's hands mercilessly pumping his cock as Jeff slammed into him, the need, the hunger so intense he truly felt as if he *was* devouring Daniel's raw heart. Then Sean's voice came out in a low growl, filled with the words that traveled down his spine to his tight balls.

"Now, Daniel, give us all you got, show us you know who you belong to. Give yourself over and come for us. Now."

When Sean bent his head to sink hard teeth in the same exact place Jeff's own teeth had left a red mark on Daniel's throat, Jeff froze, his orgasm pouring out of him just as Daniel cried, hips bucking wildly, come spurting all over as Jeff filled him with his seed, Sean's hand still tugging gently at his cock to keep him shuddering through a wave of aftershocks, his grip on Daniel's throat never loosening until the small body collapsed against Sean's chest.

Jeff let himself fall forward, his cock still buried deep in Daniel's warmth. Two sets of arms immediately rose to wrap him, to keep him close, and he almost drifted into a contented sleep, the smell of their sex, the smell of *them* so strong, so good, so strangely entwined to form a new entity that hadn't existed before, that he was sure they were an altogether new thing themselves. An exotic species, whole and unique in its complexity, three hearts pounding away to feed a single soul.

Jeff shifted a little to pull his cock out of Daniel, his sweet lover whimpering at the loss. He moved to kiss the abused lips, whispering soothing words. "Shhh, my precious little cub, I'm yours, I'm not going anywhere."

Deep green eyes pierced him with a look so full of meaning that Jeff felt his whole body aching with the most delicious, burning pain.

"I love you, Jeff."

"I love you, too, Daniel, more than life."

Daniel's eyes filled with tears, his sweet face turning to meet Sean's hot gaze on them. "Sean...." Daniel's voice broke, a big hand coming up to stroke his delicate features.

"I know you love me, little cub, as you know I love nobody else but you and that wildcat you captured."

Daniel nodded and tilted his head to reach Sean's lips. They kissed tenderly, Jeff's hands unable to stay still, moving on their own to touch their linked mouths. Two tongues came out to lick his fingers, the sensation so good his cock would have started filling again if he hadn't been so completely drained and boneless.

"Sean?"

"Yeah? What is it, pretty prince?"

They spoke between lazy kisses, Daniel's head turning to take both their mouths, one kiss at a time. It was so sweet, so tender, so good.

"I still want to feel you inside me, Sean. Please."

Jeff froze, his cock definitely giving an interested twitch, Sean's eyes so wide his blue irises were all framed in white, broad circles. Yeah, that was unbelievable—theirs, the sweetest, sexiest cub any pair of wild lovers would ever have. When he spoke, Sean's voice was all husky.

"You make me need, sweet angel, but it might be too much for you now, don't wanna hurt you."

Daniel tried to frown, but his face was so relaxed it turned into a cute pout. "I'm not that fragile."

"Nope, you're strong."

"Then why...?"

He never got to end the sentence, Sean's mouth closing on the teeth marks on his neck and sucking hard. Daniel yelped, his lean back arching in the tight space between his lovers' pressing bodies.

"Because," Sean growled, "you're already mine, pretty cub, and I'm gonna enjoy you as the exquisite delicacy you are... very, very slowly."

Sean's tongue came out to lave at Daniel's throat and Jeff couldn't help himself, his tongue meeting Sean's on the sweet, flushed, marked skin.

"Mmm, yeah, Jeff and I, little cub, we're gonna devour you little by little, day after day, every inch of that sweet, tender flesh, till there's no part of you we haven't touched, marked, claimed."

Daniel moaned, his body relaxing into their wet caresses, his eyes closing, his expression one of utter bliss. Sean gave Jeff a wide smile he answered easily, their bodies moving as one to settle their precious lover more comfortably on the mattress, hands reaching to pull sheets over them, arms, legs entwining to build a nest where their love would rest safely.

"Now sleep, sweet prince, and we'll meet you in your dreams."

Daniel smiled, his lips forming the words without opening his eyes, drifting into sleep even as he said them. "You are my dream. Don't... need... any other...."

Jeff chuckled and snuggled even closer, warmth and happiness seeping deep into his bones. He burrowed his head in Daniel's neck, listening to the soothing rhythm of his heartbeat. When Sean's hand settled on his throat, Jeff could feel both their pulses slowly calming to match Daniel's. Yeah, they were an amazing creature now, the three of them, nature's true wonder, evolution's latest miracle: love's emergence.

H. J. BRUES lives in Spain, enjoying the hot weather, the brisk language, the warm-hearted people, and the thousands of books of the library she works in. She has a degree in medieval history and loves castles, knights in shining armor, and barbarian warriors with no armor at all. She practiced fencing till her knees started complaining, took archery till her elbow almost fell off, and then, wisely, switched to the less martial of the martial arts, tai chi.

Check out these M/M/M titles from

DREAMSPINNER PRESS

www.ingramcontent.com/pod-product-compliance
Lightning Source LLC
Chambersburg PA
CBHW051631260626
47170CB00004B/1122